Dedicated to 135

# Chapter One

"Well, it's official." Mrs. Sawyer beamed at me across the service counter of my newly opened cider shop while half the town danced the funky chicken behind her. "You've impressed me, Winona Mae Montgomery, exactly as everyone promised you would." She fished a narrow envelope from her heavily beaded clutch and passed it my way. "This is for you. You've earned every penny."

I accepted the check with a warm smile.

Three weeks ago, Mrs. Sawyer and her daughter, Elsie, had come to see me about an outdoor wedding at my granny's orchard. They'd wanted a simple ceremony for Elsie and her fiancé, Jack, preferably in the meadow between our field of wildflowers and rows of apple trees. They'd requested a reception to follow at my cider shop just across the property. Something simple and elegant. Fun and memorable. I'd accepted their offered deposit, marked my calendar, and vowed to do my best.

Fast-forward a few frantic weeks and Elsie Grace Sawyer married Jack Robert Warren, among the wildflowers today at high noon. It was a small, modest country ceremony so beautiful I'd cried.

I tucked the envelope beneath my cash register's till and locked the drawer. "Y'all made it easy," I said. "You knew exactly what you wanted, and you were gracious at every turn."

She nodded, accepting the compliment. "Elsie was glad to have found such a perfect location on such short notice. Though I can't say I'm sorry there was an issue with their previously booked venue. A West Virginia woman's heart never travels far from home, so it's fitting she fell in love here and that this was where she was married. Besides, there's nothing like Blossom Valley in June."

I couldn't disagree. In fact, Blossom Valley, West Virginia, was unspeakably gorgeous any time of year. A national park ran through it. The Ohio River wound along it, and all things wild and wonderful lived in it, my family and friends included. Our quintessential small-town community was nestled among the Blue Ridge Mountains with views to die for at every turn. And my Granny Smythe's orchard was no exception.

The music changed, and the crowd broke into applause. Exhausted two-steppers fanned smiling faces as they made their way off the dance floor and navigated the tightly packed space. The renovated Mail Pouch barn that housed my cider shop was historic and beloved. A piece of our local history. A source of our town's pride and my personal

victory beacon. Opening the cider shop had saved
Granny's failing orchard last Christmas. The shop
allowed us to sell Granny's produce and baked
goods all year long, not to mention a little light
lunch fare and my eight-and-counting flavors of
cider. As an added financial bonus, the barn could
be rented for events like this one.

Mrs. Sawyer smiled at a group of bridesmaids in
shimmery chiffon. They'd broken away from the
crowd to take selfies with Elsie. The ladies cheerfully circled the bride, striking poses from serious
to silly, genuine smiles on their lips and an array of
cowgirl boots pecking out from beneath their
gowns.

"She certainly looks happy, doesn't she?" Mrs.
Sawyer asked softly, a prideful curve to her lips.

"Yes, ma'am," I agreed, though I suspected the
question had been rhetorical.

Truthfully, everyone in sight seemed downright
blissful. Folks chatted animatedly around tables
I'd draped in white linens and centered with wildflowers. Friends rocked with laughter in chairs I'd
tied with massive burlap bows. And the sweet scent
of cider hung thick in the evening air.

I offered Mrs. Sawyer a bottle of water from the
metal washtub of melting ice on the countertop.
The day had been long and hot, even for mid-
June. The setting sun had provided some relief,
but I mentally added an air conditioning unit to
my list of potential shop upgrades—once I'd made
enough cash to pay for it.

Mrs. Sawyer guzzled her water, then sighed as
her daughter twirled across the dance floor.

I smiled at the unfettered joy on Elsie's face, her

chin tipped upward, eyes closed. She was a pin-wheel of white satin beneath rough-hewn rafters wrapped in twinkle lights. Thick floral garlands hung in ropes from above, each handcrafted to match the soft pink-and-white color scheme. Combined with the twinkle lights and setting sun, the overall look was ethereal, even in a hundred-year-old barn.

Elsie was several years younger than me, and I didn't know her personally, but I'd seen her around before she'd left for college. She'd met her husband at West Virginia University and moved to Kentucky following graduation. He didn't have much family as far as I could see, but Elsie had plenty to spare. The couple ran a wellness shop together in Louisville, where she sold essential oils and he used his botany degree to recommend holistic approaches to healthful living, like eating kale and taking garlic tablets. *To each her own*, I thought, but I preferred a burger and fries. The shop kept them busy, so Elsie didn't travel often. Her mother was over the moon to have her home for the weekend, so she'd extended an open invitation to the town last week and had made a mighty effort to see the news spread. All of Blossom Valley was welcome to attend the reception any time after eight. The formalities would be over and folks would have a chance to see Elsie before she climbed aboard the old farm truck I'd decorated as the getaway vehicle, and left again. I wasn't sure a barn, even one the size of mine, could accommodate the entire town, but there was plenty of space outside and I was thrilled for the added exposure.

I filled and distributed a few more cups of cider,

then took a beat to bask in the glory of my blessings and achievements. Six months ago, my granny's orchard had been deep in the red, but together with a lot of prayers and elbow grease, we'd renovated the barn, opened a cider shop, and turned things around. So far, the results were far better than I'd imagined.

I kept a framed portrait of Granny and Grampy behind the counter. They'd purchased this land with money from their wedding. They'd built a legacy and raised a family here. Then when their teenaged daughter had a baby and ran out, they'd stepped up and raised me too. I'd gotten my dark hair and eyes from Granny, but my go-getter attitude and big mouth were all Grampy. The latter two were the qualities that had made my cider shop possible.

The recent renovation had replaced the original slatted flooring with high-gloss wide-planked pine. The former hayloft had been transformed and repurposed into much needed storage space, a potential expansion area for cider shop seating and a lovely overlook for anyone wanting a bird's-eye view of the area below. At least that's what I'd been told. I didn't make a habit of leaving the ground more often than absolutely necessary.

At a booming round of howdy-dos, Mrs. Sawyer peeled away from the counter with glee. "Marvelous!" she squealed, setting her empty water bottle aside. "Welcome!"

I squinted curiously at the silhouettes moving through the open barn doors and morphing into folks I recognized beneath the warm cider shop lights. Thanks to a decade of waitressing at the Sip

N Sup, I knew just about everyone in town by sight, if not by name.

I felt my grin growing as I motioned for my best friend, Dot, to join me behind the service counter.

She arrived with an armload of discarded plates and crumbled napkins. She dumped the collection into a former wine barrel turned trash bin, then flicked on the sink to wash her hands. "Look out," she said. "Business is about to be jumping." She dried her hands and put her game face on. The billowing material of her scoop-neck satin blouse did little to conceal the athletic figure beneath. Dot was an outdoorswoman by day, a ranger at the national park and animal rescuer on the regular, but tonight she was my fellow barkeep.

I grabbed a fresh stack of cups and righted them on the bar. "Let's hope all these folks are thirsty."

Dot pulled jugs of cider from the refrigerator and lined them behind the counter for quick access.

If there was anyone in town who hadn't visited my new cider shop yet, they were probably on their way now. And nothing was better for business than word of mouth or a good experience. Since everyone loved a wedding, I was counting on tonight to provide both.

I pulled the little countertop chalkboard back into view for the benefit of our new arrivals and waited while they made their way over for a look.

"What'll it be?" I asked the first man who made eye contact. I recognized him from the local shoe repair shop, but couldn't recall his name.

"House special, for me," he said, "and a champagne cider for my wife."

"Coming right up." I filled a cup with Honeycrisp and ginger cider for the man. Then I whipped a plastic flute off the counter and dipped it top-down into a shallow dish of caramel sauce. Next I pressed the sticky rim into a bowl of brown sugar and gave it a twist. Hunks of dark crystals clung to the edge as I righted the flute, throwing delectable scents into the air.

He watched with eager eyes as I filled the flute halfway with champagne, then topped it off with cider and a few chunks of chopped green apples. "Outstanding."

"Thanks." I wiped my hands into a towel behind the counter and set the empty champagne bottle beside my last full one. I'd need to get more soon.

"What do I owe ya?"

"Not a thing. Tab's on Mrs. Sawyer tonight," I said.

He nodded approvingly, then pressed a generous wad of ones into my tip jar before vanishing back into the crowd with his drinks.

Dot and I worked diligently for several more minutes before the newcomers were satiated and I could catch my breath.

"You throw one heck of a wedding," Dot said, digging her hands into my tip jar and removing a pile of crinkled bills. "Remind me to call you up when it's my turn." She arranged and smoothed the money, then worked it into an already bursting envelope tucked beneath the counter. "Folks sure are generous once you get them all liquored up."

I bumped my hip against hers with a laugh. "No one is liquored up. Aside from the champagne ciders, nothing back here is alcoholic. Just good old-fashioned sugar highs all around." I hooked a fingertip on a tray of Granny's mini turnovers and tugged it in Dot's direction, eyebrows wiggling.

She nabbed a flaky, icing-drizzled treat and nibbled slowly, attention fixed across the room. "What do you suppose the groom's drinking?"

I turned to catch sight of Jack hoisting a silver flask to his lips. His face was ruddy, and his posture slack. Both seemed accentuated by the bright white of his tuxedo, a sharp contrast to the traditional black attire of his best man, Aaron. Aaron patted his shoulder and leaned in close, hopefully to tell Jack to pull it together.

Jack made a sour face and gave him a shove.

I tensed, searching the crowd for Elsie and hoping she hadn't seen.

"Uh oh," Dot said. "Bride's mad."

I watched in horror as Elsie carried the weight of her skirt in both hands, heading straight for her groom. Her fair skin was flushed, her eyebrows pinched.

Aaron stepped back as she approached, then cast the groom a grin before retreating onto the dance floor, immediately enveloped by a round of ladies in chiffon.

Dot sucked frosting from her thumb. "He's cute," she said. "The best man, not the groom. Jack's a mess."

My gaze drifted back to the man in question. Elsie stood on her tiptoes, palms against Jack's cheeks, successfully blocking my view of his face. I couldn't tell if they were kissing or talking nose-to-nose, but given his hands cradling her hips, I was confident the tension had been diffused.

I gave the room another long look and felt my shoulders relax. Everyone seemed happy and no one appeared in need of a drink. The bridesmaids had formed a circle around the best man and were clearly showing off for his benefit. Dot was right. He was cute. "How's it going with Jake?" I asked, turning to watch her instead. Dot had been seeing Jake Wesson, a junior loan officer at the bank, for a few months now, but it never seemed to evolve beyond coffee or a movie. "You haven't mentioned him in a while."

She wrinkled her nose and lifted one shoulder. "He's a nice guy."

"Something wrong with nice guys?" I asked.

"No. I just don't think he's the one for me."

"Fair enough," I said, selecting a fat chocolate-dipped strawberry from a platter down the bar. I bit into the heavenly fruit and scanned the crowd for someone who might be the right guy for her.

My attention caught on a far too familiar face and I groaned. My ex-boyfriend, Hank Donovan, leaned casually against the far wall, his forearm resting against the wood above his head, his face buried deep into a bridesmaid's hair. Whispering in her ear? Kissing her cheek or neck? I instinctively made a thick gagging sound.

Hank had broken my heart in deep and complicated ways not so long ago. Though to hear him tell it, the whole thing had been a misunderstanding. Regardless, he'd spent the last six months trying to make it up to me. I'd been warming to the possibility I might've overreacted last year, but seeing him lost in the golden curls of a too-young-for-him bridesmaid had me rethinking things.

Dot slid against my side. "Who is that with your man?"

"Bridesmaid," I said, unable to recall her name or if I'd even been introduced. "She seems nice, huh?"

Dot barked a laugh. "I'd say. Only a truly charitable individual would allow Hank to eat her hair like that."

I grabbed a rag and busied myself wiping pastry crumbs and water spots off the heavily lacquered reclaimed-wood countertop. "Hank isn't my man anymore."

She nudged me playfully with her elbow. "So where's your new fella?"

I rolled my eyes, but didn't bother responding. I knew who she was referring to, and Sheriff Colton Wise wasn't my fella. He was barely a friend. More like an infinitely frustrating acquaintance who'd shown up last fall when I found a dead body and called for help. He'd gotten under my skin, accusing Granny of murder and me of conspiracy. He'd eventually dropped that nonsense, bought me a chocolate malt, and saved my life, but he still made me crazy. "I'm going to get more champagne. Hold down the fort?"

She nodded and I slipped away. The air grew heady and thick as I passed the crowded dance floor where perfumes and colognes collided with heat from too many moving bodies and an abundance of fresh-cut flowers. I wiped my brow and shimmied as a bead of sweat cruised the valley between my shoulder blades.

A rumble of angry voices registered in a beat of silence between songs, and I craned my neck in search of the source. My jaw dropped as Hank and the groom came into view overhead, posed in the former hayloft, features hard and bodies tensed.

"Hank?" I called. When he didn't respond, I cupped my hands around the sides of my mouth like parenthesis and tried again. "Hank?"

He pushed a finger at the groom's face and barked out words I couldn't understand through the bass of a Luke Bryan song. A moment later Jack gave him a shove. Hank stumbled back against the loft railing, arms flung wide.

"Hank!" I screamed.

A few guests rushed to my side. I raised a hand overhead, pointing and speechless.

Jack took notice of the gathering crowd and stormed away, knocking his shoulder into Hank as he headed for the steps. I moved back as Jack jogged past me, his unbuttoned white tuxedo jacket flapping at his sides. Several people called after him, but he didn't stop.

Elsie whirled in his wake and gave chase as he exited the barn.

Her bridesmaids followed her, and Hank followed them into the night.

I gaped, motionless and stunned, while the clutch of guests at my side disbanded. They flowed easily back to their tables or the dance floor, seemingly satisfied with the dramatic resolution.

I, on the other hand, wanted to know what on earth had gotten into Hank and why Jack had pushed him.

I grabbed a case of champagne from the walk-in refrigerator and headed back up front to see if Dot had heard anything.

She lifted her eyebrows when I approached. "Did you see the groom, the bride, her bridesmaids, and Hank blow out of here?"

"Yep." I set the box on the bar. "Any chance someone has had anything to say about it? Like what happened? What started it? Or how Hank is involved?"

"Nope."

I bit my bottom lip, torn. I hated to get involved in something that was clearly none of my business, but I also didn't want the dispute to end in fisticuffs on Granny's property. Then the sheriff would hear about it, or worse, come out to deal with it himself, and my cider shop might get a bad reputation for being a rumble spot. "I'm going to find out what happened."

Dot grinned. "Good luck."

I hurried outside before the group got too far away or the men started fighting again. The night beyond the bustling barn was quiet. No signs of anyone, just innumerable stars in an inky black sky and the scents of spring flowers on the air.

I tried not to think about the meaning behind Dot's silly smile. I supposed she thought I was nosy, but I was the hostess. I had an obligation to see that the guests were all right.

I slowed as a familiar truck tore out of the parking lot, tossing loose stones and kicking up tufts of grass in its wake.

*Hank.*

I sighed. At least if he was gone, he couldn't cause another commotion, but I would've liked to ask him a few questions. I turned back for the barn, moderately disappointed. Why had he argued with Jack

Warren? Had they even known one another before tonight? I pulled my phone from my pocket. I could always give Hank a call to make sure he was okay. If he felt like talking about what had happened, all the better.

A bloodcurdling scream froze me in place and stilled my thumb above the phone's illuminated face. My heart seized briefly before jolting me into a sprint.

"Help!" a chorus of women cried as I rounded the barn toward the bulbous old farm truck I'd decorated as the bride and groom's getaway vehicle. Tin cans littered the ground behind the idling truck, each tied to the rear bumper with twine. The words *Just Married* were scripted across the back window.

A line of bawling bridesmaids stood before the hood. Their faces jerked uniformly in my direction as I skidded to a stop.

"What's wrong?" I asked, forcing an encouraging smile.

Their gazes swept silently away, turning their collective attention to the ground before them and the idling truck.

I crept forward, drawn by quiet sobs and a fist of apprehension clenching in my stomach.

Elsie was sprawled on the ground in a heap of white satin, her narrow body trembling with every gut-wrenching cry. "Help him! Please! Help him!" Her desperate fingers clawed at a pair of shiny white shoes and matching tuxedo pants just visible beneath the truck's rusted old bumper.

# Chapter Two

I moved slowly through the clusters of reception guests gathered outside my open barn doors. The sheriff had divided folks into groups, then assigned his deputies to interview and dismiss them. Dot and I had decided to divide and conquer as well. I'd chosen to help the outdoor guests while Dot remained inside. Mostly, we were handing out bottled water and eavesdropping, but given the situation, our behavior seemed excusable.

"Water?" I offered the next group waiting to speak with a deputy. They waved me off, and I turned slowly away, surveying the scene. I waited for them to resume their conversation, and I wasn't surprised when they did. So far, the same sentiments were present on every guest's lips.

*I just can't believe this is happening. Who would do something like this? And on his wedding day!*

Hopefully Dot was having better luck inside.

I set my tub of water bottles on the ground after

making my rounds. "Feel free to help yourselves," I told the nearest guests.

Several people nodded in acknowledgment.

I selected a bottle from the melting ice and headed toward the sheriff.

He stood hands-on-hips, scrutinizing the cloud of remaining guests as I approached. Sheriff Wise was toned and bronzed from his love of the outdoors, tall and lean by nature, and handsome to a fault. I could only attribute that kind of luck to award-winning genes. At five-foot-four with an average face and build, I hadn't been as lucky.

"Water?" I asked, raising the drink in Colton's direction.

He accepted after a long, slow appraisal that started at my head and ended at my toes. "Pretty dress," he said, returning his eyes to mine.

"Thanks. Nice hat."

He touched the brim of his big sheriff's hat with a fingertip and smiled. "You don't think it's too much? It came with the outfit, but I wasn't sure."

I smiled.

In addition to being fit and fine, Colton Wise was charming, thirty-four, and single, a rare combination in our town and it hadn't gone unnoticed. Superficial facts aside, he'd also done some impressive things before settling in Blossom Valley last year. Three tours with the marines, a stint as a detective in Clarksburg, and participation in a joint task force that worked with the FBI for starters.

I tried not to envy his genes or success, though I wouldn't have minded being a little taller. My height had some serious disadvantages for a gal who wasn't a fan of ladders. "Any luck with the guests' interviews?"

"None." He opened the bottle and drained half its contents before stopping to take a breath. "What about you?"

I pulled my chin back. "What about me? You interviewed me first." I hadn't known much then, and I hadn't learned anything since.

"I saw you pretending to hand out waters," he said. "What'd you hear?"

"Nothing," I squeaked. "I wasn't pretending."

Colton didn't look convinced.

My shoulders sagged. "Fine. I was listening, but I didn't hear anything new or useful," I admitted. "Apparently everyone here thought Jack was a saint, and they're all equally shocked by his murder."

"What did you think of him?" he asked.

I blew out a long breath, unsure. "Honestly, I barely spoke to him. I worked with Elsie and her mom to organize the wedding. I didn't meet Jack until this morning. We were both too busy for more than a quick greeting and a handshake."

Colton finished the water, then crossed his arms. "Let's go another route. In our initial interview, we talked about the moments surrounding Elsie's scream. Maybe you should tell me what else you remember about tonight. Anything unusual about Jack or Elsie's behavior that made you take notice."

I considered the question, easily recalling Jack's ruddy face and slack posture, then his outburst in the loft. The way he'd withdrawn from the party to argue with Hank, then stormed off when they were interrupted. "I saw Jack drinking from a flask and picking fights tonight," I started. "I had champagne and cider cocktails available, but he must've wanted something stronger. I saw Elsie and her bridesmaids follow him outside. I heard her scream a short while later."

Colton raised his attention to the barn several yards away.

I turned to follow his gaze.

Elsie sat blank-faced on a chair inside. Her elegant updo was a disheveled mess. Gnarled fingers of black mascara stretched over her cheeks to her chin. Her designer gown was filthy, littered with bits of dried grass and dirt from where she'd eventually passed out beside her husband's body. Thankfully, the paramedics had gotten her up and into a chair for an exam.

"Has she said anything?" Colton asked. "Given some kind of reason or excuse for his behavior? Made any speculation about who would want to hurt him?"

"No," I said. "She was barely coherent when I found her, then she fainted. EMTs treated her for shock and now she's like that." I lifted a hand in her direction, indicating the distant, unseeing expression on Elsie's face.

I turned back to Colton, curious again. "She was alone when she found him," I said, repeating information from our initial interview. This time, I watched him more carefully, gauging his reaction. "Her bridesmaids said they arrived seconds before me but after the scream."

I didn't mean to make assumptions, especially

since I knew firsthand that finding a body didn't make someone a killer, but wasn't the spouse usually the main suspect? Wasn't there a small possibility that Elsie's reaction to Jack's death wasn't strictly made of grief? Couldn't there be a truckload of guilt in there too? "I wonder if Elsie lashed out at him and did something she couldn't take back?"

Colton shifted his weight. "Anything's possible. For now, I'd like a written statement from you."

"Of course."

An image of Hank swam before my eyes. The way he'd pushed his finger at Jack's face had frightened me a little, and the way he'd run off moments before Jack's body had been discovered hadn't made me feel any better. As much as I hated to think that someone I'd once loved was capable of hurting another human being like this, I couldn't ignore the facts or my lingering questions about his quick departure. "Colton?"

A pair of headlight beams flashed over us before he could answer. The little pickup rocked to a stop several feet away and Granny jumped out. "Heavens!" she called, hustling in my direction. "What on earth is going on?" Her dark brown eyes were wide with fear and she opened her arms as she ran, ready to draw me in.

Granny's friend Delilah hurried around from the driver's side. "Was someone hurt?" Delilah asked, her naturally husky voice in direct contrast to her tiny stature.

"I'm okay," I said, not completely sure the words were true.

Granny stroked my hair while Delilah patted my back. The pair had met in elementary school then lost touch after high school when Delilah married a military man and began to journey around the world. Delilah had returned to town a few months ago, following the loss of her husband. She and Granny had been thick as thieves ever since. A fair expression given that the pair usually looked as if they were up to something.

Colton gave them a rundown on the situation and Granny went still as stone.

I squeezed her arm in reassurance. "I'm okay," I promised.

She released me suddenly and pressed her fingers against her lips. "I saw the emergency lights and all I could think of was—"

"I know," I whispered, fighting my own horrible memories of the night *I'd* faced a killer.

I'd been luckier than Jack.

Granny wiped her eyes and straightened on a deep inhalation of breath. "What can we do?" She moved to stand with Delilah. They were dressed in matching blue and gold T-shirts. TWISTED THREADS, the name of their needlepointing crew, had been meticulously stitched across the front. Both women had arranged their hair in loose buns and their jeans were dark and bootcut. Basically, they were adorable, but outfits aside, they were opposites in the extreme. Granny was all heart with shocks of gray through her dark brown hair and eyes that always looked innocent to folks who didn't know better.

Delilah was no nonsense, narrow as a matchstick

with a sleek silver bob and sharp blue eyes. After forty or so years as a military wife, she wasn't to be trifled with despite her diminutive size. "Maybe we can help in the barn while Winnie and the sheriff investigate," she suggested.

Colton turned hard eyes on her. "Actually, I've got things covered here. Winnie's going to give me a written statement, then she's leaving. You can wait for her at your place."

I bristled at his tone and bit my tongue against the urge to tell him I did what I wanted.

The lingering concern in Granny's eyes cooled my temper. "He's right," I said. "The last time I tried to help, I wound up causing trouble."

Delilah's thin silver brows drew together. "That's not how I heard it."

Colton shifted. "Exactly how did you hear it?"

The older women exchanged a look.

Granny moved her attention to me. "We'd better go."

"You'll walk her home, won't you sheriff?" Delilah asked. "There's a killer on the loose after all."

I lifted a palm. "I can get there on my own. Whoever did this to Jack probably doesn't know I exist. I don't have any reason to worry."

Granny frowned. "Well, at least have Hank walk you."

My lids closed automatically. When I opened them, Colton had one brow raised. "Where is Hank?"

"Hmm?" I asked, instinctively buying some time.

"Uh-oh," Granny muttered, clearly recognizing my tell. She grabbed Delilah's arm. "We'll come and pick you up when you're ready, Winona Mae.

Just let us know. Good night, Sheriff," she called as they ran away.

Colton took a step in my direction. "You're hiding something."

Delilah's truck revved to life, and an image of Hank driving wildly out of the parking area rushed back to mind, along with a new question. "How did the killer get a key to the getaway truck?" I asked. It wasn't as if the vehicle could've started on its own. A jolt of realization shot through me. "The best man was the designated getaway driver," I spun in search of him among the remaining guests. "Have you spoken with him? His name is Aaron. He had the key."

Colton nodded slowly. "I have."

I waited for him to say more, but he didn't. "The best man is the only one who could've started the truck," I said. "If he isn't the killer, then surely he knows who had the key." I tried to imagine the tall, attractive man from the dance floor as a killer, but failed.

"The key was left in the truck," Colton said flatly, his blue eyes narrowing. "Caught between the visor and the roof. Any other theories you'd like me to follow up on for you?"

I gave him my business face. "Actually, yes."

"Sheriff!" A man called from the distance, turning our faces in his direction. A portly deputy in his late fifties crossed the space between us at a clip, his short strides covering ground much faster than I would have imagined possible.

Colton lifted his chin when the deputy arrived. "What do you have?"

The man glanced at me. His badge said Lehman, but he didn't say anything before angling his back to me and leaning conspiratorially toward Colton.

I recognized Deputy Lehman from the diner. Apple fritter, coffee with cream and sugar, five days a week. He always sat in Reese's section.

"Lehman?" Colton prodded.

Lehman gave me a look over his shoulder, then lowered his voice as he spoke. "I gathered statements from the bridal party," he said under his breath. "Several of them claimed to have seen the groom arguing with Hank Donovan tonight, and the best man thinks he saw Hank leaving the party just before Elsie screamed."

I groaned, and the men looked at me. "Sorry. I thought that was internal."

Colton pressed his lips into a thin white line and his face went red. Frustration and betrayal darkened his eyes.

"I was going to tell you," I said.

Colton pulled a set of keys from his pocket. "You and I are going to talk later. Right now I need Hank Donovan's address."

I rattled off the street name and house number, then watched as Colton climbed into his cruiser and reversed out of the lot.

I headed back to the barn, dialing Hank's number as I went.

My stomach tightened as voicemail picked up. The creeping notion that Hank could have gotten himself into something big and dangerous was taking root in my mind. He didn't have to be the killer to have reason to run. Maybe he'd seen the killer and that person went after Hank!

I left a voicemail asking Hank to call me, then I went to take a look at the crime scene.

A pair of spotlights had been erected near the truck, illuminating the space alongside the barn. Jack's body was gone, already removed by the coroner, but the truck was still there. A man in a black windbreaker and blue latex gloves was crouched outside the open driver's-side door, scanning the floor mats and dashboard with a small handheld light. Processing the crime scene. I'd seen it done before on television, and once in the outbuilding where Granny kept the cider press.

I ducked under the yellow crime scene tape, dragged along by my insatiable curiosity and the need to help any way I could. I cleared my throat when I got close.

The man started, then stretched onto his feet.

"How's it going?" I asked. "Anything I can do?"

"You're not supposed to be on this side of the tape," he said, looking wholly confused. "How did you get back here?"

I gave the flimsy plastic barrier a skeptical look before extending my hand in apology. "Sorry," I said. "I'm Winnie. I own the cider shop. I just wondered if I could be helpful. Maybe get you a bottle of water?"

"Wayne," he said, accepting the handshake. "I'm fine. Thank you. No water."

"Have we met before?" I guessed, suddenly certain we had, though I couldn't recall how.

Wayne's gaze flicked briefly away. "I believe we met last fall. Inside your press house."

I cringed. "Right." He'd processed the scene of the last body I'd found too. I took a step back, prepared to leave the ugly memories behind, when my gaze caught on the driver's seat. "Did you roll that seat forward?" I asked, moving around him for a closer look. There was a distinctive gap between the back rest and rear window. There was no way anyone as tall as the average man could've been behind the wheel. His knees would've been pressed against the dash.

Wayne bobbed back into view, opening his arms and wedging himself between me and the open truck door. "I'm sorry, Winnie, but you need to get behind the yellow line." His brows furrowed with uncertainty. "I'm not trying to give you trouble," he said. "It's the same for everyone. Authorized personnel only back here. Plus, Sheriff Wise gave explicit instructions."

I made a sour face, but flipped my hands up in surrender. "I understand. Sorry for overstepping. I'll see myself out."

Wayne relaxed visibly. "Thanks. I appreciate that."

I hurried back the way I'd come, feeling hopeful but agitated. Hopeful because the fact that the truck's seat was so close to the steering wheel confirmed there was no way Hank could have been driving. Agitated because the look on Wayne's face suggested that Sheriff Wise's "explicit instructions" had included my name, specifically.

I rounded the corner and darted into the cider shop.

Dot took notice immediately and filled a flute with champagne as I approached. "Well?" she asked, pushing the drink in my direction. "Did you learn anything out there?"

I lifted one finger while I gulped the bubbly drink.

Feeling slightly less frantic, I gave Dot the skinny on all I knew, which was admittedly not much. "Hank ran off and I don't know why. He's not answering his phone, so I can't ask him. And Colton heard about Hank's fight with Jack, so he went to find him."

Dot's stared, open-mouthed. "Do you think Hank had something to do with what happened to Jack?"

"I'm not sure." I finished the champagne, then shook my head. "I don't think Hank's a killer, but he was darn cozy with that bridesmaid earlier, and I think it was a woman driving the truck."

"Really?" Dot asked, moving in close. "You think it might've been the blonde bridesmaid?"

The best man appeared in the threshold of the open barn doors before I could answer, then he made his way in our direction.

He dropped his bowtie on the bar and unfastened two buttons of his tuxedo shirt. "Hit me." He tapped the counter then collapsed onto the stool beside mine.

Dot set a flute of champagne in front of him. "You okay?" she asked.

"Nope." He raised the glass in a silent toast, then sipped the contents.

The pained expression on his face broke my heart. I couldn't imagine losing Dot, especially not like this. I swiveled to face him and worked up an encouraging smile. "I'm not sure if you remember, but we met this morning. I helped you with your boutonniere. I'm Winnie. This is Dot."

He nodded. "I remember. I'm Aaron."

"Nice to meet you," Dot said softly.

I wasn't sure where he was from, but his slightly too long blond hair and striking blue eyes suggested it was somewhere in my dreams. He carried himself like a professional, but his confident gait and posture screamed athlete.

"I'm sorry about what happened," I told him. "You and Jack must've been close."

"We were college roommates," he said, winding long fingers around the narrow flute. "I can't believe he's dead," he whispered, more to himself than to Dot or me. His gaze fixed, unseeing, on the sparkling champagne, and he pulled in a ragged breath.

Dot passed him a napkin.

He raised his eyes to hers, confused. "Who do you think could have done something like this?"

She shook her head. "I don't know, but Jack will get justice. You can count on that."

Aaron frowned. "How?"

"The local sheriff and his deputies are very good." I said.

Dot wrinkled her nose. "That's true. Plus Winnie and I will do all we can to help out. We were here when it happened, and between the two of us we know just about everyone in town. Plus Winnie helped crack another murder case last Christmas, so she has experience."

Aaron's brows knitted tightly, obviously processing her insane declaration. "I thought you guys planned weddings."

"No. This is my cider shop," I corrected. "Elsie

and her mother rented it for the wedding. I helped coordinate the details. Dot's a park ranger."

He turned back to his champagne, understandably confused by my muddy distinction.

"Never mind that," I said, shooting Dot a warning look. "I'm going to check on the remaining guests and see if there's anything I can do to make them more comfortable."

I slid off my stool and stepped away. "Holler if you need anything." I walked backward until I caught Dot's eye over Aaron's shoulder. Then I sawed a finger across my throat a few times, hoping she'd get the message. She and I had no business making promises to a grieving man, especially ones we couldn't keep. Plus, Colton would have six consecutive strokes if he thought I was investigating another murder. I'd nearly gotten myself killed last time.

I moved into the recesses of the barn, away from listening ears, and dialed Hank.

I bit my lip as I waited for the call to connect. What was Colton saying to him? What had Hank seen or heard that made him run?

Several rings later, his voicemail picked up.

I glanced at the handful of guests beyond the open doors. I should probably have made my rounds again, offering cold water and warm condolences, but I didn't have it in me. The one who really needed my help was Hank, and he was in trouble. I could feel it in my bones.

I dialed his phone twice more with the same outcome. Hank wasn't picking up, and Colton hadn't returned.

I gnawed the tender skin along my thumbnail and paced, nervous habits I'd acquired after my too-recent near-death experience.

Questions piled on my heart and constricted my chest. What had happened tonight? And why? Had Colton arrested Hank? Did he deserve it?

I needed answers. I was helpless without them.

But I refused to stay that way for long.

# Chapter Three

I walked myself home after the last guest and deputy had gone. I didn't bother calling Granny like she'd suggested. I'd made the quarter-mile walk across the orchard from my cider shop to my home many times, and I trusted the grassy moonlit lane to get me there again tonight. Plus, I needed the exercise and silence. I had a lot to process.

The night was beautiful, warm and eerily quiet after the long day of controlled chaos and a horrific tragedy. I savored the sounds of a distant owl, of crickets and bullfrogs singing the evening score. I sipped the sweet mountain air and tried to be "in the moment." That was what all the stress relief websites had suggested I do last month when I'd struggled through the pressure of finals. After taking classes one by one, all year round, for a decade, I was finally a senior. I'd planned to catch my breath during the two weeks before my summer class started, but it seemed like plans had changed. Now I had another murder on my hands.

Not *on my hands* exactly, but in my lap for sure. Outside *my* barn and during a wedding reception *I'd* hosted. Worse, it looked as if my ex-boyfriend Hank had played some role in the mess. I took a series of deep breaths. In through my nose. Out through my mouth. Then I sent Colton a quick text to see if he'd arrested Hank. Colton was notoriously tight-lipped about his investigations, but arrests were public record, so he had no reason not to answer me. I stared at the little screen.

Colton didn't respond.

I gripped my forehead and tried to refocus on the gorgeous summer night, but a wave of intuition set my senses on alert. I picked up my pace as fear settled in.

Granny's modest farmhouse was aglow up ahead, complete with a gleaming porch light and faux candle in every window. Delilah's truck waited patiently in the drive. Across the field, my home was dark. I'd forgotten to turn the porch light on when I left this morning, and I hadn't been back since.

I slowed my approach as intuition came again, this time whispering against the nape of my neck in the dark. Suddenly whatever awaited me in the shadows of my porch seemed a whole lot less scary than whatever was causing the fine hairs on my arms to stand at attention. I hurried up the steps, key in hand and ready to dart inside. Something moved on the wicker chair beside the door and I stifled a scream. An orange cat arched and yawned then leapt at my feet and waited by the door.

"Kenny Rogers!" I laughed in relief. "Are you trying to give me a heart attack?"

His sister, Dolly, appeared a moment later, and the pair circled my legs as I unlocked the door. I reached inside to flip the switches on the wall before entering. The porch and kitchen lights snapped on simultaneously, and I followed the cats inside.

I secured the deadbolt, then flicked on the television, desperate for familiar white noise.

Kenny Rogers and Dolly called to me from the kitchen, mewing and pawing at the lidded container where I kept their kibble.

Dot had rescued the kittens from the national park last fall after finding them with their fatally injured mother and siblings. The kittens had been only about six weeks old and still transitioning from their mama's milk to solid foods when Dot convinced me to take them in. The decision hadn't been hard. She'd named them both Kenny Rogers, after her favorite singer of all time. It was the same name she gave every animal that came into her possession. Dot was on a mission to find every injured or abandoned animal in West Virginia a forever home, and calling one name at meal times was easier than calling two dozen. Plus the generic moniker helped keep her from getting too attached. I owed her one more adoption after a promise I'd made at Christmastime while trying to do three nice things in a pay-it-forward move. I could only imagine what she might deliver to my doorstep next.

"There," I said, filling the little bowls and stroking their fur as they ate. "Eat up, then let's snuggle. I've had a day."

I tossed my keys onto the counter and kicked off my shoes. I sent Granny a text to let her know

I'd made it home safely, then collapsed onto the couch, thankful to sit down. I'd finally convinced Granny to get a cell phone last month, and every time I didn't have to track her down on the twenty-five-acre grounds, I was thankful. The fact she enjoyed texting was all the better.

Grampy had converted the old outbuilding for me when I'd decided to save money by commuting to college rather than moving away. Attending the local community college instead of a major university had allowed me to work full time at the diner around my class schedule and pay cash for my classes instead of going into debt. Living at the orchard had meant I could help my grandparents as needed and that Granny hadn't been alone after Grampy died. There was no price tag for that.

My phone buzzed with a text and I dropped it on the floor trying to turn it over and see who it was. Was it Hank saying he was okay? Was it Colton saying he'd arrested Hank?

The message was from Granny. I swiped the screen and sighed. She thanked me for letting her know I was safe and wished me sweet dreams.

I tossed the phone onto my coffee table and tucked my feet beneath me on the cushion. I hated having questions without answers. It didn't make sense for Hank to argue with Jack. They didn't even know each other before tonight. And what was Jack's problem anyway? This should've been the happiest day of his life, but instead he'd been miserable, and he'd brought a flask! Clearly whatever was bothering him had started before he'd dressed for the ceremony.

Assuming I was right about a woman being behind the wheel of the truck tonight, it seemed possible that infidelity had been a possible motive in Jack's death. Maybe Jack had been caught cheating and Elsie found out. She might've been mad enough to run him down, or maybe she'd known and forgiven him, but the other woman wasn't happy to see him wed.

Kenny Rogers leapt onto the couch and rubbed his face against my cheek. I stroked his fur and let my eyes close. Dolly stretched out along the back of the couch and chewed my hair.

I pulled the locks away and groaned as they fell past my nose. No wonder Dolly was after me. I smelled like fried chicken, not to mention a hearty mix of all the other dishes I'd helped serve at the reception dinner. Barbecue ribs. Roasted potatoes. Baked macaroni and cheese.

I forced myself upright and headed for the shower.

My mind and muscles unwound easily in the steamy heat, quickly replaced by utter exhaustion. I toweled off, feeling lighter and smelling less like fried foods, then took my time preparing for bed. I applied body lotion and night cream at a snail's pace. Blow-dried my hair to ten times its natural size. Then slid into my comfiest cotton pajamas and went to make a cup of hot tea.

The cats were curled together on the couch when I returned. Two ginger lumps atop my favorite patchwork quilt. I longed to join them and cuddle until morning, but I also wanted to crawl into bed and sleep like a starfish. I decided to make the decision after tea.

My living space was bright and cheery, drenched in a rainbow of colors, patterns, and fabrics. It raised my spirits to look at, which was exactly the point. I wanted anyone who entered to feel welcomed and encouraged, as if the room had given them a hug. That was the way people felt at Granny's house, though it helped that she literally hugged everyone who entered.

I lumbered into the kitchen and hopped when a clump of something stuck to the bottom of my bare foot. I shook it off with a groan. "Kenny," I whined. "Dolly. That had better have been dirt from outside and not from your litterbox." I gagged internally at the unpleasant possibility, then stepped on another hunk of something dark and cool. "What the devil?" I crouched to inspect the mess and clean my floor. Bits of compressed dirt dotted my otherwise clean linoleum. I gave the sleeping kittens a long look. Had they been *this* dirty when I'd let them in tonight? I stretched to my feet and headed for the broom closet.

The distinct creak of a porch floorboard stopped me mid-step. The sensation of being watched returned, and fear gripped my heart.

Beyond the window, a storm was brewing. Trees swung their branches in the moonlight and wind ruffled my curtains. A jolt of panic squeezed my heart as I watched the sheer fabric dancing against the glass. I hadn't opened my window.

I shut and locked the frame in one fluid movement then yanked Louisa, my prized Louisville Slugger, from her corner beside my front door. Louisa had taken me through four seasons of baseball on the boys' all-state team and put me in the local record book for most high school home runs.

I had no doubt she'd take me straight through anyone who got in her path.

I dialed Colton's number, then hesitated, hover-
ing my thumb over the screen without pressing
SEND. Colton hadn't answered my text before. What
made me think he would answer now? Maybe I
should call the sheriff's department's main line instead? Or 911? Or maybe no one at all. What exactly did I plan to report? That I had two outdoor
cats and found a little dirt on my floor? Or that my
kitchen window was open, but only by a crack? Was
I positive I hadn't forgotten to close it the last time
it was open? The way I'd forgotten to turn on my
porch light? I wouldn't have called the sheriff over
these things before today.

I rolled my shoulders then shook out the tension in my arms and hands. Someone had died on
my property a few hours ago, awful, yes, but I hadn't
known him. I had no reason to be afraid that I
would be targeted next. Whoever had a beef with
Jack had nothing to do with me.

I hoped.

Still, I found my feet carrying me toward the
door instead of taking me through the house to
check for intruders. My toes hit the cool porch
planks, and I spun for Granny's house, gripping
Louisa to one shoulder and pressing the phone to
my opposite ear.

My heart pumped wildly as I sprinted across the
field, listening to long bleating rings on Colton's
end of the line.

A new and terrifying possibility hit like a load of
bricks crashing through my mind. What if I'd been

right about Hank being a witness? What if he'd seen what happened to Jack and was in life-threatening trouble now too? *Killers weren't big on leaving witnesses,* I reasoned, *and they probably weren't fans of nosy women who asked too many questions and confronted the crime scene crew either.*

"Granny!" I screamed, taking her porch steps two at a time. "Grann—"

The door swung open and Granny appeared with Delilah close at her side. "Winnie?"

I jumped into her kitchen and pressed the door shut behind me.

Then turned and stared through the window in horror as a shadow moved into the tree line beside my house.

# Chapter Four

Twenty minutes later, I was curled on the same kitchen chair I'd escaped to for meals, homework, and comfort all my life. I sipped a steamy mug of sassafras tea while Granny and Delilah stood watch at the front window.

"I don't understand what's taking so long," Granny complained. "How much time can it take to check one little house for burglars?"

Delilah glared through the glass at her side. "Ridiculous. I could've cleared the entire area ten times already and I'm twice that man's age."

I traced a fingertip around the rim of my mug, feeling strangely numb. The result of a past trauma and too many competing emotions, I assumed. I wanted to concentrate on the moment and breathe, but my brain refused to focus at all. Despite the familiar sights, scents, and sounds of Granny's kitchen, I was mentally adrift.

My gaze skated across brightly painted cabinets

and shelves stuffed with mismatched plates and bowls. A refrigerator papered in my old drawings and outlined with recent dean's list certificates. My eight-year-old fingerprints smudged permanently into baseboard paint. My miniature handprints fossilized in the cement countertop. Rows of cookbooks and walls of framed photos. Granny and Grampy. My mother. Me. The story of my life was written in this room, on the chipped cups I'd dropped and in the grooved floorboards beneath my feet, carved slowly by two dozen years of restless nights of heartache or homework.

I pushed the last shortbread cookie between my lips and wondered how long my strangely disconnected mood would last.

"You doing okay, Winnie?" Granny asked, turning to check on me from her guard post at the door.

"Yep." I sucked crumbs from my fingertips and took another long drink of steaming tea.

What had I really seen out there? Did a shadow move away from my home, or had the reception's nightmarish events and a brewing storm played tricks on my mind? Couldn't a swaying tree easily throw shadows in the moonlight? Couldn't fear make a person see, say, or do almost anything?

"Finally!" Granny huffed. She set her beloved rifle, Bessy, back into position by the door, then swept the barrier open.

Sheriff Wise strode inside. "Ladies." He gripped his big hat to his chest and nodded as he moved.

"Well?" Granny asked. "What did you find?"

My stomach rolled in anticipation. Which would it be? An intruder? Or paranoia? I wasn't sure which to hope for. I was too young to lose my mind but didn't particularly want to be murdered either.

Colton approached me slowly, ignoring Granny's question for the moment. He crouched before my chair and scanned my tear-stained face with kind and knowing eyes. "How are you holding up?"

*Not great*, I thought. I'd fled my home, barefoot and in my high school gym clothes, possibly for no reason, then I'd eaten my weight in shortbread. "Great."

His lips twitched at one side. "Good. May I?" he motioned to the chair beside mine.

I nodded, and he sat, upturning his hat on the table.

Granny and Delilah joined us with another tray of cookies and a hot cup of tea for the sheriff. "Sheriff Wise?" Granny pressed. "You want to tell us just what the devil is going on?"

"Was someone in Winnie's home tonight or not?" Delilah asked.

I waited, breath held and lungs burning, for the answer.

Colton swept his gaze over the other women before setting his attention back on me. "I didn't find anyone in your home."

Breath whooshed from my chest, and I realized I would rather be losing my mind than in bodily danger. Lots of crazy people lived long, full lives.

"All the windows and doors were closed, nothing was out of place," he continued. "I took your keys from the kitchen counter before I left, and I locked up on my way out. I'll walk you home when you're ready, unless you'd feel more comfortable staying somewhere else tonight."

Granny gripped my hand across the table. "You're always welcome here. You know that."

"I'll stay too," Delilah said. "Your Granny has Bessy and I've got my Beretta in the glove box. We'll take turns keeping watch."

Colton whistled the sound of a falling missile. "That's a big no," he said flatly. "I can assign someone to keep watch over the property if you all feel that uncomfortable, but the last thing I need is a bunch of armed and antsy civilians staying up all night expecting trouble. That's how folks get shot."

Delilah leveled him with a stare. Whatever she was thinking, she kept it to herself.

Granny folded her hands. "Then tell us what we can do. Surely there's something."

"You're already doing it," he said. "Remaining calm is paramount. I also have a couple lingering questions. Where were you today while the reception was going on?"

I turned to look at Colton. The question sounded suspiciously accusatory.

"We were in Morgantown," Granny said. "At the Knitwits convention. They put us up at the Motel 6 all week and gave us a table at the event to showcase our needlepoint."

"You weren't around at all today?"

"No. We were traveling." Granny looked from Colton to me, then back. "I wanted to be here to help, but my plans to attend the convention were in place long before Elsie Sawyer decided to get married at my orchard."

He nodded. "I was hoping you might've seen

something everyone else missed. Maybe provide another perspective."

I sagged in relief, thankful he hadn't planned to accuse Granny of something crazy again.

"This is your work?" he asked, waving a hand at piles of their completed needlepoint stacked on the table.

Granny and Delilah had been sorting and organizing their remaining stock to see which patterns were sold out and which hadn't sold at all.

"That's right," Granny said, a punch of pride in her voice. Granny loved to quilt, sew, and perform any kind of needlework. It was a trade her mother and grandmother had taught her. One she'd tried to teach me, but the effort never took. I'd preferred to be outside with Grampy.

Colton tugged a stack of the thin white cloths in his direction and flipped through them.

Granny had grown up stitching Bible verses and proverbs, but times had changed, much to her dismay. People had different preferences and a collectively darker sense of humor these days. Meaning her perfectly executed floral borders no longer circled scripture.

"One cat short of crazy," he read, turning the product to face me. A small orange cat was stitched beside the words.

"And I already have two," I told him.

He showed me the next sample with a grin. A dainty wreath of purple posies surrounded five thick navy words. "Come back with a warrant."

I laughed.

"That one was a request," Granny said on a sigh.

She truly missed stitching nice things, but no one bought those anymore. "Viola Covington's grandson is attending the police academy in Winchester."

Colton set her work aside. "They're very good," he said. "The women in my family do their share of needlepoint as well. None as good as this."

Granny and Delilah sat a little taller.

My knee began to bob beneath the table and my spine stiffened. "Did you talk to Hank tonight?"

Something flashed in Colton's eyes. "No. Why?"

"What do you mean?" I mentally calculated the hours he'd been gone and refusing to answer his phone. Time had blurred after Elsie's scream, but that was just after nine and it was after midnight now. "I thought you went to his house to question him."

"I was unable to locate Hank Donovan," Colton said. "I'd planned to call you in the morning for ideas on where he might be."

"What do you mean you couldn't locate him?" My heart sputtered an erratic rhythm and my ears began to ring. "Trace his phone," I said. "Or his truck. He could be in trouble or hurt." *Or worse,* I thought, unable to speak the words.

Granny checked her watch. "It's late, but I could call his mother."

"No need," Colton said. "I've been there. She claims not to know where he is. Same for his sister." He turned cool blue eyes back on me. "And there's no need to track his phone or hunt down his truck. Both are at his house. Phone on the table, visible from the porch. Truck in the driveway."

I collapsed against the chair back. None of that made any sense. "Why would he leave without a vehicle or cell phone?"

"We think he's on the run," Colton said. "Witnesses saw him argue with the deceased and flee the scene of a murder. It's likely that he ran home to get a change of clothes, supplies, and cash, then left the phone and truck so he couldn't be followed."

"That's ridiculous." I planted my palms against the table. "He can't just live on the lam. Hank's not stupid. He knows that."

Colton watched me. Unmoved. "I don't expect someone like Hank to live off the land and sleep in caves. I think it's more likely he intends to solicit help while he formulates a plan."

He was right. Hank had grown up in Blossom Valley with the rest of us, but he'd always been more interested in celebrity gossip than camping. He was clever and ambitious, and he'd probably had a plan in place before he'd ever reached home tonight.

"I want you to help me find him," Colton said.

"What?" I squeaked.

"Your lifelong relationship with him and more recent romantic involvement give me reason to believe he'll reach out to you. I need you to let me know when he does."

Granny shifted in her seat, looking more than a little uncomfortable. She turned serious eyes on Colton. "Hank Donovan isn't a killer," she told him. "I understand things look bad right now, but I've known that boy all his life. He's a good kid who wouldn't break bad."

"Innocent people don't run," Colton said.

Delilah rubbed narrow fingers over thin lips. She knew the Donovans too. Had gone to school with Hank's grandma. "Something else is afoot here."

"He didn't do this," I whispered, unable to find my full voice.

"Maybe not," Colton allowed, "but I won't know until I talk with him, and right now he's nowhere to be found. I believe he'll contact you. I need to know when he does."

I wrapped trembling arms around my middle, numbness fading fast. The possibility that I was wrong about Hank sent ice shards through my veins. There had to be another explanation. "What if his truck and phone were left behind because the person who killed Jack came for Hank too?" I asked softly. "Maybe he saw something he shouldn't have."

"Unlikely," Colton said with his usual over-confidence. "His bedroom curtains weren't fully closed. I could see his closet doors were open, along with some drawers. He probably grabbed some essentials and took off. I doubt an abductor would've given him time to pack a bag."

I lifted my tepid tea in one shaky hand, gripping my middle more tightly with the other. My thoughts darted in a new direction, unable to deal with the possibility Hank was a killer. "You said no one was inside my home. Is it possible someone had been there and gone?"

"Yes." Colton nodded stiffly. "The place was empty when I arrived, but there was mud on the floor, windowsill, and porch."

Delilah scoffed. "Not a very cautious intruder."

Colton nodded. "Someone in a hurry, I would guess."

Anger sparked in my core. "When were you going to tell me?"

"I was getting there," he said. "I think your intruder was Hank."

"You said he'd reach out to me. Breaking into my place isn't how people make contact with one another. Besides, why would he come over, lurk around, scare the bejeezus out of me, then leave?"

"Maybe he changed his mind. Felt guilty for dragging you into his mess and decided not to get you involved yet. Maybe he used your place as a temporary hideout until my deputies left the grounds and the coast was clear. Maybe he was already gone when you got there. I don't know yet, but I will find out."

A small measure of relief swept through me. If Colton was right, then I wasn't crazy or in danger. I liked those possibilities a lot. "I think I'm ready to go home." If the house was clear and locked up, then there was no reason to stay with Granny, and Colton was getting under my skin again.

Three chairs scraped across the aged kitchen floor with mine. Granny and Delilah met me at the door.

Colton loomed silently behind us.

When I'd collected Louisa, kissed the women's cheeks, and stepped into the brewing storm, Colton was at my side.

"What are you doing?" I asked, pulling wind-blown hair from my face.

He lifted a hand. My key ring dangled from one finger.

"Oh." I marched woodenly forward, unwilling to reach for my keys, in fear he'd pull them away and make me kick him.

"You always run off, you know that?" he asked. "You get mad and leave, then I end up chasing after you."

"I don't want to fight with you."

"Then, let's start over because I have more questions for you, and I need you to see this as a conversation, not an argument."

I shot him a sideways look.

"Nice bat," he said.

"Thanks, but you don't have to make small talk. I get it. Just ask your questions."

Colton kept pace at my side. "Good, but I meant what I said about the bat. I love baseball. I didn't realize you were a fan."

I offered Louisa to him for inspection. "I took a play from Granny's book and got the bat out of storage. Now she stands by the front door in case I need protection."

Colton accepted the bat and gave her a few swings as we moved, then rolled her over to inspect the inscription branded into her. "State champs?"

"Mm-hmm. Not bad for a town with a four-digit population."

"Don't girls usually play softball?"

I stopped short and leveled him with a glare. "Yes, but Blossom Valley High didn't have enough girls to make a decent cheer squad let alone a whole sports team. If I wanted to play ball, I had to play with the boys, which meant I had to be twice as good so the coaches couldn't find a reason to keep me from making the team." Folks liked to say

I got a fair chance because our school was so equitable, but I knew it was because the guys wanted to win. Plus, I suspected a few had hoped we'd share a locker room.

"Impressive."

"Agreed," I said. I examined his carefully guarded expression in the moonlight. Something didn't feel right about him. There was more tension in his brow than usual and a fresh distance in his eyes. "Everything okay?" I asked.

"You mean besides today's murder?"

"Yeah." I cocked my head and narrowed my eyes. "There's something off about you. You're more brooding than usual, and you seem distracted. Why?"

He stole my signature move and started walking without me. "I don't know what you're talking about."

"So you admit it," I said, easily catching him as heat lightning flashed in the sky.

He didn't speak again until we'd reached my porch. He unlocked the door and motioned me inside. "Why don't you take a look around. See if anything is out of place, missing, or new."

"New?" I asked. "Like a present?

"Like a threat. In case I was wrong about who was in here."

I checked the rooms thoroughly, moved the shower curtain aside, and peeked behind my doors. "Nothing new or missing that I can see," I announced, making my way back to Colton.

He'd taken a seat on my couch, feet wide on the ground and forearms planted against his thighs. "I don't like this, Winnie."

"I could've been wrong," I admitted. "Maybe no

one was here. Maybe the shadow was a figment of my imagination."

"And the mud on your floor?"

I took a seat on the armchair across from him. "Cats?"

Colton shook his head, sharp blue eyes narrowed with concern.

"If you're right about Hank, then I was never in any danger."

"And if I was wrong?" He lifted dark eyes to mine.

I wet my lips, mind scrambling for a better option. "You interviewed reception guests, but Mrs. Sawyer gave an open invitation to the whole town. What if whoever killed Jack never stepped foot inside the barn? Maybe no one even knew the killer was here tonight."

Colton's head bobbed thoughtfully. "A crowd and music make good distractions."

I tried to imagine someone coming to a wedding with an intent to kill the groom, then happening upon him alone, outside, away from spying eyes. What were the odds? "This had to be a crime of passion," I said. "No one plans to hit another human with a truck outside a party. That would take too many stars aligning."

"Maybe. Maybe not," Colton said. "I've seen crimes far more convoluted than this one. The killer could have called Jack's cell phone to lure him outside or into position. Tech services is looking into it now, but the phone was damaged in the incident."

I wasn't convinced all that was necessary. "Have you spoken with the bride?" I asked. "She's the right size to have been behind the wheel, and she was the first on the scene of the murder."

Colton's eyes narrowed. "What do you mean, she's the right size?"

I bit my lower lip and braced myself for his complaints. "After you left to find Hank, I stopped to ask Wayne if I could get him anything, and I noticed the truck seat had been rolled forward." Which brought me full circle on another thought. "Hank couldn't have driven the truck like that."

Colton pulled his phone from his pocket and stared at the screen. "Doesn't mean he wasn't involved." He pushed onto his feet and headed for my front door. "I've got to go. Lock up behind me. Keep your bat by your bed and call if you need me."

"What happened?" I asked, hurrying behind him to the door. "Did they find Hank? Was someone else hurt?"

Colton tucked the phone into his pocket and ignored my questions. "Do me a favor," he said, "Don't open the cider shop tomorrow and try to keep folks away from the area."

"Of course." It would have been callous to go on so soon as if nothing had happened.

Wind rushed inside as Colton stepped onto the porch. Summer storms in Blossom Valley were torrential. They often caused flooding and lobbed limbs or treetops onto roads, houses, and powerlines. He popped the collar of his coat and stuffed his big hat onto his head. "I'll be back to take another look around the barn tomorrow. I meant what I said about locking up and calling if you need me."

His phone buzzed again, and he jogged down my steps and into the night.

I flipped the deadbolt, then triple-checked the locks on the back door and all the windows.

"Come on Dolly, Kenny Rogers," I called, shaking their treat bag and clutching my phone and Louisa to my chest. "We're all sleeping in my bed tonight."

I closed my curtains and wedged a chair against the bedroom door before locking it too.

I didn't know who'd been inside my house earlier, but no one was getting in tonight.

# Chapter Five

I dragged myself out of bed at dawn the next morning, cranky and exhausted. Each time I'd drifted off to sleep during the night, a random clap of thunder or flash of lightning jerked me awake once more. Add to that my already ragged nerves and a pair of cats sporadically racing over my head, and I'd given up all hope of rest.

I lumbered to the kitchen, then fed the cats while my coffee brewed. Several cups of liquid enthusiasm later, I was wide awake and anything seemed possible. I dressed in my softest pair of jean shorts and the red V-neck T-shirt I loved, then wondered what to do with myself. It was too early to intrude on Granny or head to the cider shop, especially considering I wasn't allowed to open for business today anyway. I scanned the room and decided there was plenty to do right where I was. I started with the kitchen, then moved systematically through my house, tidying and sprucing like it was a competition. I didn't stop until it looked like someone else lived there. After that I wrote out checks to pay my bills. Balanced my business accounts. Cuddled the cats, then made a second pot of coffee.

At well past ten, there was no more denying the obvious. It wasn't too early to go out. I was stalling. Avoiding the thing I'd been trying not to think about since I'd holed up in my room last night. I didn't want to go outside because the feeling of being watched was still with me. Regardless of the logic that swaying trees created shadows, I knew what I saw. Someone had been in my yard, moving away from my home and into the dense tree line.

From the looks of things outside my window, the storm had been more bark than bite. A few twigs and small branches were scattered over the ground, but the world was otherwise bright and dry. Good news for Colton's investigation and my nerves. The sooner he figured out what really happened last night, the better. Jack needed justice. His family needed closure, and I needed to know I hadn't once been in love with a man who'd willingly live on the run and was wanted for questioning in a murder. So far that last one wasn't looking good.

My stomach tightened as selfish fears of my cider shop's demise came to mind. That shop meant everything to me. It was my dream business and the reason the orchard had stayed out of foreclosure. I'd even sold two of Grampy's prized Mustangs for the money to renovate the barn. Losing business over a second murder on orchard property, one right outside my cider shop doors, would ruin everything. How could Granny and I even come back from a black spot like this? What if my dream was over and I'd barely gotten started?

I poured another cup of coffee, then dialed Hank's number on autopilot, I hung up when I remembered he'd left his phone behind. The mounting questions returned and poured over me like an avalanche. Why would Hank intentionally abandon his phone? Had he been abducted? Was he in cahoots with a killer or hiding from one?

I'd spent half my sleepless night speculating to the point I worried I might go mad.

I pressed the refilled mug to my lips and let my gaze wander to my window.

Outside, a pair of finches landed on the narrow perch circling my cylindrical bird feeder. The unit swayed with their weight, dangling securely from a hook on my porch roof. They pecked merrily at the food until they'd drawn the attention of several others like them. It was a relaxing sight, until my attention drifted to the tree line beyond.

My thoughts traveled instantly back to the movement I'd seen in the dark last night. Even now, in the sunlight there seemed to be an unusual shape tucked among the thick leafy branches. Something human-like leaning against a tree trunk, motionless and still. I stared. Waiting for the strange shape to move, willing my eyes to discern it clearly, and praying it wasn't a killer. I rubbed my eyes and looked again. A small glow appeared near the shape in question along with spots from pressing my eyes too hard.

I shut the curtains and took a step back. Familiar fingers of dread tickled a path down my spine.

Maybe it was time to visit Colton and his deputies at the cider shop. I could offer them something to drink or snack on, then see if one of them wanted to check the tree line near my home for evidence of a creeping stalker.

I tugged worn-out canvas sneakers onto my bare feet and headed for the door.

A broad shadow appeared on my porch and I stumbled backward, as the breath caught in my throat. The shadow grew nearer, broader, taller. Then knocked.

I crept forward, hoping anyone who'd come to kill me wouldn't be polite enough to knock. Just in case, I pressed my back to the wall beside the door and used one fingertip to pull the curtain carefully away from the window.

A massive bouffant of platinum blonde hair came into view and my heart rate plummeted back to normal. I'd only ever known three people to have hair like that. Marie Antoinette, Dolly Parton, and Gina Donovan, Hank's little sister. None of those women would want to hurt me, and I suspected I knew which one it was. The woman suddenly spun in my direction and Gina's wide blue eyes met mine. "Open up!"

"Sorry!" I called, springing into action and hauling open the door. "I wanted to see who was out there first."

"Well, it's me," she said, marching into my living room on four-inch heels and collapsing onto the couch. "I can't believe what's happening with Hank. It's absolutely bonkers." Her pale blue eyes were rimmed in red, and I guessed her night hadn't been much better than mine. She gnawed her petal pink lips and fussed with the hem of her vintage sun-dress where it fell across her knees. "I've just come from church and everyone's talking about last night."

I took the seat across from her, unsure how to respond. In my sleep-deprived state I'd completely forgotten it was Sunday, but Sundays were good news. Granny and her ladies faithfully attended weekly worship services at the chapel, and they were sure to have some fresh gossip when they returned. I made a mental note to visit her after lunch. In my experience, most gossip was rooted in truth, then twisted and manipulated, sure, but if there was a chance someone knew something about what had happened last night, I wanted to know. That original truth could be the nugget I needed to find Hank. "Can I get you anything?" I asked Gina.

"I'd love to know where my brother is," she said with a sniffle. "Otherwise, no."

It was hard to believe the poised young woman before me had been an extremely awkward teen. In fact, it wasn't until Hank and I had started dating that she'd broken free of her ugly duckling stage and turned into a swan almost overnight. She'd taken an interest in photography, which had led to research on fashion and eventually to hours of playing with her hair and makeup as a creative outlet. She'd excelled at all of it, but most importantly, she'd stopped letting boys' comments about her lack of curves hurt her. Instead, she'd started standing taller and embracing the runway model's figure she'd been blessed with. Now most of the town kept standing appointments for family photos at her home studio and half the boys from her graduating class were still kicking themselves for not treating her better when they'd had the chance.

"I'm sorry this is happening," I told her. "I'm sure it will all be sorted soon."

Gina rolled tear-filled eyes to meet mine. "Folks are saying Hank killed a man. Why on earth would he do that? I'd never even heard of anyone named Jack Warren until now."

"I know," I said, wishing there was something more I could offer her. "Are you sure I can't get you anything to drink? Cider? Coffee? Ice water?"

A sob burst free from her pretty face, and I crossed the room to her side, scooping the box of tissues off my coffee table as I sat.

"It's going to be okay," I assured, wrapping an arm across her narrow back and offering her a tissue with my free hand. "We'll figure this out."

"Oh, Winnie." Her eyes cleared and hope slid over her tear-stained face like sunshine after a rain. "Thank you!" She wrapped me in her arms and squeezed me hard. "I knew you'd help me."

"Uhm." I leaned away. "What?"

Gina popped onto her feet and swung her handbag over her shoulder. "Let's start at the Sip N Sup. Is that what you're wearing?"

I gave myself a long look. "Yes."

She tipped her head to one side, reevaluating. "Fine. Let's hurry before the lunch crowd is gone."

I climbed into the passenger side of Gina's little white pickup, and we bounded down the long gravel lane toward the county road. The sheriff's cruiser stood outside my cider shop beside a gray truck and a trio of men apparently deep in discussion. Colton's head lifted as we rocketed past.

It'd been years since I'd ridden with Gina, and I'd completely forgotten she was a lunatic at the wheel. I concentrated on the classic country music floating through her dashboard speakers instead of the trees blurring outside my window. Everyone had their vices, and Gina's had always been speed.

She slowed at the intersection outside Sip N Sup. "Excellent," she cooed, lowering the radio to a barely audible drone. "We haven't missed a thing."

She eased into the crowded lot, circled the building once, then double parked behind a Jeep in the employee section. "This looks like Reese's Wrangler," she said. "No way she's leaving here before us with a crowd this size."

Reese was a young blonde waitress with a fearless temperament and plucky personality. Easily one of my favorite people.

I followed Gina around to the front of the building then inside to the last pair of empty stools at the counter. Sip N Sup was Blossom Valley's most popular hangout. Folks of all ages came to share burgers, shakes, coffees, and gossip. The PTA held meetings there. Birdie Wilks brought her card club and no Little Leaguer in town had ever finished a season without enjoying at least one ice cream chaser from the kitchen.

The booths and tables around the perimeter were full. I recognized many of the faces. Local families dressed up from church. Couples in hoodies and jeans who'd probably enjoyed their morning off and slept in. There was an unusually high energy in the room, and it was on days like this that I missed running miles around the checkered floor in my little blue uniform the most.

Gina produced a silver hook from her handbag, placed it on the counter's edge, then hung her bag from it. "I hate to put things on the floor," she said. "I wouldn't want anyone to trip."

"Hey, y'all," Reese appeared before I could comment on Gina's handy purse hook. "What can I get ya?" She didn't bother with a pen or paper. This wasn't her first rodeo.

"Coffee for me," Gina said. "Scrambled eggs, fruit, and yogurt."

"I'll have a cheeseburger with Swiss cheese and onions," I said. My stomach growled with enthusiasm at the thought. "A side of sweet potato fries and a . . ." I opened my mouth to say chocolate malt, but thought better of it. I wasn't putting in nearly as many miles around my cider shop as I had while waitressing here, and my pants were a little snugger for it. "Diet soda."

Reese nodded. "Be right back." She jetted away, her blonde ponytail bobbing in a perfect corkscrew behind her.

Gina scanned the crowd slowly, her gaze catching briefly here and there before moving carefully on.

"Are you looking for someone?" I asked. "I can help."

She turned back to me, expression hard with determination. "Yeah. I'm looking for anyone who might be talking about Hank. I figure if they know him, they probably know me, and they're going to look my way while they talk about him. That's basic psychology."

I wasn't sure what I'd expected Gina to say, but that hadn't been it. I gave the room a careful scan of my own. No one seemed to be looking our way, and a surprising number of the faces were unfamiliar to me. "I'm not sure we'll hear much with all this noise."

Gina spun to face me. "Well, something has to happen. Folks sought me out at church this morning just to say they were sure Hank was on the run for a good reason." She let her jaw sink open. "Can you believe that? They said he was on the run. What's a good reason for that exactly? And others assured me they didn't think he killed that man." She used her fingers for air quotes around the last five words. "Which of course means they do believe it, or at least that they're willing to be persuaded that way. We've got to nip this mess in the bud before it goes to seed."

I didn't disagree. I just wasn't sure how to stop the gossip when we couldn't even find her brother.

Reese manifested before us with a broad smile and brown plastic tray in hand. She transferred the plates and drinks onto the counter then produced two sets of silverware rolled in napkins and a straw from her apron pocket. "If you need anything else, just holler," she said, vanishing before I could thank her.

"She's good," Gina said. "Fast too."

I slid my straw into the cup and paddled ice around my drink. "She ran circles around me and everyone loves her."

Gina speared a hunk of fruit with her fork and dragged it through low-fat vanilla yogurt. "Why don't we start with you telling me everything you know about what happened last night," she said. "Then we can tear it apart and analyze it."

"Believe me. I've done that. A thousand times," I promised. "I don't know anything useful." I sunk my teeth into the best burger in West Virginia and let my eyes flutter shut.

"Something else then," Gina pressed. "Maybe he said or did something odd before the wedding that makes sense now. Was something bothering him earlier this week or when he arrived for the reception?"

"I don't think so." I took another bite and considered her question while I chewed. The greasy, salty, juicy burger made my taste buds do a happy dance. "I hadn't seen much of Hank before the wedding," I said. "I was busy all week finalizing details and decorating. Honestly, I barely spoke to him last night either. I saw him fight with Jack, and I saw him drive away, but I can't even be sure he knew something happened to Jack before he left. He might not even know now."

Gina rolled her eyes. "He'd have to be dead not to know now." She dropped her fork and slapped both palms over her lips. "I didn't mean that."

I checked the tables and stools around us for listening ears. No one seemed to be paying any attention. "I know it's a lot to deal with," I whispered, leaning in close, "but Hank's smart. Whatever's going on, he'll be okay." I hoped the words sounded truer to her than they did to me. I was worried to my marrow about Hank and wished more than anything that I could help him out of whatever he'd gotten himself into. "I wish he'd just reach out to one of us," I said. "Then we could just ask him what's going on."

Reese reappeared with a coffeepot to warm up

Gina's cup. "I've only got a minute before my next order's up," she said, "but I had the closing shift last night, and I heard about what happened. There's been a few variations on the story since, but I gathered the gist. I'm real sorry about all this," she told Gina. "Are you guys here to see if you hear anything?"

I said, "No," at the same time that Gina said, "Yes."

Reese nodded. "If I see him or hear any mention of where he might be, I'll let you know."

"Thanks." Gina said, her voice cracking on the little word.

"Just don't hold your breath it'll be today," Reese warned. "Most of these folks aren't from around here, so they won't know anything."

"Who are they?" I asked, giving the booths of strangers a long curious look. They were all dressed for hiking in comfortable clothes, long pants, and boots. There was a fair mix of genders, ages, and skin tones represented. I couldn't guess the multitude of other differences, but they didn't look like a family in the traditional sense. "Some kind of tour group?" I guessed.

"Something like that. More like some New England–based hippie crew down here hunting mushrooms all week." She shot me a droll expression. "Hunting. Mushrooms. Let that sink in a sec."

I snorted.

"Mm-hmm," Reese said. "Gets better." She leaned a hip against the counter and flattened her lips for a long beat, as if gathering her strength or patience. "One of them told me they even brought in some special pigs. Called them truffle hogs. Said the animals are trained to root out expensive mushrooms."

Gina barked a laugh, then wiped the smile off her face with a napkin. "Sorry. Please go on."

"The lot of them are staying up in Carpenter's Run, hoping to hit the mushroom jackpot or some such nonsense."

The order bell rang and Reese peeled herself off the counter. "I'll reach out if I hear anything."

Gina and I finished our meals in silence. When I moved my napkin from my lap to the counter, she spoke. "Lunch was good, but gathering clues here was a bust. What should we do next?"

"I don't know," I said truthfully.

"Well, what did you do last time?" Gina pressed. "You cleared your granny's name in a couple of weeks. We need to do that for Hank."

Dread swelled in my chest. "Last time my meddling got Granny hurt."

"I don't care if I get hurt." Gina gripped my hand, her fervent expression softening. "Right now, my mama is scared to death. She's sitting by her phone, waiting for the worst. I can't stand to see her like this. I have to find my brother. I can't let people think he did this awful thing. My mama's poor heart can't take it."

Gina had scored the lead role in her high school's annual theatrical production nearly every year. At times like these, it wasn't hard to see why.

"We can try," I said, not feeling very hopeful. "The last time I looked into something like this, I had clues to follow. This time everyone in town seems to know the same amount of nothing." *Ex-*

*cept the killer,* I thought. The killer knew everything and that left Gina and me at a severe disadvantage.

I pressed a palm to my middle, wishing I hadn't finished my burger. "I don't think we can find Hank without Hank's help. How's that for complicated?"

Gina's eyes went wide and she squealed. "That's it!" She dropped a wad of cash on the counter then dragged me off my stool.

"Where are we going?" I yipped, tripping over my feet as we ran for her truck.

Gina gunned the little pickup to life and reversed wildly out of the lot. "We're going to ask Hank for help."

# Chapter Six

We pulled into an unfamiliar driveway several minutes later and Gina jumped out. According to her, Hank lived here now and had given her a key. I ignored the nonsensical jab of betrayal. He hadn't mentioned it to me. I'd assumed he was still renting the townhome I'd helped him move into in January.

Gina slid her key into the tumbler and the lock rolled smoothly. "Here we are. Now, let's see what we can learn."

I moved cautiously into the space, feeling a heady mix of emotions tug on my heart. "He moved."

Gina lowered herself onto the floor beside a coffee table littered with papers and empty cups. "Yeah. He's fixing it up after work and on weekends."

I moved carefully through the room, taking note of lumber and staining supplies stacked neatly in a corner. The kitchen had seen its share of updates already. A new tile backsplash. A cream and tan speckled quartz counter. Oil-rubbed bronze knobs, faucets, and hardware. Stainless steel appliances and a deep undermount sink. "He's done a nice job," I said.

Gina offered me a sad smile. She sifted through stacks of loose papers on the table before turning her attention to the laptop. "He wanted to finish the work before announcing he'd bought the place. The location was good and the structure was sound, but there's a lot to be done."

I moved back into the open two-story family room, reminding myself that where Hank lived was none of my business, and he could keep all the secrets he wanted now that we weren't together anymore. I admired the soaring pine ceilings and massive cobblestone fireplace, flanked by equally impressive windows on either side. The black leather living room set I'd helped move into Hank's townhouse now centered the log cabin family room, each piece angled to take in the magnificent views beyond the glass.

"Help," Gina said, motioning to Hank's briefcase and the papers on his coffee table. She stared at the open laptop. "I'll figure out his passcode. See if you can learn something from the paperwork that could help us find him."

I moved a little closer, but stuffed my hands into my pockets. "Are you sure we should be intruding like this? Won't Hank care that we're here uninvited?" It felt like an invasion of Hank's privacy just to be there. I didn't think I could paw through his things. For all we knew, he'd vanished for a perfectly understandable reason and didn't want to

be found. Maybe we were messing up his plan by
forcing ourselves into his business.

"Hank doesn't get a choice," Gina said. "He's
my brother and he's missing. He could be in danger, and I surely hope he'd be looking for me if
the situation was reversed."

"I think I'll look around first, then I'll come back
here and see about the papers," I said, putting off
her request. Roaming the halls seemed somewhat
less invasive than digging into his personal life.

I climbed the stairs to the loft overlooking the
family room and took in the beautiful view, then
moved along the narrow hall toward two small
guest rooms and a bath on the second floor. The
rooms were empty aside from a set of weights, a
sports bottle, and a towel in the first.

I headed back the way I'd come. The home's
craftsmanship was top notch, and I longed to drag
my fingertips over the massive logs that made up
the exterior walls. But I thought it best to keep my
hands to myself.

I found the master bedroom on the first floor, two
doors down from the kitchen, past a half bath and
laundry room. The bedroom ceiling was vaulted
with a ceiling fan spinning over an unmade bed. I
wrapped my arms around my center as I moved, reminding myself not to touch anything. *If Hank
turned up like Jack, then his home could be considered a
crime scene.* I pulled in a steady breath and braced
myself for the possibility. If the worst happened, I
didn't want my prints everywhere. It would be different for Gina. She was family, and she'd been
given a key.

I shuffled to the dresser, imagining Hank there,

preparing for work or bed. Castoff ties had been draped over the mirror beside cologne bottles and tiepins. Stacks of folded undershirts and piles of socks stood before a small frame. The photo inside was nearly invisible behind the clothing, but I recognized it immediately. Gina had taken the photo of Hank and me on her nineteenth birthday. We'd surprised her with a white-water rafting trip down the Shenandoah River. I'd been exhausted afterward, soaking wet and sunburnt, but Hank had just told me he loved me for the first time, and my world had gotten brighter. Gina had snapped the photo as Hank kissed my nose, and I looked like a heap of euphoric goo in his arms, completely melted by the idea that I was loved by someone other than Granny or Grampy. Until then, I hadn't believed it was possible.

I was nearly as surprised to find Hank had kept the photo. More than kept it, he'd taken the time to set it out on his dresser. Did he always do that? What did it mean? My chest tightened at the possible implication.

Then I remembered his face buried in the golden curls of a barely legal bridesmaid and the warm, confusing emotion fizzled away.

"Winnie!" Gina screamed.

I spun for the living room and burst into a sprint, glad to put the photo and its memory behind me. "Coming!"

"I'm in!" she said, eyes wide as I approached. "I did it! I cracked his password. I tried a million variations before it hit me, but I got it. Now look." She turned the laptop's screen to face me. Hank's email account was up and open.

"You cracked his email account too?" I gasped, certain that wasn't okay. I sank onto the couch at her side, torn between worry and awe.

"Of course not," she said. "His other passwords were already saved. I only had to get past the lock screen. Now let's see who my big brother has been chatting with these days."

"Wait!" I pushed one hand between Gina and the screen. "Maybe we shouldn't be doing this. When we got here, I assumed we'd find a clue out in the open that could put us on the path to finding him. I thought we might find a big calendar taped to the refrigerator with a name and time circled in red or a printed receipt for a local hotel on the counter. Then we'd leave. Now we're taking liberties with his privacy just because he trusted you with a house key, and I don't think that's right."

Gina scowled. "Hank gave me that key for emergencies. He's missing, Winnie, and accused of murder. That constitutes a major emergency in my book. Now get on board or close your eyes." She pulled the laptop onto her knees and sank back against the couch at my side.

I closed my eyes and listened intently while she clicked around.

"There's a bunch of recent emails from Sarah Bear Twenty-two," Gina said. "Ever heard that name before? There are at least a dozen from her in his deleted folder too. They were all sent this week. Maybe she knows where he is."

"Or maybe it's spam," I said, sneaking a peek with one eye. "Sarah Bear Twenty-two sounds like one of those phishing accounts that prey upon lonely people then start demanding money to free them from their homeland."

"I don't think so," Gina said. "Hank's smarter than that, and he's been corresponding with her. I wish she'd put her last name in the address instead of twenty-two. What does that even mean?" Gina sucked in an audible breath. "Good grief, you don't think twenty-two is her age, do you? That's younger than me!"

"The number could mean anything," I assured. Like, perhaps, the number of times she'd been arrested, her present number of children or ex-husbands.

"These emails are flirty," Gina said, her mood severely deflating. "Why wouldn't Hank have told me if he was seeing someone?"

"Hank likes his secrets," I said, lifting and dropping one shoulder in a pathetic shrug. "I didn't even know he lived here."

Gina's bottom lip jutted forward. She stretched an arm across my shoulders and tugged me to her side. "He wanted to surprise you with this place after it was finished. The plan was to invite you for dinner and woo you."

That sounded like Hank. His love of surprises was nearly as strong as my need for advanced warning and inclusion. His so-called surprises had once been the catalyst for our breakup. I'd told him so at Christmas, and he'd claimed to understand, but here we were again, and this time his secrets might have put him in serious danger.

Gina straightened on the couch and hit reply to one of Sarah's emails.

"What are you doing?" I squeaked. "You can't

reply to her from Hank's email. She'll know we hacked in! We're not even supposed to be here."

"I'm not going to tell her I'm me," she said. "I'll pretend I'm him and make arrangements to meet up. Once we get there, we can tell her what we're up to and see what she knows. Surely someone who traded this many emails with him knows more than we do about his life."

Beads of sweat gathered on my forehead and under my arms. "That's called catfishing," I whispered. "You can't do that."

Gina stopped typing to glare at me. "I don't care if this isn't nice. It's not illegal, and Hank needs help. He could be hurt or worse. If you have a better idea, I'm listening."

I pressed a palm to my temple and stared at the laptop screen, begging my brain to work.

And then I saw it. "SarahBearTwenty-two@ BVCC.com!" The address burst from my lips and set me on my feet. "I know how to find her!"

Gina started beside me. "How?"

"B-V-C-C," I said. "Blossom Valley Community College."

Gina jumped up to join me. "We can find Sarah Bear through your school."

I nodded, and Gina pulled me back out the door to her waiting race truck.

We arrived at the college in record time, thanks to Gina's driving and the lack of traffic. I frowned at the beautiful scenery outside my window. Normally, students were everywhere along the winding roads through campus. Walking. Reading under trees. Playing catch on the lawns. Instead, the whole place was empty, save a few ducks by the pond and a couple walking a dog.

"Sunday," I said, feeling stunned by the fact all over again. "That's why it's so quiet around here, and we're between semesters." Not great news for our search for Sarah Bear.

Gina drove to the main building and parked in visitors' parking. "Now what?"

"Now, we go inside," I said. "We came all this way, and the lot's not totally empty. We might as well go in and see what we can do. All we need is someone to recognize the email address." Or preferably someone we could convince to look it up.

"If this doesn't work, we should talk to Elsie next," Gina said. "She was the first on the scene. Maybe she knows something useful and doesn't even realize it."

I suppressed a shiver. Elsie's weird catatonic response to Jack's death gave me the creeps.

Gina climbed out and pocketed her car keys. "What?"

"Nothing." I took a deep breath, then forced images of Elsie out of my mind. "She just freaked me out last night." And as far as I knew, she hadn't spoken a word since being dragged away unconscious from her new husband's lifeless body. I doubted she'd come up with an epiphany in her current state or that she'd be willing to share it with me if she had.

I led the way into the main building, then stopped at the reception area. "I'm looking for a friend," I told the guy at the welcome desk. "We had a class together last semester, and I found her book in my car. I think she lost it after we studied for finals. Any chance you can help me find her?"

"Probably not," he said. "I'm just covering for my buddy. Maybe someone out there can help."

Gina and I leaned across the desk, following his line of sight down a hallway. "Someone's there?" Gina asked. "You aren't closed today?"

"Classes aren't in session right now, but a bunch of staff and students are setting up for an open house right now."

"That's perfect!" I nudged Gina with my elbow. "Let's go."

"Thank you!" Gina called, but the guy behind the desk had already refocused on his cell phone.

We cut down a narrow hall between conference rooms and through a lounge designated for student teachers, then across the atrium separating the various wings. Long hallways stretched from a central hub like spokes on a wheel. Every school of study had its own hall and most of the general courses were housed in separate buildings, connected externally by flagstone paths. After ten years, I knew the layout better than almost anyone, and I'd been here longer than most professors.

We stopped at a set of open double doors with blue and white helium balloons on either side. Round tables dotted the room inside. The tables were covered in blue linens, and old-fashioned nurse's hats acted as centerpieces.

"Hello," I called to a pair of women dragging chairs toward the tables.

They stopped to smile. "Need some help?" the taller one asked.

From the sweat stains on her shirt, it looked like she was the one who needed some help.

"I'm Winona Mae Montgomery. I'm a student her in the School of Business. This is my friend Gina."

Gina and the ladies exchanged pleasantries, while I scanned the faces of a group of new arrivals. The newcomers were also pulling chairs. All but one was male, and the woman was at least Granny's age. "We're looking for a student who goes by the name of Sarah Bear Twenty-two," I said, projecting my voice for everyone to hear. "Do you know her?"

The group looked at one another, but no one answered.

Gina grabbed a yearbook from the closest table and fanned through the pages. "Is this the entire school?"

"That's everyone," the first lady said. "Are you thinking about applying?"

"Oh, no." Gina shook her head. "I'm a photographer. No degree required." She handed out her business cards.

The closest guy in the group made his way in Gina's direction. Red-headed and in his mid-twenties, he pulled a set of chairs up to the table where we stood and grinned. "What's your friend look like?" he asked. "I don't know everyone by name, but I never forget a face." The adhesive nametag on his shoulder identified him as Van. "You look familiar," he told me.

"I've been going to school here for years," I said. "I'm like one of the desks at this point." I forced a tight smile. I had no idea what the woman I was looking for looked like. She could be a student or a teacher. Eighteen or twenty-eight. I had no idea. How could I explain that?

Gina's hand clamped around my wrist. "Winnie. Look." She turned the yearbook around and pushed it in my direction. "Sarah Burrie. That has to be her, right?"

My stomach dropped. "That's the bridesmaid I saw Hank with last night." He hadn't simply been flirting with a pretty girl for the night. He'd been seeing her before the reception. Were they romantically involved? For how long? How did they meet? Was it serious?

"I think that's her!" Gina yelped, tossing the book aside.

A blonde woman stared back at us from the open doorway, her cheeks were flushed and her eyes wide.

"Sarah!" Gina called. "Sarah Bear Twenty-two!"

The look of horror in the girl's expression struck me momentarily speechless. Surely Gina and I didn't frighten her. Did we?

Gina took a step toward the doorway, and Sarah broke into a sprint. "Why is she running?" Gina complained. "What is wrong with everyone?"

Van moved into the space at my side, clearly mystified by the entire scenario. "Was that the woman you're looking for?"

I gave her retreating form a careful look. "That's her." She'd traded layers of pink chiffon for jeans and a sensible blouse, but I'd recognize those blonde curls anywhere. Sarah Burrie was the bridesmaid who'd had Hank's full attention last night.

And she was getting away.

# Chapter Seven

I burst into the courtyard, wishing I was in better shape. My sides hurt, and I'd lost track of Sarah around the last interior corner. I'd taken a guess at where she might've been heading, but clearly I was wrong. Gina and I were the only two souls in sight. The bubbling fountain and grassy knoll beyond were empty as well. "We lost her," I panted, bending at the waist to grip my knees, secretly thankful I could stop running. "Why would she take off like that?"

"I don't know," Gina said, pressing a palm to my shoulder for balance. "I think she was already on the run when we spotted her." She levered an adorable pink pump off one foot, then switched sides and repeated the process.

I turned around to stare at the building. "Running from whom?"

"We might as well add that to our growing list of unanswered questions." Gina moved onto the carpet of thick green grass, adorable heels dangling from her fingertips. She wiggled her toes against soft Kentucky bluegrass and sighed. "These shoes were meant for admiring and moving slowly over short distances, not for hiking miles of college corridors or a three-hundred-yard sprint."

I looked at her red, swollen feet. "But you kept up anyway. That's impressive."

"Thank you. Now what? We didn't see where she went or what she drives."

I hooked my arm with Gina's and started the return trip to her truck. "Now we know her real name is Sarah Burrie, and Hank was apparently seeing her before the wedding. That's good news. We'll find out where she lives and stop by for a visit."

Gina didn't look convinced, but she accepted my plan. She drove me home barefoot and at a speed very close to the posted limits. I was impressed on multiple levels. "Call if you learn anything," she said, reversing away from my house before I'd reached my front door.

I agreed, waved, collected my cats, and headed for the cider shop. Gina had been in a hurry to get home and change clothes, then try to get a bead on Sarah Burrie, preferably a phone number or address. I, on the other hand, needed some busywork so I could think. Considering that the cider shop was still covered in wedding reception decor, I had a good idea where I could go to stay busy.

Kenny Rogers and Dolly swarmed my ankles as I moved, occasionally breaking away to roll and tumble over one another as we made the trek across the orchard to my shop. The sheriff's cruiser, gray truck, and trio of men were gone, but the barn doors were open and a Johnny Cash song drifted into the sunny day. Granny belted the lyrics alongside her favorite singer. I picked up my pace.

Delilah's laughter reached my ears a moment before I stepped into the barn.

I stopped in the doorway, struck momentarily speechless by the meticulously cleaned space. Then I laughed at the kooky duo before me. Granny and Delilah were losing a wrestling match with a giant box.

"What are you guys doing?" I asked, heading their way.

Granny shook a packing tape gun at me. Tears streamed over her red cheeks. "Help."

Delilah burst into laughter and nearly rolled off the box. "We're packing the decorations, but we need more hands. The box is winning!" She struggled to stay upright, pull herself together, and pin the cardboard arms into place.

I pressed my palms against the cardboard, then joined them in a round of laughter.

Delilah rolled onto her stomach across the big box. Her short legs stretched for the ground. Her arms extended forward like Superman. "We've got it now!"

Granny wiped her eyes free of tears, then pulled a line of tape down the box's center, careful not to stick her friend to the cardboard.

Delilah stood and clapped as Granny ran three additional rows of tape in a crisscross pattern for good measure.

I set my hands on my hips and admired their

work. "This place looks amazing. How did you have time to do all this? I expected to be here all night."

Granny dropped her packing tape on the counter and took a seat at the bar. "Teamwork and determination," she said. "Plus, Mrs. Sawyer called to say she'd left a few things here last night and wanted to drop by and retrieve them after lunch. She didn't give a specific time, but when I came up to look for her things, I saw all the decorations and didn't want them to be up when she got here. I thought the visual reminder might make things more difficult for her or for Elsie if she came along with her mother."

"Was the Sheriff still outside when you got here?" I asked.

"For a bit. I told him about Mrs. Sawyer, and he understood. He asked me to wait while he and his men finished combing through the barn, then they moved outside and I was allowed in. Delilah dropped by later to invite me to Sip N Sup, but I offered her free reception leftovers if she'd help clean up the decorations."

Delilah nodded. "You know what they say. No one gets a free lunch."

"Well, let me see what I can get started for you." I moved behind the counter and opened the refrigerator. Dot had packed up most of the food and sweets while I'd been outside eavesdropping on the guests. I had no idea what I might find.

"I've spoken to the rental company," Granny said. "They'll swing by later to pick up the tables, chairs, and all these boxes."

"Perfect." I filled a plate with cornbread, ribs,

and chicken, then grabbed a second plate. "I appreciate your help more than you know." I piled baked macaroni and cheese beside a pair of drumsticks on a second plate, then nuked both plates until they steamed.

Delilah took a seat beside Granny at the counter. "Now, this was worth the work. I love ribs and cornbread."

I delivered their plates, then poured two glasses of cold cider splashed with lemon and ginger. "Voilà!"

The women dug in.

My heart soared with appreciation as I took in the spotless space around me. Wildflower bouquets sprouted from old milk glass pitchers at the center of my beloved wooden table sets. Mismatched chairs and assorted tableware from local estate sales completed the perfect picture. Much of the glassware and many of the pitchers and towels inside my shop had been donated by Granny and her friends. The pieces were originally found in bags and boxes of laundry soaps, flour, or puffed wheat. Apparently, lots of things came free-with-purchase in the 1960s, and folks in Blossom Valley had kept them.

I wanted my shop to be an ever-evolving tribute to Blossom Valley through the years, so I'd done my best to include the town's memories wherever I could. There were stacks of old magazines and newspapers in bins and on my sideboards. Dented metal sifters and vintage cookware lined cabinets behind the counter. Aged recipe books overflowed from shelves set around the room. Photos of horse-drawn wagons bringing bread to local farms were framed on the walls. And large fabric sacks that had once held flour were arranged in a collage beside the window. According to Granny, once the flour had been used, women turned the fabric into simple dresses or tops for their daughters. I loved my displays of times gone by. They made me feel like a part of my town's long, proud history.

"We should take the rest to the shelter," Granny said, wiping cornbread crumbs from her lips. "We can feed a lot of people with the amount of left-overs in that fridge."

I grabbed a stack of carryout containers and smiled. "Good idea."

Granny routinely gave as much as possible to local families in need. She'd been adjusting her prices according to a customer's ability to pay for decades, and she'd never turned anyone away over money. Now that the orchard had recovered from its recent financial peril, she been able to give more to the community than ever before. Truck-loads of apples and applesauce were delivered to local schools every Monday from Granny's stores, along with breads, muffins, and treats. While supplies lasted, kids would get Granny's homegrown cherries, blueberries, pears, and peaches as well. Her generosity was good for the soul, the community, and business. Folks loved knowing that their patronage of the orchard and cider shop kept kids from going hungry, so they came back often and left enormous tips that I turned over to Granny's cause. We were on a mission to ensure that any student without a lunch would always have something to eat. We hoped to expand our reach throughout

Blossom Valley one day, providing fruits and baked goods to all shelters and shut-ins as well.

I had faith that we could make that happen.

"So," Delilah started, then paused, presumably for dramatic effect. Her eyes twinkled with mischief as she dotted a napkin to her lips. "Have any reporters been out to talk to you about what happened last night?"

"No." My gaze flicked to the open barn doors, thankful not to find any reporters waiting there. "Why? Were there reporters here today? Has someone called from the paper?"

"Not that I'm aware of," Delilah said, still looking strangely impish. "I just thought a specific reporter might've stopped by."

Granny narrowed her eyes and chewed more slowly.

"Who?" I asked, looking from Delilah's smiling face to Granny's stern one. "What am I missing? Is someone bothering you?"

"Delilah," Granny warned.

"Only if you consider being given flowers, notes, and invitations for tea being bothered," Delilah said.

Granny set her fork aside.

"Who is doing those things?" I asked. No reporter I'd ever known.

"Owen Martin," Delilah said.

I tried and failed to place the name. I shook my head as an indication.

"Owen has had a crush on your granny since high school, and we ran into him last weekend at the Knitwits convention. He lives over in Morgantown now, but he's offered to drive all the way to Blossom Valley just to take Penny to tea."

I looked to Granny, unsure how to respond. Instinct said it was wrong. Granny was married. Except, that wasn't true anymore. She'd been a widow nearly four years now. And for the first time, I wondered if she was lonely. She'd married Grampy as a teen, giving her a live-in best friend every day of her adult life. Now she only had me. "Do you like Owen Martin?" I asked.

"He's fine," Granny said, her tone harsher than the response required, "but I don't want to talk about him."

"His wife, Martha, passed last summer," Delilah said. Clearly, she wanted to talk about him.

My heart broke for him. Maybe life owed Granny and Owen a cushion after what they'd been through. Another chance at a deep and binding friendship, if not something more. "I think it's nice you ran into one another," I announced, having made up my mind. Granny had been sad long enough, far longer than she deserved. "It might be fun to have tea with someone you went to high school with. Reminisce about the old days. Did you know him well then?"

Granny blushed. "Can we please change the subject? I'd rather talk to you about the grass," she said.

I wrinkled my nose at the strange expression. "Are you saying Owen Martin is a snore fest?"

"No!" Granny said. "I'm telling you we need to deal with the grass. It's grown far too tall to take the riding mower over, and I can't find the time to hook up the tractor for lawn work. We might have to hire someone to keep the grass cut this summer. There's too much ground to cover and too many other things to do. I made grass cutting a priority the last few years and the business nearly failed. I've got to prioritize, and I can't be everywhere at once."

"I'll help," I said. "Once we get it under control, I can run the riding mower every few days for maintenance."

Granny rolled her eyes. "Between schoolwork, studying, owning and operating your cider shop, and helping me with all the business and marketing aspects of my orchard? Sure thing. Why not add mowing five or six acres of grass to the list?"

I considered making a remark about sarcasm being rude, but she was right. Even if we subtracted the acreage claimed by apple trees, wildflowers, outbuildings, the cider shop, and our gardens, there were still quite a few acres in need of mowing. Once my summer class started in two weeks, I'd have to trade sleep for the chores already on my plate. "I'll call around," I said. "There are plenty of landscaping businesses in town and even more kids home from college looking to make some summer cash. I'll see what I can do."

"We can split the calls," she said, "but I need to pick my blueberries and cherries first. There's still a stack of orders from the convention that need filling, but I can talk on the phone while I do that."

"I'll help with the berries," Delilah said, "and the group can help with the needlework. Don't worry about that. Oh," she snapped her fingers and turned my way. "That reminds me, Miss Honor Roll College Student. I've put together a letter I want to send from our needleworking group to our counterparts in Harper's Ferry. I want them to consider teaming up with us for the state convention. We can cut our costs by sharing a double-sized booth and creating a themed selection of items to represent the region. There's no sense in making two competing displays when we can work together."

"Smart," I said. "What can I do?"

"Read the letter?" she asked. "Let me know if I made any typos and how you'd feel if you received something similar from another cider shop before a big cider festival."

"Sure, anytime." Writing was never my strong suit, but I loved to read and frequently found typos in published work. Sometimes in books by my favorite authors. "Do you have my email?"

"Don't need it." Delilah pressed a tri-folded paper onto the countertop. "Got the letter right here."

I opened the paper and read carefully. It was short and sweet, covered all the points she'd said it would, and sounded as professional as anything I'd ever read. "I think this looks great."

"Fantastic. I'll run it to the mailbox today." She tucked the letter into her purse and looked at me. "Now that you've got the day off, I guess you'll be going to the post office too."

"Why would I do that?" I puzzled over her words. My bills were paid. I didn't have a major marketing mailer going out. "Is something going on at the post office?"

Granny dragged my tattered copy of *Cider Wars* magazine down the length of the bar then slid it my way. "I believe there's a big deal cider contest going on."

My cheeks heated and I mentally kicked myself for having mentioned the competition to them last month. "I know. It's just that I've been so busy with the wedding."

"Wedding's over," Delilah said. "Your school's still out and there's no time like the present. So, which sample are you going to send? I can take it with me when I go see the postman. Save you a trip into town."

I squirmed. "I'm not ready. I haven't decided what to send."

"Send anything," Delilah said. "The judges would be fools not to give any of your ciders a blue ribbon. Just pick your favorite and let's pack it up."

I stepped back from the counter, distancing myself from the pressure until my backside bumped against the workstation behind me. If the only thing at stake was a ribbon, I'd have sent in my new summer blends for feedback. The *Cider Wars* contest was huge. The first-place winner got a spot in a national advertising campaign, and promotion in the magazine with a list of national vendors. Even the last-place winner would be featured in the magazine and every winner got a thousand-dollar cash prize. I could easily pay a local kid with a mower to tend our grass all summer with that kind of money. So I couldn't send just anything. I had to send my best. Only I had no idea which of my ciders was the best. The whole thing was subjective, and winners would be chosen by a set of judges I knew nothing about.

It was a paralyzing decision. So, I'd decided to circle back to it some other time.

Movement caught my eye at the open door, and

Mrs. Sawyer stepped inside, saving me from the stress of disappointing Granny and Delilah further. "Hello," she said softly. "Is this an acceptable time?" Her simple black dress and flats were paired with black stockings, a matching handbag, and a tiny veiled hat. The ensemble looked like something out of another era or a Hitchcock movie.

After Grampy's death, Granny and I had moped around in jeans and his old flannels.

Granny slid off her stool and rushed to meet Mrs. Sawyer. "Of course. Come right in. What can we get you?"

"Just my daughter's things, thank you. I'm afraid I don't have much of an appetite." If her oversized sunglasses and slumped shoulders were any indication, Mrs. Sawyer hadn't gotten much sleep and had likely been crying again. She'd been a wreck last night while trying to comfort Elsie, who'd been barely coherent. I imagined not much had changed.

Delilah shoved her and Granny's plates in my direction. Scents of Elsie's reception dinner wafted up my nose in response.

I tucked the plates behind the counter, struck by a senseless pang of guilt about eating her daughter's leftovers.

I rounded the counter to greet Mrs. Sawyer with a handshake and encouraging smile while Granny pulled out a chair for her at the nearest table. "I'll grab your things," I said. "Give me just a moment."

I looked to Granny for help. She and Delilah had cleaned the place spotless. I had no idea where to begin looking.

Granny pointed toward the back room. "I've put

the keepsakes into one box for easy transport. Cake cutter and server, guest book and pen, the unopened favors and leftover programs. Elsie's bag is right on top. You can't miss it."

I hurried to the storage area that had temporarily doubled as a pre-ceremony dressing room for the bridal party and periodic crash pad where the bride and bridesmaids could catch their breath throughout the day. I flipped the light switch and found my storage area returned to its former simple glory. The dressing mirrors and sheets of pink and white tulle were gone. No more makeup stations and padded chairs. Just walls lined with sturdy bins waiting for the fall harvest.

Elsie's things were front and center just as Granny had promised. I slung the bag over one shoulder and hefted the box into my arms. A pair of muddy Zig Zag sneakers sat on the floor nearby. It was lucky for their owner that I was an honest person because the shoes were exactly my size and a brand I loved to look at but would never dare spend the money on. I turned them over like a true glutton for punishment, admiring their signature diamond-shaped tread. I consoled myself with a reminder than I too could indulge myself with fancy sneakers soon. Just one more year or so of classes, and I'd finally be done with college. Then the cash I put aside each semester to pay for classes could finally go into my bank account or out for the occasional indulgence, like Zig Zag sneakers.

"I think this is everything," I said returning to the dining area. "I'm guessing these are Elsie's sneakers? Or maybe one of the bridesmaids'? They were with the other things, and they aren't mine."

But I could've used them earlier when I was chasing a bridesmaid through my school.

Mrs. Sawyer rose to meet me. She ran a handkerchief under the rims of her big sunglasses. "They're Elsie's." She pressed the monogrammed white linen to her nose, then reached for the box. "Thank you."

"How's Elsie holding up?" I asked.

Mrs. Sawyer's mouth fell open, as if I'd asked the dumbest question she'd ever heard, which I had.

"I can't imagine what y'all are going through right now, but if there's anything we can do to help lighten your load, just let us know," I added, hoping to soften the stupidity of my question.

Granny and Delilah added their hearty agreements.

Mrs. Sawyer stood motionless for a long beat, then leaned against the table at her side. "I'm not sure what to do for Elsie. She's barely spoken since last night. When she does talk, she only repeats his name." She straightened then, her spine going stiff. "I should go. She's alone and might need me."

Granny took the shoes from my fingers. "I'll carry these out for you. I would've put them in the bag if they weren't so dirty."

I followed Granny and Mrs. Sawyer outside. My gaze fixed on the sneakers. "Has Elsie been hiking?" I asked.

"No," Mrs. Sawyer said, beeping the locks on her car open. "Not since she got home last week. She and Jack were busy with wedding things every day."

"Any idea where she got her shoes so muddy?" The weather had been hot and dry for the better part of two weeks before last night, and I couldn't imagine her leaving the fancy shoes muddy if there had been time to tend to them. I also couldn't help wondering if the mud from her shoes could somehow be related to the mud left on my floor. It seemed an odd coincidence at best, given the recent murder so close to both her discarded shoes and my kitchen.

Mrs. Sawyer loaded the box and bag onto the floor of her backseat then turned to me, hands on hips. "What's this about?"

"I'm not sure," I admitted. "Do you know Sarah Burrie?"

"Of course. Sarah's a lovely girl. We've known her family for years. Elsie babysat for the Burries when she was in high school. The four-year age gap never stopped their friendship." Her clipped tone warned me she was losing patience. Her long strides around the car hood toward the driver's door told me I needed to get to my point fast.

"I saw Sarah at my school today. Does she live near there?" I asked, hoping to sound casual despite the frantic beating of my heart. If I could get an address, I could stake out her place until she agreed to talk with me about Hank. She couldn't run away if she was already home.

Mrs. Sawyer opened the driver's door and stopped. "Why do you ask?"

Granny and Delilah moved into view, looking equally ill at ease. "Winnie?" Granny asked. "What's going on?"

I forced a shaky smile. "I saw Sarah with a friend

of mine last night, and hoped to get to know her better. Do you know Hank Donovan, Mrs. Sawyer?" I stepped forward, a sincere plea in my heart. "He's gone missing and I'm worried. I saw him with Sarah, and I'm hoping she can tell me where he is."

Mrs. Sawyer pulled the sunglasses off her face, revealing red puffy eyes. Her expression morphed smoothly from pensive distrust to an angry scowl. "Hank Donovan is the man suspected of murdering my son-in-law. If I knew where that rat was hiding, I'd have gone hunting for him already."

# Chapter Eight

I spent the rest of the day replenishing my diminished gourmet cider stocks and wishing Hank would resurface. He never showed, but I made solid progress on the ciders. Each of my specialty flavors started with one of three standard Smythe Orchard varieties. From there, I handcrafted the gourmet blends a few gallons at a time, adding berries, spices, and flavorings to the base ciders as they warmed.

I poured gallons of chilled cider into large pots on the industrial range inside my shop and turned the burners to medium-low. Then I arranged the ingredients on my counters as the base liquids warmed. I'd only been making my specialty ciders in the shop since the barn had been renovated last Christmas, but it was already a well-polished routine. These days I could make double batches with ease, which cut my production time in half. A good thing considering my sales were up. It was hard to believe I'd ever gotten the job done at my place on an apartment-sized hand-me-down stove-top.

Within minutes, the easy rhythm of the work erased anxiety from my day. I measured brown sugar and vanilla extract into bowls. Piled fresh berries to be mashed with a pestle and mortar. And I hummed along to my favorite songs, occasionally belting the lyrics of artists who made my days brighter. Together, the music, warm night air, and sweet scent of Granny's homegrown apples made the act of breathing an exercise in nostalgia. Precious memories of my life floated easily to the surface of my mind, as tender and lovely as the days I'd made them. Walks with Grampy. Baking with Granny. Chasing fireflies and butterflies. Eating watermelon off the vines.

I stirred the ingredients into the warmed ciders, letting the new flavors take hold and simmer before securing lids to the pots while they cooled. I prepped half-gallon jugs with appropriate labels and lined them up for filling.

By ten o'clock, I was on my way home, satisfied with all I'd accomplished and dreaming of my soft, downy bed.

I crossed the threshold, petted the cats, then changed into my pajamas before putting a kettle on for tea. I grabbed my laptop while the water heated and searched for Sarah Burrie's social media accounts.

I scrolled through photos of Sarah, marveling at the way she, like so many, put their lives online to be studied. My accounts were locked down tight, but Sarah's were public. There were photos of her at school, on vacations, and at parties. I stopped on an image taken outside the apartment complex near our campus. Was this where she lived?

There was only one way to find out. I cancelled the warming teapot and went to see my favorite girl, Mustang Sally.

Sally was my 1968½ Ford Mustang 428 Cobra Jet. She was one of three classic Mustangs that Grampy had painstakingly restored during my childhood. I'd spent hours bent over their hoods at his side, and in the end, he'd left them to me. I'd sold the other two to his best friend, a local vet who loved Grampy and the cars as much as I did. The money had paid for most of my cider shop's renovations, but I couldn't part with Sally. She was the one who sang to me.

I made a couple of passes along the street in front of the apartment building from the photo before heading home. There was no one outside to talk to, and I had no way of knowing if Sarah even lived there. Still, I reasoned, it was something I could pursue later if needed. I made a mental note to call Gina in the morning and see if she'd located an address for Sarah.


Heavy knocking woke me from a dream I was enjoying the next morning. I squinted against the offending light and dragged myself upright, aggravated with whoever was at my door. I shuffled into my kitchen, then slowed as a shadow came into view on my porch. I peeked reluctantly through my kitchen curtain, hoping Gina hadn't returned for another day of amateur investigation. It had occurred to me during the night that if Sarah had been on the run from someone inside the college yesterday, as Gina had suggested, then whoever that was had surely seen us give chase, and being caught in the crossfire was never a good idea.

If I let anything happen to Gina, I'd be the one hiding from Hank instead of the other way around.

Sheriff Wise turned his gaze to meet mine the moment I shifted the curtain. Busted immediately for peeking, just as I had been with Gina, I opened the door.

I really needed to invest in a peep hole. Or one of those surveillance doorbells from the news.

I smoothed a palm over my hair and wished desperately that I wasn't wearing the same pajamas, aka high school gym uniform, I'd had on two nights ago when I'd called about the mud on my floor. "Colton," I said in greeting, hoping my morning breath wouldn't knock him over. "What brings you here so early?"

He frowned, then checked his watch. "It's after nine. Can I come in?"

I stepped back uneasily, hoping he didn't know about my late-night drive-by stalking, and simultaneously making plans to casually check the street again today.

"Everything okay?" Colton asked, removing his big hat and giving the room a long, careful look. "You seem a little edgy. Anything you want to tell me?"

"No." I pulled a hoodie from the coat closet and slipped it over my stupid pajamas, then zipped it to my chin. "Can I get you a cup of coffee?" I headed toward the counter without waiting for his reply. I needed a caffeine boost whether or not he did.

"No, thanks."

I started the coffee, then slid my backside onto the counter beside my sink to wait while the pot brewed.

"I've been up most of the night," Colton said. "I've had so much coffee I might not sleep for days."

"I wish it had that effect on me," I said. "I think I've grown immune."

His lips quirked into a lazy half smile. "I've had days like those. When I could fall asleep standing up. Not good times."

"Nope," I agreed.

The long pause between us rattled my nerves. I pushed my mug under the coffee drip to fill before setting a pot in place to catch the rest. "If you aren't here for coffee, what brings you by, Sheriff?"

He circled my living space and leaned an ear toward the hallway where my bedroom and bathroom were located. His uniform was slightly rumpled and the dark crescents beneath his eyes were disturbingly large. "I wanted to give you a couple updates, on the mud from your floor and on the crime scene situation. I'd like one more day to sweep the barn and general area, but you can open your cider shop tomorrow if you'd like."

I sipped coffee as he made his way back to me. I wanted to ask what he was so obviously looking and listening for inside my home. An intruder? An overnight guest? I doubted I'd get a straight answer, so I stuck to the script he'd started. "Another day closed won't hurt. Half the town was here when tragedy struck. They'll expect me to take a few days off in respect."

"I know how much the business means to you,

and being closed costs you income, so I'll do my best to wrap it up by nightfall."

The compassion in his eyes softened my core, and I slumped from the weight of the last two days. "Honestly, I'll be lucky if anyone ever comes in again. I know it's a completely selfish thought, but this whole orchard is headed for one of those urban legend books if another bad thing happens here."

Colton shook his head. "They'll get over this once there's closure. You can't help what happens on your property any more than the next person. We'll get this sorted and free your name of any association with the killer. Things will go back to normal from there."

"Have you confirmed the cause of death?" I asked. Gruesome as it sounded, there was always the possibility that driving a truck over Jack's body was meant to hide another injury.

"Not yet. The county coroner's practically a one-man show, but he promised to take a look as soon as possible." He glanced through the window at my side. "I should probably get back out there."

"Okay." I wrapped my fingers around the warm ceramic mug, not ready for him to leave. "But, if you have another minute, I could use a little help."

He raised a brow in question.

"I want to enter a cider contest but can't decide which flavor to submit. You've had enough caffeine, but how do you feel about a couple cider shooters?"

He set his hat on my counter and rubbed his big palms together with a smile. "I'm your man."

I hopped off the counter and lined a row of tiny plastic cups where I'd been sitting.

Colton moved closer and lifted his gaze to the window above my sink once more. "Grass is getting long."

"Yeah. Granny and I need to figure that out."

"Are you thinking of hiring a crew?" he asked. "A grounds manager might be even better. You could trade room and board, maybe meals and a stipend, for someone willing to do general maintenance, tend to the buildings and land."

I filled the final sample cup and put the cider jugs back in my fridge. "Where on earth am I supposed to find someone like that?"

He lifted the first shooter and shrugged. "Ask the guys who come to do the harvest this fall."

I made a sour face. "That's another problem. Apparently, Granny couldn't find the contact information for the team Grampy always used, so she hired someone else to do the harvest the last three years. When I ran the numbers against the inventory sheets for taxes this spring, I realized they'd been stealing from her. When I called to question them, they refused to return my calls, and when I started looking into their references, I found they were all fabricated. Those men have been taking advantage of women like Granny for a decade. They change the name of their business every time they get caught. Until then, they routinely charge for work they didn't do and take a percentage of apples with them each night, which they bag and sell for personal gain." And I'd been none the wiser until it was too late.

Colton ground his teeth, jaw popping and clenching. "So you need a whole new crew for harvest this fall, one with good references and fair rates, plus an orchard manager." He swallowed the first sample in one gulp. "Let me see what I can do."

His eyes widened. "I've had this one before. You served it warm last winter."

"Correct. Honeycrisp with cinnamon and nutmeg."

"This one's my favorite."

I handed him the second sample. "You have to try them all before you say that. This one is lemon and ginger."

He sipped and swallowed. "This is good. It's lighter. Refreshing. I don't think I've had cider like that before."

"I've been trying new things."

"You should send this sample," he said. "You'll blow the judges' minds. Remind me who the judges are."

I handed him the third sample. "I don't know. The contest is for *Cider Wars* magazine. It's printed in Boston, but it's national. The judges could live anywhere. A mention in their pages could be a huge boost to my brand and create a positive long-term impact on the financial security of Smythe Orchard."

Colton smiled. "You're smart, and I like it. Have I told you that?"

"Mostly you tell me to leave your work alone."

He grunted. "Do I need to tell you that today?"

"Nope." I handed him another shooter.

"What's this one called?"

That was an excellent question. The paperwork for the contest required names for flavors, and I didn't have any. I hadn't even named my cider shop. My head fell forward. I was terrible at naming things, and these names were too important to mess up. I shoved the thought out of my mind and raised my head. "I don't know."

The cup was already empty, and Colton's gaze was searching mine. "You okay?"

"Yep. Thoughts?"

"I can taste the berries," he said. "Are those grown here too?"

I nodded. "We grow everything except the sugars and extracts."

"Impressive." He turned to lean against my counter. "Have you considered what you're going to do when you wind up in a national print campaign and folks start placing orders from all over the country?"

"That sounds like champagne problems. I should probably worry about which sample to send first."

"Champagne problems are real problems," Colton countered. "You can be blessed with abundance and it can still be a problem."

I handed him the fourth sample, fighting against the truth in his words. How would I handle a sudden and extreme demand? I wasn't sure I could. Not long term anyway. "I'm not trying to be a household name. I just want to carve out a small, respectable legacy like my grandparents have. If my town, my home, and my roots get a little recognition in the process, all the better. If you ask me, Blossom Valley, West Virginia, could use a moment in the spotlight."

"Blossom Valley won't be in the spotlight. You will."

I narrowed my eyes at him. "Which sample should I send?"

He handed me the fourth empty shooter. "I like them all."

I pitched the cups into the sink to rinse and recycle. "You're no help, you know that? I don't suppose you've gotten any leads on Hank? It might make up for drinking all my cider."

He eyeballed the four little cups, then laughed. "Hank Donovan is smoke," Colton said. "It's like he fell off the face of the earth or into a storm bunker and hasn't come up for air. No vehicle. No telephone. No activity on his credit cards or bank accounts. I don't know how much cash he had on him when he ran, but that's got to run out eventually."

I considered telling him about Hank's connection to Sarah and the fact she'd run from me yesterday, and maybe from someone else as well, but he'd only complain I was being nosy. Which I was, but for a good reason. I was afraid for Hank and possibly for Sarah as well. Though, I couldn't ignore the fact that she was the right height to have driven the truck that hit Jack.

The mention of his phone brought another idea to mind. Gina had gotten into his laptop, but she hadn't gone through his phone. "What about before Hank ran? Any idea who he'd been in contact with before that?"

"I'm working on a warrant for his place and phone records."

I raised my brows, interpreting the *but* he'd intentionally left out.

"I have the bride's phone."

"Elsie's? She's talking?" A dozen questions flooded my mind faster than I could order or sort them. "What did she say? Is she acting normally now? Does she have a guess about what happened? How did Jack know Hank? Did she see who was driving the truck?"

"Elsie was sleeping when I stopped by her mama's place yesterday," he said, raising a palm to slow me down. "Mrs. Sawyer let me have a look at Elsie's cell phone when I asked about photos taken at the reception. There's always a chance something unintentionally caught in the background could become a clue as the investigation goes on."

"Clever. How'd you get into the phone with Elsie sleeping? No password?"

"Her password was Jack," he said. "Not exactly Fort Knox. I kept the search quick. Didn't see anything useful at first glance, but I asked to keep it just in case. Her mom gave permission."

In other words, Mrs. Sawyer didn't have any reason to think her daughter was keeping a murderous secret.

"How long had Hank known Elsie?" Colton asked.

"He didn't," I said. "Not really." I scrutinized Colton's unreadable expression. "We all grew up here, but she's a few years younger, and they didn't have any relationship that I know of. They weren't neighbors and didn't run in the same crowds. I've never seen him speak to Elsie in all the years I've known him."

"Huh."

I crossed my arms defensively. "What?"

"Funny that he'd called her a half-dozen times in three days before the wedding then."

The chill of intuition slithered down my spine. Hank and Elsie had been in communication several times before Jack died and Hank fled. Elsie's muddy shoes. The mud on my floor. Someone her height had driven the murder weapon. A bridesmaid ran. She was seeing Hank. It was all connected, but how? "Have you asked Elsie about it?"

"I've tried. According to her mother, she's always sleeping when I call or drop by, and I don't have enough cause to compel her."

An unspoken *yet*, hung in the air.

I couldn't help wondering how long a killer could play crazy to avoid being interviewed. Not indefinitely, I hoped.

"You're fidgeting again," Colton said. "You looked downright stunned when you saw me on your porch this morning, and you were hanging your head in the kitchen a few minutes ago. Now, you're twisting the hem of that sweatshirt as if it did something to wrong you."

I dropped my hands away from the hoodie's hem and pulled my fingers up inside the sleeves.

"You want to tell me what's got you on edge?"

"The causes of those behaviors are unrelated," I said.

"Why don't you pick one and tell me about it."

I decided to go along with the request, given his unusual willingness to share with me about Elsie's phone and the calls between her and Hank. "I'm surprised to hear Hank called Elsie before the wedding, but I have reason to believe he was seeing one of her bridesmaids, so it's possible the calls were made by or on behalf of Sarah." I could only pray that Hank hadn't been seeing the bride romantically as well. Though that would explain what had Jack so worked up at the reception.

"How do you know he was seeing Sarah?" Colton asked. "Did he tell you?"

"I saw them together at the reception," I said, stuffing the edge of one thumb against my teeth and biting down on the tender flesh along my nail. "Also his sister and I visited his place yesterday and she saw some emails between them."

Colton's expression hardened, but he didn't complain like I'd expected. "I'll talk to Gina again. Anything else?"

"Well, if Hank was flirting with Elsie, it could explain why he and Jack argued at the reception," I said, wincing as I tugged on a hangnail. "Or maybe we've got this turned around and it was Sarah who was seeing Jack. Then Hank found out, tattled to Elsie, and confronted Jack. Either Elsie or Sarah would fit nicely behind the murder weapon wheel." A rush of enthusiasm jolted through me. "I'd say that gives you two strong suspects."

Colton retrieved his hat from the counter and stuffed it onto his head. "I wasn't looking for theories. Just facts, but I appreciate the heads up on Gina. Maybe she'll let me into Hank's place. She has a key I assume?"

I made a sour face. "Well, we didn't break in."

Colton opened my front door and grinned at

me over his shoulder. "Thank you for the cider. Let me know when you win that contest."

I followed him onto the porch, enjoying the fragrant summer breeze and recalling the bride's muddy shoes. "Hey," I called as Colton jogged down the front steps. "You didn't tell me what you learned about the mud from my floor."

He wrinkled his nose, mystified, then laughed. "The lab said there were heavy traces of mushrooms through it. I don't suppose you know where I can find a bunch of wild morels?"

Nope, but I knew how to find out.

# Chapter Nine

I watched politely as Colton made his way toward the grassy lane that would take him to the cider shop. His cruiser and the gray pickup were in place outside the barn's closed doors. My heart thundered noisily as I waited for an acceptable amount of time to pass before racing inside to grab my phone.

Dot answered on the first ring. "What's shakin' bacon?"

My knees for one thing. I eased onto the couch and started with the news from Colton. "Sheriff Wise stopped by to give me the lab results from the mud I found on my kitchen floor."

"Don't tell me it was from a pet cemetery, Winnie Mae Montgomery, or I will freak out," she said sharply. "I mean it. You know I can't take that level of creepy."

I rolled my eyes despite the fact she couldn't see me. "No. I swear you're superstitious enough for ten people. This has nothing to do with a pet cemetery."

"You can't call me superstitious when things are real. Pet cemeteries are real."

"But haunted ones are not," I grouched. "No cemeteries are haunted. Nothing is haunted." I stopped myself from rehashing a twenty-year-old argument. "You know what. Never mind. Are you working right now?"

"No. I was reading."

I rolled my eyes again. Reading Stephen King, no doubt. "Do you remember how to get to Hank's family's cabin? And can you recall if there were any wild mushrooms out that way?"

"I don't know about the mushrooms, but I could probably find the cabin if I tried. Do you think Hank's hiding out there?"

"Maybe." It certainly made sense since very few people knew the cabin was still standing, or at least it had been several years ago when Hank and I had hiked to it for some extreme privacy. It was easily as old as my Mail Pouch barn and in one hundred percent worse condition. It was one of many relics peppering the mountains, evidence of times passed, when folks settled where they could, before towns shot up and industry prevailed. The odds that the cabin was registered on current records was slim to none. The fact Gina hadn't mentioned it already told me that even she had forgotten about it.

"Smart. No one would look for him there," she said. "Let me grab an old map of the area and I'll pick you up in twenty minutes."

I disconnected and leapt from my couch, propelled by a jolt of adrenaline all the way to my bedroom. I pulled on a pair of yoga pants, a long-sleeved

T-shirt, and my worn-out sneakers. Then I filled two sports bottles with water and headed to my porch, too wound up to stay inside. I pulled my hair back and put on a baseball cap while I waited for signs of Dot's Jeep in the distance.

Fifteen minutes later she arrived looking like a million bucks in her denim capri pants and little pink tank top. Wild auburn hair flowed from her headband in thick beautiful waves. She'd removed the Jeep's top and doors, going "naked" as she and her fellow Jeep lovers called it, through the beautiful summer day.

I ran down the steps to meet her.

She shifted into park and frowned. "Why are you dressed like a cat burglar? There's not going to be a soul at that cabin. The closest thing Hank Donovan has done to camping since Boy Scouts is stay at a Days Inn."

"I'm trying for nondescript," I said, swinging onto her passenger seat.

"If you wanted to blend in you should've worn camouflage."

Sadly, I didn't own any camouflage that wasn't pink. "I brought you a water."

"Oh, thank you!" Dot accepted the offering and dropped it into her cupholder. "I never remember mine, and it's going to be a scorcher today." She waited for me to buckle in before heading back down the gravel drive at a sensible pace. "You're going to sweat to death in that getup."

I kicked my legs out in front of me, examining the outfit. "I'm protecting myself from ticks and briars. Besides, I didn't want to stand out. If Hank's at the cabin when we get there, he might take off if he sees us."

Dot pulled her lips to one side. "You probably should've mentioned this was a stealth operation. I wouldn't have worn pink."

"It's fine. You can put your jacket on when we get out." I hooked a thumb over one shoulder, indicating the thin brown park ranger button-up lying across her back seat.

"Okay." She waved congenially to Colton and his men in the distance before pulling onto the main road. "I take it the sheriff doesn't know about the Donovan family cabin."

"Not unless one of the Donovans mentioned it."

She smiled. "And how do the mushrooms fit into all of this?"

"The lab said there were heavy traces of mushrooms in the dirt on my floor, and there were a bunch of New England mushroom hunters at Sip N Sup yesterday. Reese said they were camped out in Carpenter's Run. Since that's not far from the Donovans' cabin as the crow flies, I guessed it could be where Hank's hiding."

"So, you're assuming it was Hank who left the mud on your floor."

"Better him than any alternative."

We floated along the winding ribbon of road at just below the speed limit. I let my head rest on the seatback and stretched one hand outside the empty door's frame, opening and closing my fist against the beating wind. It was hard to believe bad things ever happened in a place as beautiful as this, but I supposed bad things happened everywhere.

Dot stopped at the traffic light downtown, then hit her blinker. We were headed away from civilization, toward the national forest's edge where farmland, private property, and boundary lines blended seamlessly along the river. She pulled dark sunglasses down to the tip of her nose and peered at me over the top. "You think Hank broke into your house and got the floor muddy? Then went to his family cabin?"

"Maybe."

She frowned. "But if you watched him flee the reception, then when did he go walking on mushrooms? Because those were already in the mud left inside your house."

"I have no idea," I said. "Colton thinks whoever it was waited at my place while the officials cleared the crime scene and interviewed the guests, then slipped away when he and the deputies were gone. I don't know about that, but I think the dirt is a clue. The timeline makes it too coincidental. So, if we find mushrooms near the Donovans' cabin, I'll know it was Hank. I prefer that to a killer having been in my house."

The light turned green, and she pushed the sunglasses back onto her nose. "That's good enough for me, plus I love a new adventure. I brought a map of the area around Carpenter's Run. Hank's family cabin isn't far from there, and this will help us find any old roads that have been grown over or forgotten."

I just hoped we could find the cabin. The structure had long ago been forgotten by locals and time. Beyond that, I hoped we'd find Hank. I wasn't sure what I'd do first if I saw him. Hit him for scaring me like this? Hug him from the immense relief of knowing he was okay?

What if Sarah was hiding with him? Worse, what might they be doing when I arrived unannounced? I suppressed an internal gag.

"What are you thinking?" Dot asked. "You look like you just sucked a lemon."

"The bride's shoes were muddy." I forced my mind away from unpleasant images and onto the issues at hand. "And Colton said she'd received calls from Hank on the days leading up to the wedding. Do you think it's possible the mud from her shoes is the same mud from my kitchen? And it's all mud from outside the Donovans' cabin?"

"No," Dot said flatly. "Every man, woman, child, and animal in Blossom Valley has mud on at least one pair of shoes, but most of our muddy paths will never cross. For it to be all the same mud, way out here in no-man's-land, would be unthinkable."

I nodded. It was the logical response, but I was looking for connections anywhere I could find them, and what if it was the same mud?

Dot turned onto a gravel and dirt pass outside of town. Carpenter's Run was a secluded hollow between two mountainsides with a small creek running through it. The pass ended abruptly a half-mile up the hill, but it was a popular spot for camping and parking, especially during hunting seasons.

Dot shifted into four-wheel-drive, and we crawled passed a line of strangers at the base of the hill. Folks in high-end hiking gear with logoed shirts and jack ets stared after us. "Was that an Audi SUV?" she asked, clearly befuddled. "I don't think I've ever seen one of those around here before."

I craned my neck for a look behind us, but it was too late. "I missed it."

I'd been drooling over the red Range Rover Autobiography that cost more than my entire college experience.

Several minutes later, Dot brought the Jeep to a stop. The expanse of rocks she'd chosen for a parking spot was also the place where the wilderness officially overtook the road. "Now, we walk," she said cheerfully before hopping out of the Jeep.

I climbed down and rounded the hood to meet her.

"How do I look?" She threaded her arms into the sleeves of her ranger jacket, completely covering her hot pink and white tank top.

"Stealthy," I said, repeating her word from earlier.

She blew me a kiss then marched ahead. "Let's do this." She peeked at her watch as she strode up the mountain.

"Do you have somewhere to be?" I asked, wondering how she planned to make that happen when we were facing a multi-mile hike up the hill and back, then a thirty-minute drive back to civilization. "Are you going into work later?'

"No. I'm just thinking about Kenny Rogers," she said, looking suddenly forlorn. "I want to be home in time for their dinner."

"Which Kenny are we talking about?" I asked.

Dot had a lifelong habit of locating and rescuing sick or endangered animals. It was how I'd gotten my kittens and why her four-acre hobby farm looked more like an overpopulated petting zoo than anything else. Being a park ranger and natural animal whisperer, Dot had found forever homes for hundreds of animals over the years, yet she never seemed to have an empty pen. She named all her fur babies, temporary or otherwise, Kenny Rogers. She claimed it had nothing to do with her over-the-top obsession with the singer and everything to do with convenience, but I wasn't convinced.

"Not the owl," I said, picturing the little guy's face. The eastern screech owl had stolen my heart at first sight, and I wanted him to live forever. He was tiny, about six inches long, with giant round eyes and only two distinct expressions; completely shocked and deeply judgmental. Someone had hit him with their car, and Dot found him on the roadside the next morning. He had a broken wing and distrusting spirit then. Now, he was healed and oddly outgoing. Dot had tended to his wing for too long to release him into the wild again, so she treated him like an angel and used him in her classes at the wilderness center.

"Not the owl," she said. "These Kennys are new."

"Do tell," I said, offering a warm smile. I loved Dot's rescue stories. They warmed my heart and meant everything to her. "We've got plenty of time."

"True. All right, so it started when welfare services took an elderly couple out of their shared home last week. The woman had a heart attack, and apparently the man had fallen on ice and become bedridden last winter. His wife had been caring for him until her heart attack, but she wasn't well enough to deal with their animals. She paid a couple of the neighbors' kids to feed the animals, but they only collected her money and left each week. So it was a mess. Long story short, the ambulance driver went back to check on the husband once the wife was stabilized, and he found the animals. They were nearly starved to death and both had evidence of frost bite. I'm working with Doc Austin to repair one's hooves."

"Hooves?"

"Yep." She linked her arm with mine and hurried me along. "I am now the proud foster parent of Kenny Rogers the donkey and his best friend, the alpaca. They both need a lot of attention right now, so I can't dawdle. We'll find the cabin, check it for Hank and the ground for mushrooms, then head home in time for the evening treatments and dinners."

"A donkey and an alpaca," I repeated. "Have you gone round the bend? Where are you keeping them?"

"I emptied the pen where I kept the peacocks last summer. It's a little tight, but I added plenty of hay and new troughs. I don't think they mind. Plus, they have each other and they're getting used to me."

I shook my head. "Bananas."

"A little, but I love it." Dot smiled. "I've been thinking of going back to school for my veterinary science degree."

"What?" I leaned against her as we moved, enthusiasm beating in my heart. "That's fantastic!"

"Thanks. Doc Austin said he'd help me with my studies and let me work at his office to gain experience. I want to open an animal rescue and adoption center when I finish. I love being a park ranger, but saving animals and helping them find forever homes is where my heart is."

Anyone who knew her understood that was true. "Let me know how I can help."

She gave me a side hug, then whipped a paper map into existence before us. "See this?" she asked. "I think that's the cabin, and I think we're somewhere around here right now." She pointed and circled her finger over the paper. I only saw lines and unidentifiable markings.

"So, we go that way?" I asked, pointing to the horizon over her shoulder.

"No." She gripped my shoulders and turned me around. "This way."

Thirty minutes later, a small brown cabin appeared among the leafy green trees. The sway in the peak of its ancient roof reminded me of an old mare's back.

I touched a finger to my lips in warning, then crept toward the door on silent feet.

Dot followed.

Mounds of leaves and twigs had been deliberately arranged on the ground in front of the door, dry, crisp, and ready to sound an alarm if anyone stepped on them. I approached from the side and extended an arm to knock. "Hank?" I asked softly, then repeated myself twice more, raising my voice higher with each try.

Dot jammed a branch into each leaf pile, then kicked the mess away and opened the cabin's door.

"Making sure there weren't any bear traps hidden under there."

My jaw dropped, and I was immediately thankful I hadn't stepped on any leaves hiding a bear trap.

Dot climbed into the neglected structure first, and I followed.

There weren't any signs of Hank, but it was evident the cabin hadn't been empty for long. A partially eaten sandwich sat on the corner of a sleeping bag against the wall beneath a window. Several jugs of water and a sack of camping supplies rested in the corner.

Dot peered through the back window. "It looks like someone dug a firepit out there and made a small spit for cooking. You think it was Hank?"

"I don't know." I gave the partially eaten sandwich a long look. Bologna and bread. Not something I could imagine Hank eating, but I'd never imagined him living in a dilapidated cabin either, and that was possibly happening.

"Any luck?" Dot asked, meandering back in my direction.

I don't know. "This looks like my sleeping bag," I said, searching the inside for my initials. "But I wrote WMM in fabric marker on all my camping gear years ago." And there were no tags to be found on the item in question. I supposed, much like the mud, sleeping bags were probably present in every Blossom Valley resident's home.

"Well?" Dot pressed, stopping at my side. "Is it yours?"

"No. I guess I'm just paranoid."

"Well, someone has clearly been here," she said.

"That's something. If not Hank, then a squatter. We should tell Sheriff Wise for good measure."

I pulled my phone from my pocket, unsure how I'd explain stumbling across the information without admitting I was still looking for Hank on my own, but honestly, he should know I wouldn't give up where a friend was concerned. Plus, I was helping. I frowned at the complete absence of service bars. "I'll call when we get back to the main road."

I gave the ramshackle building and pathetic grouping of survival supplies a remorseful look. "Whoever was here heard us coming and left in the middle of eating a sandwich." My chest tightened and my eyes stung senselessly. "I hate that the person who ran might've been Hank."

"We'll figure it out," Dot said, rubbing my back with one hand and pushing the door open with the other.

"I don't understand what's going on. What would cause him to choose to live like this?" Emotions from the past couple of days pressed the air from my lungs. "I'm really worried about him."

"Well, I'm not worried," Dot said brightly. "You found Mrs. Cooper's killer last Christmas and you'll find Jack's killer too."

I hoped she was right more than I hoped for anything at the moment.

I stepped back into the fresh air and shafts of sunlight filtering down through the trees. "Still feel like hunting mushrooms?"

"Indeed," Dot said. "We should gather as many as we can and take them to the folks camped out at the base of the hollow. They'll never find their way up here."

I cut along the shadiest path in sight, feeling lighter at the idea of surprising strangers with a bounty of something they wanted. Even if I thought mushrooms were gross. "Did I tell you the New Englanders brought pigs to hunt with?" I asked, realizing Dot would love this information.

"Aww," she cooed. "I love pigs."

"These are trained pigs." I smiled at the thought. "Like coon dogs, but for mushrooms. They're called truffle hogs."

Dot laughed.

I turned for a look at her contagious smile and caught sight of a strange little glow on the tree beside her head. A distinctive red dot wiggled along the bark and fear gripped my lungs. "Gun!" I collided with her as the shot rang through the hills and bark splintered from the tree.

Air whooshed from my lungs in an oof, as we bounced against the hard ground and rolled over a small embankment into more waiting leaves.

Dot swore.

I pulled her up with me, our bodies still in motion, and dragged her behind the nearest giant tree trunk. My fight-or-flight response was all-in on flight, but she looked dazed and confused. "Are you okay? Did you hit your head?"

She touched her head cautiously, but shook it, wide-eyed. "No."

I clasped her hand in mine. "Then we've got to run. Ready?"

Tears spilled over her cheeks as resolve formed on her face. One stiff dip of her chin said she was back with me.

And we were off.

A second shot rang out behind us, hitting farther away than the first. Instead of ringing my ears again, it seemed to vibrate the mountains like a massive tuning fork.

Dot squeezed my hand, but kept pace.

We held one another up as we tripped and stumbled down the mountain in half the time it had taken us to climb it.

She released me at first sight of her waiting Jeep. "Seatbelt!" she yelled as we parted ways.

I buckled up while Dot spun the four-by-four around like a stunt driver and rocketed us toward safety.

# Chapter Ten

Dot didn't stop until we reached Main Street and caught the red light behind a souped-up Thunderbird. She released the steering wheel and frantically patted herself down as if checking for injuries. Or a bullet hole. "Holy smack!" she said, wide-eyed, hands back on the wheel. "Did that just happen? Did someone shoot at us? Twice?"

I nodded. Unlike her, I was having trouble finding my voice. It didn't help that my swollen tongue was stuck to the roof of my pasty mouth.

"Why would someone do that?" She eased forward when the light turned green, blending seamlessly into the normal flow of traffic despite the fact she was nearly panting with residual panic. "Was it just because we were at the cabin? Did the shooter think we were trespassing or that we might've taken something while we were inside?"

I raised and lowered my shoulders, then looked at the cell phone in my white-knuckled grip. "I have to tell Colton," I croaked.

Dot passed me one of the sports bottles I'd brought along, then chugged the contents of the other as we crept through town at the posted speed limit.

I concentrated on breathing, deep inhales and even longer exhales. In through my nose. Out through my mouth. Slowly, my heart rate returned to normal.

Someone called out to a friend on the street and I nearly swallowed my tongue. "Why doesn't this car have any top or doors?" I asked. What would stop the next bullet from going right through me while I was strapped to her seat?

"I don't know!" Dot yelled. "What is wrong with me?" She took an unexpected right at the pie shop, her attention running back to her rearview mirror every heartbeat or two.

"Where are we going?" I asked. "I need to go home. The sheriff and his deputies are there."

"I'm making sure we aren't being followed. We don't need that gun-toting maniac knowing where you live!"

I couldn't have agreed more, so I dialed Colton as she zigzagged through residential neighborhoods, and waited nervously as it rang. My insides ached with the apprehension of knowing I had to repeat everything that had happened and not wanting to say it aloud. An irrational desperation churned in me. I wanted to hide the attack. I didn't want anyone to know. If no one else knew, then maybe it didn't have to be true.

"Sheriff Wise," Colton answered, his voice thick with authority and an unconditional promise to protect.

"Someone shot at us!" I blurted, suddenly eager to talk. Colton could protect us. He could keep Dot and me safe, and that changed everything. I needed Dot to be safe more than I needed air.

"When?" Colton asked. "Where? Are you hurt? Do you need an ambulance? Stay there. I'm coming to you."

"No. We're on our way back. We're coming to you. Are you still at the cider shop?"

"Yes." He blew a shaky breath through the phone's receiver, and I imagined him digging his fingers into thick sandy hair. "How soon will you be here?"

I looked at my watch, surprised to find my hands still shaking. "Twenty minutes?" I guessed. "Maybe thirty. I'm not sure. Time is passing strangely right now."

"Probably because you're in shock," he growled. "Where are you? Pull over and I'll come pick you up."

"We're in Dot's Jeep near the college, but we're heading home. She's taking a convoluted path to be sure we aren't followed."

Colton launched into a lengthy lament about my ability to find trouble in a town with a near-zero crime rate while I took a minute to assess my scrapes and bruises from our tumble in the forest. When he finished with that, and I failed to explain how to get to Hank's family's cabin in a way he could understand, we disconnected. "He's meeting us at my place," I told Dot. "We have to give written statements about what happened."

She nodded and hung another left. "Is he sending his deputies to the cabin?"

"No. I couldn't explain it right, so he's telling a

couple of his men to get ready. They're going up the mountain with him, and they're taking me as a guide."

Dot's jaw dropped. "No."

"You don't have to go this time," I told her. "I'll have three armed bodyguards. Besides, they won't find the place without me. There isn't even a decent road to follow."

Dot stopped at an intersection and rolled her head against the seatback to face me. "I think I need to lie down."

"I think you should," I said. "When you're ready to get up, you can feed and care for Kenny Rogers."

A small smile bloomed on her pale lips. "That's right. Kenny needs me." She drove on looking slightly uplifted. "I'll be home earlier than I expected. I can spend the extra time working on the donkey and alpaca's trust issues or contacting potential forever families."

"Exactly," I said, "and after a run like that, I bet we got our daily step count in. I think that was more cardio than I've done in my life."

She laughed. "First, I really need to lie down."

Good for her. I doubted I'd sleep again this decade.

Dot slowed for a group of jaywalkers and our location registered to my fuzzy brain. "This is Lincoln Street." I twisted on my seat, looking for the building I'd driven by four times last night. "Pull over," I said, finally spotting the red brick three-story across the street up ahead. "I think Sarah Burrie lives in one of those apartments." I unbuckled when she pulled over, then ran around to Dot's missing door. "Give me five minutes?"

She shifted into park, then let her arms fall limp at her sides. Her shoulders drooped and her head fell against the backrest.

"I'll be quick," I promised. "If I can confirm this is Sarah's place, I'll tell Colton, and we can stop here together after the cabin." I waited for a car to pass me on the street, then dashed across to the opposite sidewalk on wobbly legs.

The neighborhood was historic, just blocks from the community college and filled with apartment buildings from the turn of the last century. Moss grew in the shadows cast by stately oaks, and tree roots pushed the sidewalks into hills and valleys from beneath.

I hurried up the steps to the front stoop. A stack of names with round white buttons lined the jamb beside the door. Half the names were illegible, missing, or utter nonsense. Pinky Moonfry. Thomas the Tanked. A drawing of a stick man on his side.

My attention caught on the tag marked simply SB. I pressed the button and waited.

No answer.

I tried again, and the door opened.

Two little girls walked outside with a playground ball. They looked me over. "You don't live here," the taller one announced.

"I'm looking for a friend. Her name is Sarah Burrie."

"Why don't you know where your friend lives?" the girl asked.

"I know which building," I said, straightening my posture as a fresh round of aches and pains set in. "I just can't remember which apartment."

They shrugged and left.

I followed their lead, having missed my opportunity to grab the open door and slip inside.

I stopped at the corner to cross the street and spotted a BVCC parking pass dangling from the rearview mirror of an older blue sedan. Upon closer inspection, I noticed a stethoscope slung around the gear shifter and two duffle bags on the floor in the back seat. I turned around for a longer look at the building. Was Sarah home? Was this her car? Was she planning to disappear like Hank?

I pressed one palm to my throbbing temple and went back to Dot's Jeep. My body was moving on autopilot and my brain was in no shape to make sense of anything.

Dot pulled away with one arm cradled to her middle as I buckled up. "I'm not cut out for all this excitement," she said. "My pulse finally returned to normal and now I'm nauseous."

"It's shock," I said. Something I knew plenty about. The symptoms were as unique as the person experiencing them, and none of them was pleasant. "Do you want me to drive?"

"No. I'm okay."

She went directly to my place from the apartment building, looking paler by the minute. Either she was sure we weren't being followed now, or she was too tired and queasy to care.

"Do you think it's possible that Sarah was involved with Jack, and she killed him out of jealousy because he married Elsie?"

"Anything's possible," she said. "Someone shot at me today. I never thought that would happen, but it did."

"True," I said, "So, if Jack had been romantically involved with Sarah, it would be equally plausible that Elsie found out, got mad, and lashed out at him for the betrayal."

The same two theories I'd tried on Colton earlier were beginning to seem more and more possible and less and less like theories.

We lumbered along the gravel lane between the county road and my house at a crawl. Fatigue had sucked all the pep out of Dot, and I felt sick for having asked her to go with me. I'd put her in danger to satisfy my curiosity. I wouldn't let that happen again.

Colton leaned against his cruiser, now parked outside my house. His arms were crossed and his brows furrowed.

"He doesn't look happy," she said. "I'm glad I'm leaving. Tell him I'll stop by the station and give a written report when I feel better."

"Okay. I'll call when we get back to see how you're feeling."

She stared through her windshield as I climbed down. "Y'all need to mow your lawn. This is looking rough."

"I know." I let my head fall forward. "We don't have time, so I'm going to hire someone to deal with it." I gave her another long look, not liking the pallor of her skin or the unfocused look in her eye. "Maybe you should come inside and rest."

Dot turned to stare at me. "I know some guys who can help with the grass."

"You do?" I tried to think of who she could mean. Maybe someone she met through the national park? "Who?"

Colton took a step in our direction, apparently tired of waiting for me to say goodbye.

Dot's attention jumped to him.

I refocused on Dot, in no hurry to fight with Colton or relive my recent trauma. "We could use the help," I said. "Are they expensive?"

"No. They'll work for food." She shifted into drive and cut her eyes in Colton's direction. "I'll get them out here so you can meet them. Be careful today. Whoever's camping in that cabin means business."

Colton rounded the Jeep to Dot's side. "I hear you experienced a trauma." He took her hand in his and set his fingers against her wrist. "How are you feeling?"

A tear slid over her cheek.

He flashed a penlight from his key chain into her eyes, then asked her for random details about her life and a list of current physical discomforts. Gauging her injuries and mental faculties, I assumed. Eventually, he agreed to let her drive home.

"No concussion?" I asked as she drove away.

"No. Shock, but she'll be okay. How about you?" he asked. "How are you holding up?"

"Great." I was about to tell him how guilty I felt for being the reason Dot had been in the forest with a shooter to begin with when an old idea resurfaced. "I need to check on something." I made a beeline for my front door and let myself inside. I left the door open so Colton could follow if he wanted, but there was only one thing on my mind. That too-familiar blue sleeping bag.

I hurried through my kitchen, the site of the

dropped mud, and rounded the corner to a storage closet in the hallway. I dropped to my knee and pulled out the totes and boxes stacked beneath a dozen winter coats. When I jerked on the container marked "Camping," I nearly threw it over my head. It wasn't heavy anymore. It was empty!

I jumped to my feet and screamed unnecessarily for Colton, who'd appeared just inches away.

He gripped my forearms to steady me, then scowled at the orange tote in my hand. "What's that?"

"Empty," I turned the container over to demonstrate. "Someone stole my camping gear, and I think they're using it at Hank's family's cabin."

"And you're still going to tell me it wasn't Hank?"

I wavered. I didn't want to think that Hank would break into my house or steal from me, but the facts were glaring. Someone knew where I kept my camping gear, and they knew where to find Hank's family cabin. There were two people in the world with both those tidbits of information. Hank was one of them, and I was the other. Dot might also have known, but since she'd been on the business end of those gunshots, I discounted her as the shooter.

If Hank was the one camping at the cabin, did that make him the shooter?

"People aren't always who we think they are," Colton said, sounding unexpectedly compassionate, and maybe a little guarded. "Someone killed Jack Warren and took two shots at you and your best friend. That person took those shots from a cabin belonging to Hank's family. A cabin, I'm guessing, that contained your stolen camping gear."

"Let's just go," I said, suddenly feeling as deflated as Dot had looked. "I want to get this over with." Then maybe go to bed.

We took Colton's cruiser to the sheriff's department, where we met up with a pair of deputies who'd loaded two gray pickups with one side-by-side, off-road utility vehicle each. Colton and I traded the cruiser for one of the trucks and the deputies climbed into the other.

I examined the cab's interior as we rode toward Carpenter's Run, trying not to think about what had happened earlier or wonder if it might happen again. The truck was clean, almost sterile, and it still had the new car scent so many folks loved. Personally, I'd have preferred to ride in Colton's cruiser. The interior smelled of chewing gum and breath mints. There was dirt on the floorboards and his cologne had seeped into the fabric of the seats.

"You sure you're up to this?" Colton asked, turning off the main road and heading into the hollow at Carpenter's Run.

I rubbed sweat-slicked palms against my trembling thighs. "No, but I'm going to try."

He gave an accepting dip of his chin. "You should tend to those injuries when we get back."

I followed his glance to my filthy outfit. Tears in my shirt and pant legs revealed broken skin and angry red welts. "I tackled Dot," I whispered. "We rolled over a hill. There were leaves gathered at the bottom, but . . ." I pressed my mouth shut, not ready to say more.

"You were brave," he said. "The distance you added with that move could be the reason she's safe at home in bed right now. You did good, Winnie. Know that." The quiet ferocity in his tone sent goose bumps over my arms.

He was wrong though. I hadn't been brave. I'd acted on instinct, and bravery required making a choice against fear. Choosing to come with him now instead of crawling under my covers indefinitely was my feeble attempt at bravery. Colton and his men would've found the cabin with or without me eventually, but my help would expedite the process, and I needed to do what I could. The sooner the killer was brought to justice, the better. Then Dot would no longer be in danger and Hank could go home.

Colton parked in the clearing where mushroom hunters had been earlier and climbed out of the truck. He retrieved a duffle bag from behind the seat, then began to unload it.

I refocused on a pair of squirrels playing chase in the leafy canopy overhead. Was this what they felt like at hunting season? Did they know, like I did, that there was a predator in the woods?

"Here." Colton tossed something dark and heavy onto my lap.

I lifted the object, dumbstruck, as I watched him put on something similar.

"A bulletproof vest?" My ears rang and my stomach flopped. "You think the shooter is still out there. Waiting at the cabin?" I'd hoped the gunman assumed I would return with the sheriff and had since taken leave.

"Better to be safe," Colton said. "Do you need help putting it on?"

I shook my head, then repeated the process I'd

watched Colton perform. "These aren't going to stop a bullet aimed for my head," I said, recalling the small red dot on tree bark beside Dot's wavy hair.

"You're right." He cocked one hip and rested his forearm across the top of the open door. "You don't have to come any further. I don't want you to if it's going to cause you additional trauma."

"Waiting alone in this truck while you disappear into the trees is going to cause me additional trauma." I gripped the door's handle and willed my legs to cooperate. "I'm coming."

Colton went to the back of the truck and lowered the tailgate to free the side-by-side.

I continued to grip the door handle, frozen.

*Sometimes all it takes is enough bravery for the first step*, I told myself. *Just take* one *step*.

By the time the deputies had helped Colton unload the side-by-sides, I was on my feet and ready to face the forest again.

I climbed into the small off-road vehicle and waited while the men set the channel on their long-distance radios, a good idea given the lack of cell phone coverage where we were headed.

The ride was loud and sometimes rough, but we arrived at the cabin just ten minutes later, having covered the same amount of ground that had taken Dot and me more than half an hour to walk. This time, the cabin was empty. No sleeping bag. No half-eaten sandwich, backpack, or jugged water. Even the small spit Dot had seen from the rear window had been dismantled and tossed aside. The firepit had been filled in and watered down. Whoever had been hiding here was gone, and I hoped that was true for the shooter as well.

Colton and his men walked the perimeter, then examined the cabin inside and out using flashlights, metal detectors, and three pairs of blue latex gloves. They cast impressions of footprints in the dirt and tested for signs of body fluids. I stayed close, but out of the way. On another day, I might've learned something. On this day, the best I could do was try not to let Colton out of my sight and keep watch for movement among the trees.

The sun hung low in the summer sky when we finally climbed back into the side-by-sides parked on a road nearly erased by time. The deputies loaded their findings, kits, and equipment, then led the way down the mountain.

The vehicles' engines echoed through the silence, sending treetops full of birds into flight as we passed beneath. In the shadow, backlit by the setting sun, a small, familiar glow caught my eye before falling slowly to the ground.

I gripped Colton's forearm as fear constricted my heart.

Our vehicle stopped. "Did you see something?"

I swallowed hard, unable to take my eyes away from the place where I'd seen the strange light. I lifted a finger toward the trees as a wave of déjà vu struck through me. I'd experienced this all before. With the dot from the scope earlier.

*In the trees beyond my home,* I realized.

Colton radioed the deputies, then climbed out of the vehicle, gun drawn, and moved carefully away.

I watched in terror as he approached the deepening shadows, afraid of what he'd find.

Or what would find him.

The deputies returned and disembarked from their vehicle. One came to stand with me while the other moved in the direction Colton had gone.

"False alarm," Colton said, reappearing suddenly and moving swiftly back to our vehicle.

The deputies wheeled their side-by-side around once more, looking thrilled for a reason to perform the little donut.

Colton, on the other hand, didn't seem happy at all. In fact, he looked as if he'd seen a ghost.

# Chapter Eleven

I gave a written report at the station before Colton drove me home in his cruiser. Twilight had settled over the world around us, casting ethereal shades of lavender and mauve across nearby streams and fields. For the first time in hours, I felt safe, warm, and cozy, surrounded by majestic views of West Virginia's beauty and comforted by the presence of a capable sheriff at my side.

Tension bled from my neck and shoulders as I relaxed against the seat and inhaled the scents of Colton's car. Outside, the wind was starting to pick up.

"Storm's a brewing," Colton said, taking the final turn onto the orchard's long gravel drive. "I hope this won't amount to much." He leaned forward over his steering wheel and peered into the sky. "I'd like to get back out to that cabin at daybreak and take a run at the scene with fresh eyes."

"Does that mean you're planning to get some rest tonight?" I asked, examining the heavy circles beneath his sharp blue eyes. "'Cause it looks like you could use it."

"I'll worry about me," he said, shooting me a disbelieving look. "You should concentrate on not getting shot at again." He parked the car and climbed out.

I waited while he moved around to open my door. Most men didn't make the simple chivalrous gesture anymore, but I liked it. Grampy had been a door opener too. "Thanks."

He climbed the steps behind me, clearly distracted and checking his phone.

I wondered idly if whatever had been on his mind when he'd come out of the woods was still bothering him. "Want to sit and rock a minute?" I asked, delaying our inevitable parting. I had a feeling Colton would leave the minute he knew I was safely inside, and I wasn't ready to be alone.

He must've interpreted the unease in my expression because he took a seat in my red rocking chair and slipped his phone into his pocket. I sat in the gray rocker beside him. I'd rescued the rockers from a curb in town and restored them to the beauties they'd once been. Like Grampy's Mustangs, the rockers had gotten a second chance at life.

Colton and I watched in companionable silence as a growing wind raked over the orchard, swaying branches and freeing the less determined leaves.

"It didn't rain much last night," I said. "Was your crime scene still intact this morning?"

"It wasn't in bad shape. I think we got what we needed."

"What did you need?" I asked, stopping my rocker to focus wholly on his coming answer.

Colton took his time, glancing at the barn before answering, while questions erupted like popcorn in my mind.

"Another piece of the puzzle," he said finally. His blue eyes twinkled, and I knew he was much closer to naming the killer than I was. A childish, competitive streak in me took exception to the little gloat. I'd been looking for answers just as long as he had, after all. *But it wasn't a competition.* He was a sheriff and I was a cider maker. I had only a curious mind and the internet. He had professional training, a team, and a lab on his side.

"Has your puzzle got a picture forming yet?" I asked, trying to pose the question in a way he might answer.

A cocky smile teased his lips. "I think so."

"Care to share?"

"Nope." He turned his attention back to the darkening sky. "Most folks don't like a good storm," he said, swiftly changing the subject. "Storms are loud. They force folks inside and usually get everything wet, but I don't mind."

"Me either," I said, beginning to rock again. "I've always loved the rain. Never feared the storm. Granny used to have to call me in when lightning struck because I'd be lost in play. Dancing in the rain. Twirling in the wind."

He turned to me, his expression unreadable.

"That was just last week," I teased, suddenly feeling exposed. I dragged my attention back to the horizon and concentrated on the easy rhythm of my chair. The weathervane on Granny's house spun in wild circles and her wind socks stood at full mast. "I think there's something a little magical about all this commotion."

"Let's just hope my new crime scene isn't washed away." He removed his hat and scraped long fingers through his hair, a nervous habit of his I'd seen before.

"You did all you could," I reminded him. "And you gathered a lot of samples for the lab."

Colton and his deputies had taken their time combing the area. They'd flagged several sections for a second look and dug a bullet from the bark of a tree. Plus, I was fairly confident that Colton had personally taken at least a million photos on his phone and with an official camera.

"You want to tell me what else is bothering you?" I asked when he didn't respond to my comment on his work. "Don't say it's just this investigation because you haven't been yourself in a while now."

He offered an apologetic smile, then pressed his hat back onto his head and lowered the brim to shield his eyes. "I think I've got a ghost problem."

"Haunted house?" I asked, teasing.

I frowned as I realized for the first time that I had no idea where Colton lived. As the county sheriff, he might not even live in Blossom Valley, and the possibility seemed traitorous.

"Haunted by my past," he corrected, pulling me back to the moment.

"I don't understand."

"It's probably nothing." He stood and moved to

the porch's edge. "I'm just a little off my game I suppose."

I moved with him, hoping to hear what wasn't being said.

He pulled his phone from his pocket and stared at the screen. I recognized the Clarksburg area code on an incoming call, but missed the rest, and the number wasn't saved in his contacts. Clarksburg was the location of our nearest VA Hospital. I'd made the trip many times with Grampy. It was also the town where Colton had been a fast-rising detective before coming to Blossom Valley. It was the place where he'd worked with the local FBI task force.

He rejected the call and tucked the phone into his pocket. "I should leave you to it," he said. "Try to get some sleep and tend to those wounds before they get infected."

I watched as he made his way to his car, looking at his phone once more.

Colton said he was feeling haunted, but to me, he looked more like someone who was being hunted.

I unlocked my door and moved inside, then sent him a text as he climbed inside the cruiser.

CALL IF YOU NEED ANYTHING.

He buckled up, checked his phone, then smiled. A moment later, my phone buzzed with his response.

BACK AT YA.

I dropped my phone on the kitchen counter and turned for the stove. I needed a hearty dose of chamomile, a hot bath, and possibly a shot of whiskey after the day I'd had.

Something moved in my hallway, too tall to be Kenny Rogers or Dolly, and I whipped Louisa out of her corner by the door.

"Don't," the low tenor of a man's voice shot fear into my soul.

Then Hank emerged from the shadow.

"Jeez!" I yelled, dropping Louisa where I stood and moving in to hug my stupid, infuriating, idiot of an ex. "What are you doing here? Where have you been? I was scared to death!" I shoved him for good measure, then hugged him again.

Hank shrugged as I backed away, looking impossibly more exhausted than I felt. He was dressed in a pair of my plaid sleep pants and one of the oversized T-shirts I wore to bed. "I was hiding. You know where, and I'm here now because I had to go somewhere after that lunatic shot up my cabin." He tousled his wet hair and frowned. "I helped myself to food, clothes, and a shower. My stuff's in your laundry. I hope that was okay."

I made a sour face. "Well, it's not as if I can ask you to undo any of that."

He grinned. "I returned your camping gear. Sorry about tearing off your tags but I didn't want any of it to lead back to you if I was caught and it was confiscated by authorities."

I folded my arms across my middle. Typical Hank. He was so concerned about my good name that he defaced the property he'd stolen from me. Yet that same concern hadn't stopped him from helping himself to my entire house. What if he got caught here? How would that look? I pinched the bridge of my nose and tried to focus. "Did you get a look at who was shooting today?"

"No. I heard some rustling outside the cabin, so I went to check it out. I didn't see anyone, but I figured I ought to use the facilities while I was outside."

"Gross."

"Yeah, well, my bladder might've saved my life," he said smugly. "I was down the hill behind the cabin when I heard the first gunshot. I hid until I heard your screams. Then I knew you were in danger, so I ran back up to help you, but someone took a shot at me before I got there."

"I heard the second shot," I said. "I could tell it wasn't near us, so I thought we were making good time getting away." In reality, Hank had drawn the shooter's attention in a new direction.

"I hid again," Hank said. "When I came out a while later, no one tried to kill me so I gathered my things and headed down the mountain. I knew it was only a matter of time before you showed up with the sheriff."

"My things," I corrected, cranking the heat under a pot for tea. "You gathered *my* things and headed down the mountain."

"Potato. Potahto." Hank took a seat on my sofa and hooked one big foot over the opposite knee. "I noticed you and Mr. Lawman looking mighty comfy outside tonight. Hanging out in your matching rockers."

I glared at him, refusing to take the bait, and infinitely relieved to know Hank hadn't been the one shooting earlier.

"I'm glad my misery could bring the two of you closer."

"We've been trying to find you," I said, ignoring

the rest of his dumb statement. "And since you've taken liberties with my home, my shower, food, and camping gear, you owe me some repayment."

"What do you have in mind?" he asked, eagerly leaning forward on the sofa.

I rolled my eyes. "I want answers. What happened the night Jack Warren died? What were you fighting with him about, and how did you even know him? Did you see who killed him? Why did you run?"

Hank held his hands up in a T, signaling for me to take a time out.

"Talk," I said. "Now."

"I would, if I could get a word in, but you're still rattling off questions."

I made a show of taking a seat in the chair across from him and pretending to button my lips.

"For starters," Hank said with a sigh, "none of this is what it seems, which is why I ran. I knew how it would look the moment I saw Jack lying under that truck, so I took off. I needed time to prepare myself for what came next."

"You ran away," I accused. "You should have stayed to clear things up, but you didn't. I've been worried sick, your mom isn't eating or sleeping, and Gina's making hasty, off-the-cuff decisions, all in the name of finding you, while you've been hiding from your reality."

"I haven't just been hiding," he snapped. "You make me sound like a coward. I've been trying to figure out what really happened to Jack. I need to clear my name, and I know once the sheriff has me in custody, he'll stop looking for anyone else to blame. He'll waste precious time on convicting me instead of looking for the real killer. You of all people should understand," he said. "Isn't that exactly the reason you got involved in Mrs. Cooper's murder last winter? I was following your example. I've been investigating."

I held up a hand. "Start over from the beginning, and try not to point at me as your reason for any of this." I'd been Hank's scapegoat before, and I refused to do that ever again.

Late for dinner with his parents? *Winnie* took too long getting ready.

Not interested in a party invitation? *Winnie* has to work that night.

Don't want to donate to a local sports club? *Winnie's* got my wallet.

None of those things had ever been true, but I'd allowed Hank to tell people they were, thinking there wasn't any harm in letting folks down easily. It'd taken time for me to realize it was my reputation he was hurting, never his. I was always the bad guy, and he was the golden boy.

"I've been getting to know Sarah Burrie," he said timidly. "She was one of the bridesmaids. Short. Blonde. Her family is close to the Sawyers."

I rolled one hand in the air, indicating he could move ahead. "I know who Sarah is."

He shifted, then pulled in a long breath. "Things with Sarah were going great until a few days before the wedding. She started acting strangely after Jack got into town. When I pushed her for a reason, she mentioned that he'd come to her house the night before, but she wouldn't elaborate on what had happened or why it'd upset her."

"So you called Elsie," I said. "Making sure the bride knew what she was getting into?"

"No." Shock washed over his face. "I mean, yes, I called her, but I didn't tell her my suspicions about Jack. I asked if she knew why Sarah had been acting strangely, and I made sure to mention the night that something had happened to upset her. I hoped she'd look into it and find that Jack was involved somehow. I even checked back with her a few times to see if she'd made any progress, but she never did. It was too bad. No one deserves to marry a cheater or whatever Jack was. I don't know if Jack came on to Sarah, or hurt her, or what, but whatever happened between them really shook her. When I wouldn't let it go, Sarah told me not to talk to her anymore."

I frowned. That didn't mesh with the memories I had of them at the reception. "You still came to the wedding as her date."

"I took a chance," he said. "I showed up at her place that morning with flowers and an apology. I was dressed for the wedding in case she forgave me. I figured whatever happened between us, she shouldn't have to spend the day alone when she'd already planned for a plus one. She accepted my offer on the condition that I didn't mention Jack to her."

"So, you kept your promise to her, but confronted the groom instead. What did he say?"

Hank huffed. "I avoided that guy all day until I saw him grab Sarah's elbow on the dance floor and whisper something in her ear. He looked mad, and it ticked me off. His best man made it to him before I did. I walked Sarah off the floor, and we went back to our table for some water. She wouldn't tell me what happened. That's why I confronted Jack later."

"And?"

"And he said nothing happened." Hank gave a dark laugh. "He told me I hadn't seen him grab her and that Sarah was mistaken about him stopping by her place the other night."

My hackles went up on principle. Something had clearly happened to Sarah, and the man she'd accused of upsetting her was a little too angry and not enough surprised by the allegation for my taste. "He accused her of lying without even asking what she'd said?"

Hank nodded. "He tried to walk away, and I grabbed his wrist. I shouldn't have, but I lost my temper. I suggested he lay off the liquor and try to work up an apology. He told me I didn't know what I was talking about, and I told him I'd find out what really went on at her place and I'd be back to make sure he apologized. That was when you showed up, he pushed me and ran off."

I worked backward through his story, a little proud of myself for deducing the cause of the tumult was a philandering groom. "You followed him outside. What happened when you got there?'

"I saw the girls with Elsie, but no sign of Jack, so I went the other way. I didn't want to hear Elsie or Sarah complain, and I wasn't finished with Jack. When I heard an engine turn over near the barn, I knew it had to be the getaway truck because everyone else parked in the orchard's gravel lot. I thought that moron was planning to drive in his condition, so I ran around to try to stop him. The truck was running when I got there, but the door was open, and there was no one inside. I went over to take the keys so he couldn't drive, sure it was him planning to storm away." Hank's Adam's apple bobbed and color drained from his face. "That's when I saw him. Under the truck. I couldn't understand what happened. I thought it was some kind of freak accident, but the truck was in park. It couldn't have rolled over him. Someone hit him, then shifted into park." He covered his mouth, looking more than a little sick at the memory. "I heard someone coming. I knew how it looked, and I panicked. I left the keys where they were and ran."

The teapot sang, and I jumped. "I'll get that." I poured two cups of chamomile, then topped Hank's off with cream and sugar.

Wind whistled around my window frames and rattled the panes as I ferried a tray with the tea pot, fixings, and mugs to the coffee table in my living room.

"The weather's supposed to clear up tomorrow," Hank said. "Nothing but warm dry nights for the rest of the forecast."

I lifted my cup, caught off guard by his smooth change of subject from murder to the weather. "How did you hear that while you were in hiding?" I asked, allowing the transition. It wasn't long ago that I'd been dreading a difficult discussion with Colton. Maybe this conversation was just as tough for Hank.

He pointed at my television.

I shook my head. "Of course." I rested my cup against one knee as another thought popped into mind. "Have you been lurking around here at night? Waiting in the tree line for me to leave or fall asleep so you can use my stuff?"

He snorted. "No. Why?"

My stomach dropped. If it wasn't Hank in the trees, then was it my imagination, or was it someone else? "No reason."

Hank propped his feet onto my couch and flipped through the television channels, looking more at ease than I was comfortable with. "This is funny, right? You and me living together. I always thought we'd be married first."

"We aren't living together," I said. "You broke in to use my washing machine and shower. You can't stay here."

He swung his feet onto the floor and sat up straight. Disbelief spread over his innocent face. "I don't have anywhere else to go. If I'm caught, I'll be hauled in for questioning, maybe even arrested." He slid to the edge of the couch cushion, gripping his teacup between his palms and pleading with his eyes. "I can't go to jail. I'm innocent. You have to help me figure this out."

Clearly, Gina wasn't the only overly dramatic person in his family.

"I won't lie for you," I told him. "And I won't hide you here."

"I'm not asking you for that," he said. "No one is going to ask you if I'm staying here. All you have to do it not bring it up."

Colton knew Hank would come here. He'd told me so, and I hadn't believed it. "One night," I said. "You have until dawn to call your sister and your mama. Let them know you're okay and that you're going to do the right thing. I'll drive you to the sheriff's department in the morning and try to help you with Colton, but the bottom line is that you were wrong to run."

Hank frowned, swiveled, and kicked back on my couch. "Fine, but you could at least agree to help me crack this mystery like I helped you in December."

I bit my tongue against the fact that he'd simply answered a few of my questions in December, like a half-dozen other people had. None of those people insisted on getting partial credit for my work.

"Fine," I said. "Let's start with where Sarah is hiding," I said, feeling frustrated as usual in his presence and still in need of answers.

He waited for the soda commercial to end before looking my way. "What do you mean?"

What I meant was that she had risen quickly to the top of my suspects list. What I said was, "She ran away when I tried to talk to her at school, and when I stopped by the building I believe her apartment is in, she didn't answer her buzzer. So, is she avoiding me? Is she on the run? Where is she?"

Hank rolled onto his side and propped his head on one hand. "I don't know. She was supposed to meet me at the cabin today, but she never showed. I'm a little worried about her to be honest."

My jaw dropped. "Seriously?"

"I couldn't believe it either," he said, looking genuinely shocked. "I gave her perfect directions and waited all morning for her to arrive. A shooter showed up instead. Go figure." He turned blissfully, cluelessly, back to my television, never once considering that his new girlfriend had shown up as promised.

And that she'd brought a gun.

# Chapter Twelve

I woke the next morning to the sudden pounding of someone's fist against my door, and jolted upright in bed. My hazy thoughts and addled mind believed for a moment the house was under siege or being ripped from its foundation by a twister. When my phone began to ring on my bedside table and Colton's face appeared, I knew I was in trouble.

"Coming!" I called into the air, then picked up the phone and answered with the same startled cry. "Coming!" I hopped out of bed and wobbled. The urgency of the knocking had literally thrown me off balance.

"Are you up?" Colton asked, his voice strong and assured through the phone at my ear. There was an air of relief in the sound despite the previous pounding.

"No," I groaned. "I was sleeping." Like the dead apparently. Though, I supposed that was what a couple days of continuous stress would do to a person.

"Care if I come in?" he asked. "The porch is lovely, but I'd rather talk to you in person."

"Sure. Give me just a minute." I flung open my bedroom door and ran for the living room. Hank wasn't on the couch. "Uhm," I said softly, turning in a small circle before sprinting room to room. "Almost there."

Kenny Rogers and Dolly raced around my feet, meowing and attempting to corral me toward their bowls for breakfast. I hopped over them, looking behind furniture and open doors for signs of a cowering Hank. Then I made fast plans to murder him myself if I found him still in my house. He'd promised to leave and do the right thing this morning.

The cats dug their claws into my pant legs, crying for food as I hurried from one room to the next, sweeping the floor with my tabbies as I went.

No one in the laundry room, guest room, or bathroom, but there was half a pot of coffee on the counter. Steam floated from the contents. A dirty mug beside it. I ground my teeth and spun back to the empty couch in the living room. "Of course the blanket's not folded," I complained. "Ridiculous."

"Winnie?" Colton asked. "Everything okay?"

My heart sped. "Yep." I bounced the heel of one hand off my forehead. "It's just such a mess in here." I flipped the blanket into the air, folded it in half, then hung it over the back of the sofa. I righted fallen pillows and gathered discarded snack papers from my coffee table on my way to the kitchen trash. "I wasn't expecting you again so soon," I told Colton as I reached for the doorknob. Then I remembered the coffee.

I dumped the pot into the sink and tossed the cup into the dishwasher before pulling my front door open. "Hello." My breath came too fast, and my skin was on fire from my poor choice in sleepwear.

Colton looked me over. "Are those flannel pajamas?"

"Mm-hmm." I'd selected my least attractive set before bed because something about Hank being in the next room all night felt icky. "I was cold. Coffee?"

"Please," he said, still frowning. "It's pretty warm in here, and nearly eighty outside already."

I filled the kitties' bowls with kibble, then got to work making fresh coffee for the humans.

"What brings you here this morning?" I asked, only needing one guess. *Was it because I gave a near-fugitive shelter and didn't call to turn him in like I should have?* "Nothing's wrong, I hope." I dared a glance at his exhausted and strung-out expression while I selected two mugs from the cupboards.

"I'm afraid so. We need to talk."

I opened my mouth to agree, hoping I appeared calmer than I felt, but a strangled sound came out instead.

*We need to talk* never prefaced anything good, and since Colton was a lawman and I'd let Hank hide out in my house all night. "I'm so sorry," I blurted as Colton said, "My team and I found another body this morning."

"What?" we said in unison.

I covered my mouth with one hand and pointed at him with the other.

"We found a body in the forest near the Dono-van family cabin."

The hairs on my arms rose to attention beneath the too-warm flannel. I gripped the counter for balance. "Where?"

"At the bottom of a hill, just outside the perimeter I cleared yesterday."

My stomach rolled. Could the body be Hank's? Is that why Colton was behaving so strangely? I'd told Hank he couldn't stay, so he'd run back to his family's cabin and been killed? Was that possible? "Who?" I asked softly.

"Maybe we should sit down," he said, motioning to my living room.

I didn't need to be asked twice. My knees were already shaking. "Was it Hank?"

"No." Colton followed me to the living room and took the seat beside me on the couch. "No wallet. No license. We're attempting to identify him now."

I nearly collapsed onto the cushions, selfishly thankful it wasn't my friend but knowing the man was someone else's. "We were just there. I watched you go over every inch around the cabin. You left evidence that you'd be back. Tarps and crime scene tape. Someone went there anyway? Then got killed? It doesn't make any sense."

"The body was about ten yards outside the perimeter I set yesterday." He gave a humorless chuckle, then set his hat on my coffee table and returned to the kitchen. He reappeared a moment later with two mugs of black coffee and offered one to me. "Someone had covered him in leaves, but the storm blew some of those away. The tip of one boot and top of his head were visible today. Th_ coroner's up there now making some initial assessments. He'll be on his way back to the morgue soon to process the body."

"Why are you here?" I asked, confused and suddenly worried again. Did he want me to take a stab at identifying the body? "Oh, no. Do you think I know him?" I raced mentally over all the men I knew and which of their deaths might initiate a personal visit by the sheriff.

Colton returned to the seat beside me and set his mug aside. He clasped his hands and released a long, labored breath. "I came here because when I saw that body, so close to the place where someone had shot at you, I realized it could have been you. It was one thing for you to tell me about the shooting after it was over and you were okay. It was something else to see a body there."

I set my hand on his arm. "I'm still okay," I whispered, "just like I was yesterday. Just like I'll be tomorrow." I understood the crush of emotions in his eyes. I'd felt the same way when Dot had been in danger. My heart warmed with a realization of my own. *Colton cared.*

He wet his lips and nodded, seeming to pull himself out of the funk. He scanned the room then lifted his cup for a long pull on the coffee, successfully dislodging my fingers from his arm.

"No one recognized the new body?" I asked. It seemed strange in a town as small as ours, though to be fair, the local sheriff's department covered more than Blossom Valley.

"No. I even sent his picture through our department email. No one's seen this guy before, and it's bugging the snot out of me."

"You think it's related to whoever shot at me?" I asked.

"A man was killed outside a remote cabin, owned by the family of a person of interest in a recent murder. Add in the fact that someone shot at you outside that same cabin, and I'm sure it's all connected. I just can't seem to figure out how, and I don't like it."

"Maybe the shooter and this guy are related, but not Jack's death," I suggested. "Maybe the shooter had been waiting for this guy and mistakenly shot at Dot and me when we arrived."

"Maybe." Colton settled back against the cushions with his mug in hand.

"What happened to him?"

"Toss-up. Could be a fatal head trauma. Could be the bullet in his gut. I'll have to wait for the autopsy."

I felt the wind whoosh from my lungs.

Colton's exterior was eerily calm. His clenching jaw and curled fingers told me there was more. "He was dressed for hiking. The hill he was at the base of wasn't too steep, but it would only take the right rock and the wrong part of his head to connect, and that wouldn't matter."

"He was shot?" I asked, finally finding my tongue.

"Yep. Found a .45 caliber casing in the leaves. Matches the one I pulled from the tree near the Donovans' cabin. One that had been aimed at you and Dot."

My stomach rolled and heat rushed up my neck and across my cheeks. I willed myself not to be sick in front of him. It really could have been me, or Dot or Hank under those leaves this morning.

"You finally seem to be having an appropriate reaction to my news."

I shot him a sarcastic look.

I tried to imagine someone wandering all the way back to Hank's family cabin. There weren't any hiking trails out there, and it wasn't hunting season.

"Mushroom hunters!" I perked up at the idea. "Maybe he's one of those guys who came in from up north to look for mushrooms." From the short look I'd gotten at that crew, they'd seemed like people with money who'd taken an adventure together. I thought of their high-end cars and name-brand gear, their special truffle hogs. "Maybe he found some valuable mushrooms and someone else wanted them. We know there are mushrooms in the area; traces of them were in the soil on my floor."

"But we don't know where that soil came from," he said. "Do we?"

I bit my lip against the urge to tell him it was Hank who'd trailed it in here while stealing my things. "Maybe you should talk to the mushroom hunters."

"Already done," he said. "I was at the Sip N Sup looking for them. I found a few who gave me the rundown on why they moved their camp up to Archer's Knob yesterday. Seems they heard gunshots and saw two women in a Jeep come flying off the mountain. It spooked them, so they relocated."

"Guilty."

"I am aware," he grouched.

Colton unearthed his phone from one pocket and swiped the screen. "I need to read this." He leaned forward, deeply focused.

I craned my neck for a peek as he scrolled.

"Huh." He rubbed his head and wrinkled his nose, looking both baffled and determined.

I imagined that was what I looked like the first time Granny asked me to balance the orchard's failing bank accounts. "What is it?" I asked, scooting closer.

Colton put the phone away. "What are you doing?"

"What do you mean?"

One side of his mouth kicked up into an almost-smile. "Some people might think it's bad manners to read another person's messages over their shoulder."

"Some people might say the same thing about dragging a lady out of bed twice in a row," I countered. "Was that the coroner?"

He watched me for a long beat before answering.

I curled my fingers into the edge of the cushion beneath me, waiting for whatever came next.

"Yes. He and the John Doe are back at the morgue, and he sent me a copy of the workup on Jack Warren. According to the report, most of Jack's wounds were consistent with being hit by a truck."

"Most?" I asked, still wondering about the strange expression on his handsome face. "Did Jack have other wounds that weren't fatal?"

"Yep."

What on earth? I slumped against the couch to consider the possibilities. Had someone knocked Jack out before running him over? Before stabbing him? Before *shooting* him? Would anyone have heard the shot above the DJ and his music? "What kind of wounds?"

"Defensive ones. Bruises and cuts on his hands, arms, and legs. Plus a puncture wound on his left calf that had been stitched. Poorly. Possibly by himself."

He'd treated his own injuries? "Who would do that?" I gasped. "I thought people only did that stuff on television."

"People who have something to hide will avoid hospitals at all costs. Medical professionals are required by law to report all gunshots and stabbings."

"You think someone stabbed him and he stitched it himself?" I stood so I could pace. "That's crazy. I can't even remove my own splinters." I circled the coffee table, chewing the edges and corner of my thumbnail. "Maybe that was why he was drinking so heavily. He was hurting and over-the-counter painkillers weren't cutting it."

"You need to stop," Colton said, pushing onto his feet. "I came over here to tell you about the John Doe so you'd see how dangerous things have become. Being shot at didn't seem to do it for you." He dug his fingers into the muscled ropes of tension along the back of his neck and swore under his breath. "You need to let this all go, Winnie. Hear me? The next body I come across can't be yours." He swiped his hat off the table and headed for the door. "Open your darn cider shop and stay here where it's safe today. Let me do my job. You stick to yours."

I watched in stunned silence as Colton marched out the door and down the front steps to his car. Then I ran to the open door and stared as his taillights vanished down the long gravel drive.

My blood boiled at the tone he'd taken with me. And he'd marched out before I could say so! A dozen forms of retaliation pushed through my mind, but they all felt a little too immature to act on. I collected my mug and went for a refill on my coffee, despite the fact my hands were now shaking from adrenaline.

The cats headed my way, probably sensing my mood and coming to nip my socked feet. They started at a small sound that drew my attention as well. I waited, frozen, for the sound to come again.

When it did, I got my bat.

I crept toward the storage closet with Louisa perched high on one shoulder. The cats stretched their skinny arms under the door, swiping at whatever was inside. I listened carefully at the small rustling, trying to place the sound. If Hank had somehow packed a mouse in my gear and brought it back from the cabin, I was going to be livid.

The closet door opened as I reached for it, and I screamed, swinging Louisa like my life depended on it.

Hank jumped back as the wood whipped past his head. "Whoa! Whoa! Whoa!" he yelled. "Stop! It's me!"

"Hank!" I released Louisa, and she clattered to the floor. Then, I clutched my chest where the sharp pain of shock and realization hit like a hammer. *I could've killed Hank!* "What is wrong with you!" I yelled, unsure who I was more upset with, him or myself.

"Me?" he asked, incredulous. "Well, for one thing, I've been cramped in your storage closet for the last twenty minutes while you and the sheriff made sweet talk." He dragged himself free of my crowded closet with a look of intent distaste. "Do you ever throw anything away? You can't possibly need all that stuff." He straightened the hem of his shirt and brushed his palms down his sides. He was in his own clothes now, and I suspected the outfit he'd taken from me to sleep in was probably on my floor somewhere.

I shook a finger at him while I caught my breath. "You can't judge my closets. You're practically homeless at the moment, and you promised me you'd be gone when I woke up."

"I would've been," he said. "If the sheriff hadn't shown up." He plucked the fabric of his shirt away from his chest, then gave me a pointed look. "I got dressed. Made my own breakfast. Then he came and I had to hide."

"You shouldn't have hidden," I said. "You're supposed to turn yourself in. What if that body they found in the woods this morning had been you?"

Hank went to pour coffee into one of my travel mugs. "Well, it wasn't." He helped himself to plenty of my milk and sugar, then leaned comfortably against the counter. "I was listening to you, and I'm thinking those guys might've been involved in some kind of love triangle gone wrong."

"The John Doe and Jack?" I asked. "And who do you suppose was the woman in that scenario?"

Hank squinted at me over his mug. "Don't say Sarah. She isn't the bad guy just because I was seeing her and you hate me."

"I don't hate you," I said. "And I wouldn't accuse her of murder because she dated you. Though I wouldn't blame her either."

He made a sarcastic face and went back to his coffee.

Kenny Rogers and Dolly leapt onto the counter at his side and took turns rubbing against him. Traitors.

"Where are you going from here?" I asked, offering a not too subtle hint.

Hank petted the cats, then looked at his watch. "Back to the cabin," he said, overly confident as usual. "That seems to be where all the action is these days. Maybe I can find some answers there."

"If you're going in search of answers, you should try to locate your bridesmaid."

His lips pulled down at the corners. "I'll see you later."

"Don't forget to turn yourself in while you're out," I said, following him to the back door. "There should be plenty of lawmen standing by to take your confession at the cabin since you're headed straight for an active murder scene."

Hank stepped outside and gave me a dirty look as he made a run for the tree line behind my house.

I shut the door behind him and locked it.

# Chapter Thirteen

I dressed for the day in a comfortable pair of jean shorts and a red V-neck T-shirt. I slid my bare feet into plain white sneakers, then locked up on my way out. Thanks to Hank's intrusion and being woken by a worked-up lawman two days in a row, my home didn't feel cozy or relaxing anymore. Hopefully it would again soon, after the killer was found and Hank stopped hiding in my closet. I strode purposefully across my overgrown lawn toward the cider shop, and considered turning Hank in for the hundredth time since he'd appeared last night. Like the coward I was, I decided to put it off a little longer. Telling Colton I hadn't called immediately would only make him madder, and I was already angry at him for coming over uninvited and then storming out. He and I could only handle so many rifts at a time. Better to put my nervous energy to work preparing to reopen my shop for guests.

The place had already been cleaned spotless by Granny and Delilah, but there was always more to be done. I could count my inventory. Make or order more of the depleted items. Create a new menu for the day. I checked my watch. It was barely ten, which gave me plenty of time to do any of those things, but I enjoyed making new menus the most.

Opening my shop late in the mornings was perfect for a number of reasons. For starters, I wasn't a morning person. I preferred to wake up when I was done sleeping, and thanks to school and work, I hadn't gotten to do that very often in my life, until now. I liked to take advantage of the opportunity. Second, there wouldn't be much point to opening during the breakfast rush at Sip N Sup. Granny's baked goods were near-perfection, but nothing compared to the diner's homemade biscuits and sausage gravy. Their cook, Freddie, made it all from scratch. Everyone in town knew it. And everyone in town wanted it. I couldn't begin to compete.

A raucous bout of laughter drew my attention across the field to Granny's house as I passed. Several trucks sat in the drive outside her door, and the inviting scents of fresh-baked fritters wafted through her open windows.

I made a detour to say hello and see what all the fuss was about.

"Come in!" Granny called when I knocked.

"Hey." I slid inside and waved at the crowded room before me. Every chair at the kitchen table had a needlepointer in it, all hard at work over stacks of white canvas squares, Persian yarns, and cotton threads. The eight women smiled and waved. Each had a steaming mug of coffee and, as I'd hoped, the countertop was lined in hot breakfast foods and fresh pastries.

"Winnie!" Granny came at me with open arms. "How are you, sweetie? Make yourself a plate." She kissed my cheek, then checked the black cat clock over her stove. "Oh, you've got time." She turned back to the table. "She has time. Make room for Winnie."

The women inched their seats closer together, making a place for me while Granny ran for another chair from the dining room. I filled a plate with spinach and cheddar quiche, an assortment of fruits, and a fritter or two, then buttered a slice of apple bread with Granny's homemade cinnamon butter and went to take my seat. "So, what's going on?" I asked, eagerly diving in to the delicious-smelling fruit. "I heard you laughing all the way across the field."

Granny blushed. "We were just lifting Delilah's spirits."

Delilah frowned.

"She decided to email that letter to the Stitch Witches yesterday instead of using the post office," Granny continued. "Their group has a website, so she sent the letter to their contact address, and she received a phone call this morning."

"A phone call?" I dragged a forkful of flaky fritter through the oozing pie filling on my plate and tried not to moan in delight. "What'd they say?"

The women tensed collectively. Some doubled down on their work. Others glanced tentatively at Granny or Delilah.

"They weren't amicable to the invitation," Granny said.

Delilah shot Granny a sour look and tossed her stitching onto the table beside her coffee. "They told me to go to hell. That's what they said."

The other women snickered. Those in the chairs beside Delilah patted her hands.

Granny sighed. "They were unnecessarily rude."

I aimed my fork for the quiche. "So you're making plans for the convention without them?"

"We're plotting revenge," Delilah said.

I stopped my fork halfway to my lips. "What?"

"Nothing we'd ever dream of doing," Granny added. "It's all in good fun."

The small brunette beside me smiled with full rosy cheeks. She had a delicate golden cross on a chain at her collarbone and a cream cardigan draped over her narrow shoulders. The woman on her right had called her Sue Ellen, and I thought she might be the pastor's wife. "We can add diuretics to their coffees at the state convention," she said, lifting her shoulders to her ears as she giggled. "Then steal all their toilet paper."

"Brutal," I said.

The group burst into laughter.

Delilah rolled her eyes. "I think we should find out where they plan to stay and cancel their reservations, then buy up all the available rooms so they can't stay anywhere in town."

"Expensive," I said, popping a bite of apple bread between my lips.

Granny began to chuckle silently, her torso bobbing goofily across the table from me. "Now that we know the group's email address," she said be-

tween bursts of quite laughter, "I think we should
sign them up for as many mailing lists as we can
find. Overrun their email account with ads about
aging gracefully and losing weight!"

The group cackled.

Delilah smiled. "This is why you ladies are the
best. You're my sisters. I love you."

They all got up to hug Delilah, who looked impossibly smaller when surrounded by her ladies.

Granny was the first to step away. She poured
me some cider and patted my back. "We wouldn't
really do any of those awful things," she said. "We
just joke about what we'd do if we had the chance,
then we go back to being the nice ladies that we
are. It's good for morale."

I couldn't help wondering if plotting fake re
venge on Hank or Colton would make me feel any
better.

The group hug dissipated, and Delilah wiped a
few tears from her cheeks. "So, Miss Winnie," she
said, "I sent my letter. How about you? Have you
chosen the cider flavor you're going to use to woo
the judges of that contest yet?"

"I've narrowed it down," I said. Which didn't really answer her question. I'd "narrowed it down"
immediately upon discovering the contest. My
three best-selling flavors were a holiday mix with
hints of pumpkin pie spice, vanilla, and nutmeg; a
more traditional fall blend of cinnamon and clove;
and a lighter, warm-weather version made with cit-
rus and ginger. The problem was that I could only
send one. "But I'm open to opinions."

The group exchanged a moment of bright-eyed
looks, then chatted animatedly about their favorite

cider flavors while I sat back and listened. Apparently, Granny always kept a jug or two of my products on hand, and many of the ladies had tasted the evolution of my craft while they'd stitched. A few of the women had been sampling my work from the very beginning, when Granny first bragged about my ideas for manipulating the standard cider's taste.

"Whatever you send will deserve to win," the pastor's wife said. "If you don't win, it's not because your product wasn't the best. It's because those magazine judges don't know what good cider really is."

Delilah folded her hands and smiled. "It's exciting, isn't it?"

"What?"

"All this promise lying ahead of you. Sometimes I wonder what my life would've been like if I hadn't married a soldier at eighteen. What if I hadn't been torn away from my home, family, and friends, then sent halfway across the world to be an army wife?"

Sue Ellen nodded. "I had three children before most women these days graduate college. My oldest had her four-year degree before I turned forty!"

The group murmured agreements and understandings.

"I wanted to be a pilot," one said.

"I wanted to open a dance studio, but the bank wasn't keen on lending money to women back then, not without a husband to help me manage the finances," said another.

"I dreamed of being an actress and of traveling the world," Delilah said. "I traveled, but none of it was carefree or glamorous. It was all pretty scary and too often heartbreaking."

My eyes stung at the thought. The eight other women in Granny's kitchen were each more than twice my age. The bulk of their years on this earth were already behind them. They'd traded their freedom in early for wedding bands and mother-hood.

I couldn't imagine being married. Not now. Maybe never. Definitely not at eighteen like Granny and so many of her friends. I was jaded by my mother's ridiculous behavior, running off to get married as a senior in high school, then getting pregnant and divorced before she'd left her teen years. The fact that my only real romantic relation-ship had been with Hank probably didn't help.

I hadn't written off the idea of marriage com-pletely. Granny and Grampy had shown me how beautiful a true partnership could be, but it would take one heck of a guy to make me consider it.

I rose to rinse my empty cup and plate.

"Are you headed to your cider shop now?" Granny asked. "Will you need help with anything today?"

"Nope. How about you? Have you got the or-chard covered?"

Granny nodded. "Yep. My first tour bus gets here around noon for a hayride and light lunch."

"Great!" Tour buses were the orchard's bread and butter this time of year. They brought groups to tour the orchard and learn about life on our land. Some groups came from as far as New York and Chicago. The visitors tended to take a ton of apples and cider home with them too, which meant our products were traveling far and wide, hopefully along with great word of mouth. Schools had started paying to visit for field trips during the school year too, thanks to Dot's connection to the nature center. She made sure every teacher and student had a flyer for Smythe Orchard and my cider shop when they left one of her classes.

I moved toward the door, and Delilah caught me with a grin. "Owen Martin stopped by looking for your Granny. She hid, but Owen and I talked for a long while. When he left, I found his press ID on the ground. Seems like he 'accidentally' dropped it, so he'll probably have to come back around to pick it up." She formed finger quotes around the word accidentally.

Granny frowned. "If he asks about me again, say I'm busy."

"Got it," I said. "Thanks for feeding me." I kissed her cheek, then looked at the ladies around the table. "And for the laughs. I needed them. In fact, I think I'll go open the cider shop and plan some fantasy revenge to improve my mood."

"Nothing too dark," Sue Ellen called. "You don't want to harden your heart. Just release a few demons."

The others nodded.

"No fire ants in his waist band then?" I teased. "No habaneros on his ham sandwich?"

Delilah choked on her coffee. The others broke into a fresh round of wild laughter.

Granny opened the door for me. "I think you've got the idea."

I smiled as I went on my way. It was kind of fun to plan juvenile acts of revenge. If nothing else, the process reminded me that revenge wasn't something I wanted in my heart or life. In hindsight, I didn't have much to be upset about. I'd once been blind to Hank's shortcomings because I'd thought I loved him, and at present all those things were probably unfairly amplified. As for Colton, he'd been harsh but not unkind. He was rightfully worried about me and admittedly haunted by something he wasn't willing to share. He'd lost his temper and stormed out. So what? He was human after all, and while I didn't like his behavior, he wasn't mine to mold.

The sun was high in the sky and warm on my skin as I headed up the long grassy lane from Granny's house to the barn. The breeze was gentle and warm, tickling the trees and adding interest to an already gorgeous landscape. Tall green grass met a cloudless blue sky on the horizon, broken only by the occasional meandering livestock. The land beyond the barn was part of an enormous ranch that hired cowboys to tend the herd. My historic Mail Pouch barn stood tall and regal at the center of my view. Groves of apple trees filled the world on its left. A winding road and distant mountain marked the space on its right. And then there was me, thankful to soon stand before it.

It sometimes bugged me that the rest of the world reduced my life and all of West Virginia to one old John Denver song, because this place was so much more than that. But at the same time, the lyrics said it all. "Take Me Home, Country Roads" was the cry of my people.

My steps faltered as the barn drew near, all wistful thoughts erased. I wasn't sure what had changed, but my intuition insisted something had. I scanned the immediate area more closely, then looked farther, critically examining the tree line closest to the barn. Wind wiggled the leaves and bowed the grasses. When the breeze stilled, silence gonged around me.

I pulled my phone and keys from my pocket, then gave the closed barn doors a tug to confirm they were still locked. I turned the key and pulled the creaky doors apart. For a moment, I was lost in the memories of horrific things that had happened to me last winter, but I couldn't let that control me now. I forced my mind back to the present and told myself to breathe.

I inhaled deeply and a fresh gust of wind tickled my nose with the scent of something strange. In the next heartbeat, a cigarette butt collided with my shoes. Seemingly delivered from nowhere, it spun and tumbled through the gravel and grass around my sneakers.

The orange ember at the tip was still aglow.

# Chapter Fourteen

I jumped inside and pulled the doors shut behind me, heart thundering wildly. Blood whooshed between my ears as I secured the locks with trembling hands, then rushed from light switch to light switch, illuminating the space. Thankfully there weren't any threats hiding inside.

I peeked around the curtains at each window, searching for signs of a lurker, a vagrant smoker, or worse: a stalker.

No one was in sight. The barn was silent, save my pounding heart, and I had to wonder . . . was I overreacting?

Or had the strange orange glow I'd seen outside my home and again in the woods been a lit cigarette? The idea of someone smoking among the trees near my home or on the mountain had never occurred to me. I rarely saw anyone with a cigarette these days, but now that one had blown against my shoes outside the cider shop, I had to wonder . . . was it possible the butt and strange orange glow were connected?

I wiped sweat from my brow and went behind the bar to put some distance and a barrier between myself and the door. I set my phone on the counter, contemplating. Should I call Colton? 911? The sheriff's department?

Or was I crazy? Was the butt just litter? It was possible the last few days had been too much for me, and I'd finally gone mad.

I opened a bottle of water from the fridge and took long, cooling gulps. Was it possible a careless driver had flicked a cigarette from his window and the wind had carried it to my feet? How long did cigarettes stay lit if they weren't snuffed out?

I brought up Colton's number on my cell phone and imagined what I would say.

*I'd like to report a litterbug.*

Or maybe, *I'd like to report having the sensation something was wrong, followed by the scent of cigarette smoke and the appearance of a butt.*

Both seemed silly. And Colton would want more information that I didn't have.

*Did you see anyone near the barn?* No.

*Did you hear anything unusual?* No.

*Notice where the butt might've come from?* No.

I pushed the phone into my pocked and rested my head on the counter. Why was my life like this?

I went back to the window and turned the sign to OPEN, but didn't unlock the door. If anyone came and tried the door, I'd pretend to have forgotten, then I'd let them inside. As long as the door was locked, a lunatic couldn't come waltzing in on me while I was alone.

I paced the floor, peeking through the windows every few moments before heading to the stockroom. Counting inventory would keep my mind busy until I decided what to do about the cigarette. Two shelves of baking supplies later, I dialed Colton and waited as the call rang through. Several nerve-racking rings later, the call went to his voicemail.

I considered hanging up, but there was no sense. Caller ID would show him it was me who'd called. "Hey, Colton," I started as normally as I could. "I wanted to run something by you, but it can wait." I ran back to the front and peered through the windows. No strangers lurking outside. No one breaking down the door to get in. Just the paranoia of a girl who'd been traumatized one too many times in the last six months. "Yeah. It can wait . . . but call me as soon as you get this." I disconnected then tapped the phone against my forehead.

Stupid. Stupid. Stupid.

The whole thing was ridiculous. I had no reason to fear the cigarette butt. I was wasting precious time that would be better spent caring for my business or figuring out what was going on in my little town. Preferably the latter since I had no customers at the moment and would really enjoy sleeping without fear of another home invasion by my ex.

I shook out my arms and rolled my shoulders, then climbed onto a stool at the bar so I could think. An idea presented itself immediately, and I dialed Sip N Sup, then asked for Reese.

Freddie, the cook, answered, told me he missed

my face, then put me on hold while he went after Reese.

"Any new gossip on Jack Warren?" I asked the moment she said hello.

"Not a word. Just a minute." Something scraped across the phone's receiver, then Reese's muffled voice hollered for another waitress to pick up her order at the service counter. "Sorry about that," she said sounding loud and clear once more. "It's busy as all get out in here. I swear some days the breakfast crowd lasts clean through lunch, or at least until Freddie's biscuits and gravy run out."

"Sorry. I won't keep you." I'd always hated getting calls at work. It usually led to disappointed customers and reduced tips. "Just one more thing. Have you heard anyone talking about Hank or the missing bridesmaid? Maybe some gossip or a possible sighting?"

"There's a missing bridesmaid?" Reese asked. "Since when?"

"I'm not sure she's missing," I admitted. "Could be she's just avoiding me." I scrambled to recall the recent order of events. "I haven't been able to catch up with her since the morning Gina and I came in for breakfast. We tried to talk to her at school, but she ran. I've tried her apartment, I think, but she doesn't answer."

"She goes to your school?" Reese asked, concern coloring her voice. "Who was the bridesmaid?"

"Sarah Burrie. Do you know her?" Hope lifted in my chest. "Do you know how I can reach her?"

"Sarah Burrie," Reese repeated. "Are you sure?"

"I'm sure that's her name," I said, "but that's

about all. I think she knows what happened to Jack Warren, and I have reason to think she's been in touch with Hank."

"Wow. You think you know someone."

Excitement rippled over my skin. "How well do you know her?" Could Reese know what had happened between Sarah and Jack?

"We went to school together," Reese said. "Since kindergarten. We rode the same bus. Marched in the same band."

"You were in the marching band?" The statement threw me from the moment. I immediately imagined her in a polyester pantsuit with a tall hat and gold feather plumes.

"Trumpet," she said proudly. "First chair for three years."

*Wow,* her words echoed in my head. *You think you know someone.* Before I could refocus on the topic of Sarah, the Sip N Sup manager yelled for Reese to get back to work.

I hadn't missed that aspect of the job at all.

"I've got to go," Reese said. "Sarah and I were never close, and we don't stay in touch, but my mama says that Sarah's mama told her she's working at the hospital in medical records now. Maybe try there."

"Thanks."

Reese disconnected our call, and I made plans to visit the hospital's medical records department soon. Meanwhile, I needed to stay open for business. Being closed two days following a murder would be seen as respectful. Being closed for three days would look suspicious. And I couldn't afford anymore wagging tongues or bad press. The orchard was just beginning to make money again, and my business was too new to withstand more hits.

A shadow moved across the drawn curtain in the front window, and I held my breath. The form and movement were human.

I dialed 911 on my phone then hovered my thumb above the SEND button, wishing in vain that I'd brought Louisa with me.

"Winnie?" Gina's voice warbled through the closed doors as she gave them a hard shake. "Are you in there? This sign says open, but the doors are locked. Are you hurt? Are you alone?"

"I'm here!" I called, hurrying for the doors before she pulled them off the hinges. "I'm okay. Come in." I unlocked and opened the doors, then leaned outside and checked in each direction for a deranged killer before tugging her inside. I locked up behind her for good measure. I wasn't alone anymore, but Hank's one-hundred-pound little sister felt more like a liability than protection.

She cocked a brow at me. "Are you okay?"

I nodded too quickly, and my head felt light. "Can I get you a cider?"

"Water," she said. "I'm on a detox. No sugar. No caffeine. The stress from this week is breaking me out."

She looked magazine-worthy to me, but I didn't have the brainpower to convince her otherwise at the moment. I handed her a bottle of water from my fridge, then took another long pull from my bottle.

Gina fluffed her giant platinum hair and slouched. "I've combed through every last one of Hank's things, read all his emails, and talked to all his friends. I don't know any more about his location now than I did when the sheriff first told me he was missing." A tear slid over her cheek and she swiped it away. "I wish I knew a little less about his shopping habits, but you take the good with the bad, right?"

"I suppose." I smiled, ready to deliver my good news. Hank was okay, or at least he had been a couple of hours ago, but she went on.

"Mama still isn't sleeping. I go by to fix her meals and check on her, but she just sits there by the phone. It's awful."

"I know where he is," I blurted, before she had a chance to push ahead again. "Well, I know where he said he'd be," I corrected. I wasn't sure how his appearance at an active murder scene had gone over. Maybe he was in jail. "But I've seen him, and he's okay."

Tears rolled silently over Gina's cheeks as she smiled "Yeah?"

"Yeah." I filled her in on everything her brother had told me, then added the information I'd gotten from Reese.

Gina listened quietly as I unloaded the details in erratic, sometimes illogical order, then she squealed when I finally finished. She ran at me with a tackle hug and pinned me to the service counter. "Bless you! Mama's going to be so happy! I'm going to wring Hank's neck as soon as I drag him home to show her he's okay."

I knew the feeling. "Perfect. You do that, and I'll see if I can nail Sarah down after I close up tonight."

"Deal!" She raised a hand for a high-five, then slapped it against my palm. "We make an awesome team!" She practically vibrated in place as I unlocked the door to set her free.

I locked up behind her, then checked my silent phone for a missed call or message. There weren't any, so I busied myself cleaning and organizing the materials behind the bar. I erased the lettering from the huge antique mirror I'd purchased from a bar in Charleston. The entire downtown building had been set for demolition, and I knew the enormous mirror that had hung proudly behind the service counter for decades was exactly what my cider shop needed. No need to print and maintain paper menus when I could use a dry-erase marker and keep the daily offerings listed on the mirror over the bar.

My markers were red, black, white, and gold, the same colors used in the painting of the giant Mail Pouch tobacco ad on my red barn's side. I kept the cider flavors listed in red because it made folks think of apples. It hadn't been an easy decision because I'd originally thought yellow was the better choice, closer to the color of cider. Eventually red had won. Those flavors only varied slightly when I ran out of one or wanted to run a trial with something new.

It was the menu that fluctuated by season and availability.

I plucked the cap off my black marker and snapped it onto the backside, then stared at the blank spot I'd created on the mirror.

FINGER FOOD FIXIN'S
CHEESE TRAY WITH TRAIL BOLOGNA
FARM-FRESH BERRY BOWL WITH YOGURT
SPRING MIX SALAD WITH GOAT CHEESE

SWEET TREATS
GRANNY'S APPLE COBBLER
GINGER SNAPS
ALMOND POUND CAKE WITH RHUBARB JAM

There was quite a selection of Granny's baked goods in the freezer if anyone had a special request, but I tried to save those for times I didn't have fresh offerings, like when Granny and her ladies were traveling.

I turned the television on when I'd finished behind the bar. I'd had the unit mounted in the corner before I'd opened. Some nights we used it to show the words for karaoke or the questions for a night of trivia, but at the moment, my mind was on the John Doe in the woods. I checked outside again, then decided to sweep the clean floors. I flipped to the local news and hoped I hadn't missed the morning show recap that played every day just after lunch.

A small crowd of anxious people centered the screen. The lights of a nearby cruiser flashed over their shocked features. Deputies and park rangers crisscrossed the area, mouths moving, faces stern. My heart leapt. Maybe Colton hadn't returned my call because he didn't know I'd left a message. Clearly something was going on, but someone had muted the darn television.

I hurried back to the remote and flipped it around on my palm, aiming it at the screen overhead. A pretty redheaded correspondent moved into the shot.

I jammed my finger against the volume button until I thought one of the two might break.

"According to local authorities," she said, looking appropriately ill at ease, "a body was found in the woods of Blossom Valley this morning just after daybreak. This once quiet little town is no stranger to violence and crime these days. Once touted as one of West Virginia's safest cities, Blossom Valley now seems to be in a race to the bottom of that same list."

The cameraman panned out, revealing the larger picture. The reporter was clearly in the woods, and unlike the clip they'd shown a moment before, the group behind her seemed to be made up of cameramen, satellite trucks, and intently focused individuals flaunting press badges.

I dialed Dot as the anchorwoman recapped all of the other unfortunate things that our town had been through since Thanksgiving. I doubted she'd be in any mood to revisit the area near Hank's family's cabin, but she might be willing to reach out to one of the park rangers and find out what was going on. Anything they knew would be more accurate and detailed than what the news could know or share.

"Hello?" Dot whispered. Wind raked across the speaker on her end of the line and into my ear. Multiple muffled voices droned in the background.

"It's me," I said. "Have you seen the news?"

"I'm on the news," she said. As she spoke, a hunched figure near the edge of the screen turned slowly toward the camera. Someone in a park ranger's uniform, using a cell phone looked a lot like . . .

"Dot!" I yelled. "You're there!" Part of me thought she might spend the rest of the week in bed after the shock she'd been given yesterday. "I was just calling to ask you to ask another ranger what was going on. Is this about the body found by Hank's family's cabin this morning? Or has something else happened?"

"The first one," she said softly.

The hoopla was about the John Doe, then. That was understandable, and I was slightly relieved that no other catastrophes had occurred. "What are the deputies saying?" I asked "Can you hear them from where you are?"

"Sometimes."

"Hey, wait." I frowned at her image on the screen. She'd already turned away and was pretending to patrol. "Why are you there? Colton said the body was just over the hill from the cabin. Why do they need park rangers?"

"The John Doe," the newscaster's voice pulled my attention back to the television, "was found just inside the national park perimeter only moments after dawn, making this case a little trickier for local authorities."

"He was in the national park?" I whispered, taken aback by the detail. Was that possible? "Is the Donovans' cabin that close to the line?"

"Apparently so," she said. "The natural boundaries get murky way up here. We try to keep the lines posted, but hunters have a bad habit of taking down the signs so they can claim they didn't realize they were on restricted land. It's hard for us to monitor the whole park. There's thousands of acres over dozens of square miles."

"Maybe I should come down there," I said. "The killer might be hanging around to see what the police know, hoping to overhear their next steps." I wanted to do that too.

"You can't," she said. "Rangers are helping deputies monitor a row of wooden barriers at the mouth of the hollow. Folks are turning up from three counties hoping to get an ID on the body. I guess a lot of people have missing loved ones. Runaways. Addicts. Some just gone. There's a bunch of upset people down there hoping this guy wasn't their loved one. It's sad."

I agreed, and I wasn't interested in waiting with a crowd at the mouth of the hollow. I wanted on the scene where Dot and the newscaster were. "Look around you," I said. "Is anyone acting strangely? Maybe a little too interested in what the deputies are doing or saying?"

"Uh oh, I have to go," Dot said, the strain in her voice sent a stab of guilt through me as I watched another ranger approach her. She nodded her head and the other ranger left. "Hey, I'll call you later and tell you what I learn."

"Or," I said, suddenly buzzing with the thrill of a new idea. "You can tell me in person because I'm coming to you."

"Fat chance. They're only letting the press past. No one else is getting up here without a shield or a press badge."

I smiled against the receiver. "Good thing I know where to find one."

I made a quick return trip to Granny's house and collected Owen Martin's press badge from Delilah, then hung it over my head and kept my chin up. I didn't have time to deal with changing the name or picture. I just had to hope the crowd would be enough of a distraction to keep the park rangers from paying too much attention. If I held the badge just right, my fingers covered most of the name and photo, leaving the institution logo and REPORTER visible, and that was all I really needed.

It wasn't the best plan I'd ever had, but it was the only one I had at the moment. Besides, what was the worst that could happen?

Delilah agreed to watch the cider shop for me, but I doubted there'd be any customers today. Not with the sudden appearance of a new crime scene. More likely, folks would swing by Carpenter's Run, then head over to Sip N Sup to see what was being said.

I ran to the massive pole barn where Grampy had stored his vehicles, and Mustang Sally lived. I slipped my arms into one of his plaid flannel button-downs and tucked my hair into one of his navy blue Mountaineer baseball caps. Hopefully the disguise would conceal my identity and present me as a re-porter who'd gotten the call and dropped what he was doing to get there. I patted the steering wheel as we motored away from the orchard. "Here goes nothing, Sally. Let's try to blend in."

I parked along the county road outside Carpen-ter's Run and walked in on foot. Everyone in Blos-som Valley knew Sally, and there wasn't a big enough flannel shirt or ballcap to hide her. So I angled off the road, careful not to leave her some-where I'd be stuck later, then kept my head down as I threaded my way through the crowd of locals and onlookers at the mouth of the hollow. When I reached the set of wooden barricades Dot had warned me about, I looked for a distracted park ranger and went in his direction. The ranger had his hands full, attempting to control and comfort a bawling woman begging for ID on the body. The beads of sweat on his forehead obviously had more to do with his nerves than the heat, and he looked like he could use an escape.

"Press," I said, lifting the hard plastic badge on my borrowed lanyard. "What seems to be going on?"

The lady wailed. "I just know it's my Bobby!"

The ranger waved me past, barely looking at the ID and never once raising his gaze to mine. Thank heavens for small blessings because my alternative plan was to take Sally up the road another half a mile and hike in from another angle. There weren't enough park rangers in the county to cover the whole forest, so I would've gotten there eventually. Sooner and easier was my preference.

I kept a brisk pace as I headed for the cabin, assuming I'd see the commotion from there and follow it to the new crime scene. When I made it to the smattering of news crews, lawmen, and onlookers, I wound through them with open ears.

Most were actively gossiping. Reporters who weren't on camera were scouring their phones for new details and collectively complaining about the lack of cell coverage.

I moved closer to the flimsy yellow tape warning us back, then settled in to listen, letting the brim of my hat shield my face. I watched the crowd as I waited to hear something useful. I wasn't sure what had happened to Hank after he'd left my place, but there was no sign of him, Gina, who'd come looking for him, or Sarah Burrie, my top suspect as yesterday's shooter.

I moved forward a few steps at a time, tuning in to various discussions happening behind me. The reporters were speculating that the John Doe's death was related to Jack Warren's and they were working up possible connections between the men to be checked once they had Wi-Fi availability again. A park ranger broke free from the crowd and my heart seized until I recognized the sweet face beneath the hat.

"What are you doing?" Dot asked, her expression one of pure awe. "What are you wearing?"

I lifted the badge. "I'm Owen Martin," I told her. "Dad really wanted a boy."

She tugged me into the trees and away from the pack of newsies and other rangers. "You can't be here. What if the sheriff sees you? Where did you get that?" She snagged the badge from my fingertips and scoffed before releasing it to bounce off my chest. "Inconceivable. Someone at the barricade believed you were a little old man?"

"I'm a very convincing actress."

Dot shook her head. "You aren't doing a very good job of convincing me you're sane."

"I'm not trying," I said with a grin. "Have you learned anything that might help me find out what happened to Jack Warren?" I asked.

"No." She yawned. "They called me in at dawn without telling me why. I assumed it was a wildlife crisis. I had no idea what had happened, and I'd rather be anywhere else. Don't these people know I was nearly killed here twenty-four hours ago?"

I rubbed her back, feeling awful as I considered how she must've felt. First yesterday's shock, then to be awakened and brought back to the scene of the trauma, only to see someone who hadn't been as lucky. My breath caught. "You were here early. Before the body was taken away?"

She rolled her eyes. "Yes." Dot liberated her cell phone from one pocket and tapped the face before handing it to me.

A blurry photo of a lifeless body among the leaves centered the screen.

"You got a photo!"

"It's not a great one," she said. "I heard the coroner say he was ready to take the body to the morgue, and I knew my time was running out. The sheriff had already left, so I took a chance and did the best I could without anyone seeing what I was doing. I figured I'd come by your place and fill you in once they let me leave."

I sent the photo to my phone, then returned the cell to her palm.

"Summers," someone called.

Dot walked away without another word.

I moved in the other direction, heading toward Hank's family cabin. The bulk of the sheriff's department workers seemed to be gathered near the top of the hill instead of near the ravine where the John Doe had landed. All that remained there was a pair of crime scene techs and some little plastic teepees indicating places that still needed to be processed for evidence.

Colton stepped into view from behind another man, and I gasped. I pressed my back to the trunk of a broad tree and cursed my poor choice in flannels. I was a bright red flag waving in a forest of greens. I listened as he gave his men a few instructions.

"Thanks," he said when he finished. "I've missed a few calls, but I'll be back with you in just a minute." He took several steps in my direction, and I attempted to shrink, evaporate, or morph into a tree. None of that happened. Instead, I crossed my fingers, literally, and hoped he'd stop moving soon.

He whispered a cuss word then my name. I got the feeling he had listened to my message.

"Sheriff?" The word burst through the low-grade white noise of his two-way radio.

"Yeah. Go on."

"Coroner's got a name on the John Doe," a woman's voice said. "Chad Denton. Thirty-five. We're looking into him now."

*Chad Denton.* I nearly yipped with glee. I'd gotten a name and a photo from today's outing. If that wasn't worth masquerading as a male sexagenarian then I didn't know what was.

My phone buzzed loudly in my back pocket where it was pressed against the tree. I jerked the device free to reject the call and saw Colton's face on my screen.

Returning my call.

So, I ran.

# Chapter Fifteen

Miraculously, I made it out of the forest without being stopped by Colton or his deputies. I left him another voicemail on my way home, apologizing for having missed his call. I also told him I was fine, and that I'd been feeling unnecessarily jumpy when I left the first message.

He didn't call back.

He didn't wake me the next morning either, successfully breaking his streak. And despite my perfectly peaceful breakfast and several productive hours with Granny at the orchard, I still wasn't sure how I felt about the silent treatment he was giving me. On a similar note, Hank hadn't shown up since I'd tossed him out yesterday, and I was beginning to worry about him again.

"Men make women crazy," Granny said, peeling and slicing another apple from the pile on my cider shop counter. "It's part of their appeal. Plus they come in handy sometimes." She selected a fourth apple and shoved the pile of accumulating peels aside. "Men lift stuff for us," she said. "I'm all about equality, but most men in these parts are stronger than I ever was. And men are generally taller. They can reach the high shelf. They've got bigger hands. Better to open jars with, and if you're lucky, he'll know how to find his way around your roost." She grinned.

"I'm not sure what that means, but please don't explain." I turned my attention back to my laptop and swallowed a groan. "I wish I had faster Wi-Fi in here. This service is slower than 1990s dial-up."

I'd been researching Chad Denton, the name I'd heard over the sheriff's two-way radio, since I'd gotten home last night. Unfortunately, I wasn't getting anywhere because Chad Denton was as generic a name as anyone could have. I suspected the more than five hundred Chad Dentons I'd found on social media so far would agree. Add to that every online mention of Chad Denton the Little League coach, marathon runner, photographer, restaurateur, doctor, frat boy, and so on and the list never seemed to end. I'd seen Instagram photos of Chad Dentons from three different countries last night alone. A newborn in Norway, a World War II veteran in Duluth, and a university gymnast in London.

I'd trolled dozens of Facebook pages, blogs, websites, and newspaper articles from all around the English-speaking world, and come up with no one who looked like the blurry photo Dot had shown me. Despite the hours I'd already put in, I suspected it would take infinitely more to find a Chad Denton who looked like the man in the photo. I wasn't even sure I'd recognize him if I found him. I'd already accidently visited one man's Facebook page twice because I didn't realize he was the same man I'd already researched. If a living man could look so different from one photo to the next, how could I possibly match up a dead one in the woods with whatever he looked like in his life?

"Why don't you use the cider shop's account," Granny said, pointing her paring knife at a sign on the wall with a guest password.

"I am, it's just so slow." I'd only paid for the base service package at the cider shop because I doubted I'd have time to use the internet while I was here, and frankly I didn't want a crowd of people all staring at their phones. I wanted folks to interact. Be present and neighborly. The guest password was a simple courtesy.

"Try your cell phone then," Granny suggested, pulling another apple from a fast-depleting pile. "It has internet. Use that."

"I don't have an unlimited data plan, and I don't want to run over my limit," I said. "I try not to use my phone for internet unless I can get on the Wi-Fi. And the Wi-Fi here is too slow."

"Then get on the internet at your house. That's fast."

"That's too far," I said, rubbing two fingers against the building tension across my brow.

I clicked on the next Chad Denton profile, then went to put my arm around Granny while the page loaded. "I think I'm just going to have to be patient," I told her.

"That's always a good plan of action."

The cider shop door opened, and a vaguely familiar man walked in. He was tall and lean, with

light hair and eyes, wearing jeans, a T-shirt, and a
baseball cap. He approached the counter with a
weary smile. "Are you open?"

I nodded, suddenly recalling where I'd seen the
man before. Out of context and tuxedo, I barely
recognized him. "Aaron, right?" Aka Jack Warren's
best man.

He nodded. "And you're Winnie."

"Correct." I stared dumbly for a moment, a
thousand questions stacked on my tongue.

"And I'm Granny Smythe," Granny said, extending a hand in Aaron's direction. "What can
we get ya?"

Aaron took a seat at the bar and folded his big
hands before him. His gaze lifted to the menu
board. "Cider and a sandwich?"

"How about grilled cheese?" Granny asked, already pulling a pan from the cabinet. "You've had
an awful week. Grilled cheese makes everything
better."

I poured him a tall glass of traditional cider and
set it in front of him. "On the house," I said, mostly
because the poor guy had just lost a dear friend,
but also because I planned to question him.

Granny hummed as she worked, and I tried desperately to think of something to say. I needed a
little small talk to start with, then I could look for a
way to move the conversation where I wanted it to
go. "I'm surprised to see you're still in town," I
started, hoping to look polite and inviting instead
of how I actually felt, like a golden retriever waiting for him to toss a ball.

He shrugged. "Yeah. I couldn't bring myself to
leave. I've been staying with Jack's family at the

lodge and helping his mom however I can. She won't leave without his . . ."

The word body hung between us, unsaid.

"I understand," I said. Jack couldn't be sent back to his hometown until the autopsy was complete. His mother, understandably, wouldn't go without him. It seemed to me that the autopsy should be finished by now, but I had no way to know for sure and no one to ask since Colton was apparently ignoring me.

"I thought I'd get out for some air while they don't need anything. She and her sisters are crying and planning the funeral. I'm not familiar with your town, so I'm basically wandering."

"You wandered a long ways from the lodge," I said. Blossom Valley's downtown wasn't big, but the town itself was sprawling. Smythe Orchard was a good ten- or fifteen-minute drive from there.

Aaron gave an impish smile. "I might've stopped at your local diner first."

I smiled. "Busy?"

"A madhouse. Then I remembered this place doubles as a cider shop when it isn't posing as a wedding reception venue, and I headed out here thinking it might not be busy. I honestly wasn't sure you'd be open."

"We're open," I said, "And definitely not busy."

Granny moved against my side and leaned toward Aaron, delivering a white plate with a perfectly grilled sandwich, cut diagonally down the middle. She'd added a scoop of fruit salad along the side. "There you are. You'll feel better once you eat."

He smiled. "Thanks, this is perfect."

Granny put her apple slices in a strainer and rinsed them, then began to roll each one in a thin pastry dough. She'd soon pour melted butter over them, sprinkle them liberally with cinnamon and sugar, then bake them until the sauce was bubbly and the dough was golden brown.

I watched Aaron take his first stringy bite of Granny's gooey grilled cheese.

"Would you like the television on?" I asked. "For background noise?" And maybe a look at the news, which would be a perfect segue into my questions.

He shook his head, still chewing, then set the triangle down and wiped his mouth on a napkin. "I may never watch television again," he said. "The news has taken over everything, and they're making Jack's death into a total circus. Don't they get that his family and friends are out here watching? That it's not a story to us?"

"No," I said softly. "I'm sure they aren't thinking of the people who are hurting. They're thinking of ratings and promotion and business as usual. I don't think they do it to be callous. It's just too easy to become desensitized." That was the thing about studying business for a decade. I'd started thinking of everything in terms of return on investment years ago. Every action in business has a purpose, and most actions are meant for gain. It was how companies stayed afloat and how a lot of people lived their lives. But Aaron was right, we were all guilty of forgetting that our actions impacted others sometimes. My heart pinched with guilt for attempting to set him up so I could selfishly pry information from him.

"They show those same clips again and again,"

he said. "And now, someone else has died and it's just this constant horrible drone."

"It was a little crazy," I said, "to have another death in Blossom Valley so soon after the first. Things like this don't usually happen here."

"Now you sound like the news people," Aaron said, forcing a tight smile. "Do you think the same guy could've done this? Some unhinged, traveling psycho? I mean, the hiker was alone, but there were at least a hundred people in here that night. Were we all in danger? Should we be glad the nut behind the wheel of that truck didn't drive it straight through the barn?"

"You don't think the deaths are related?" I asked, curiosity piqued. I'd never considered the murders were random. I still didn't, but I supposed the mere suggestion by Aaron meant that he, like everyone else, couldn't believe anyone would want to hurt Jack.

Aaron dropped his forearms against the counter. "I don't know who it was, and I'm not as present in Jack's life as I used to be, but everyone who came to town for the wedding is accounted for as far as I can tell. So, if the guy in the woods was a friend of Jack's, and he wasn't from this town, then why was he here but not at the wedding? Why assume they knew one another? Why make things bigger and more complicated than they already are?"

I nodded in slow agreement, though I'd need more time to think it all through. Since we were on the subject, I decided to ask another question before his sandwich was gone. "Have you seen

Elsie since the reception?" I asked. "I've been thinking of her a lot."

I'd considered dropping by her mother's place a dozen times, but hadn't. I wasn't sure how it would look or if she'd even want to see me. It wasn't as if we were friends.

"I stop by in the mornings to check in after breakfast, but she's still not talking. Sometimes when I talk to her, she cries. I'm never sure what to say, so we just end up sitting there. I think Jack would want me to keep looking in on her."

I couldn't get past the fact she still wasn't talking. It seemed oddly convenient for the woman who'd found Jack's body to still be silent four days later. The sheriff couldn't question someone who was incoherent. "Did you know her bridesmaids?" I asked. "Sarah's from Blossom Valley."

"I just met her last weekend," he said. "Jack, Elsie, and I had gone to college with a few of the other bridesmaids, but I didn't know Sarah or any of Elsie's friends from home."

"I saw Sarah at school the other day and she ran off."

Aaron set his sandwich down and looked at me carefully. "Is this how you investigate?" he asked. "I remember your friend saying it's what you do."

"Sorry," I said. "I don't mean to be rude."

He lifted a fork to his fruit salad. "Do you consult with the police? Or are you a private investigator?"

I laughed. "Neither. I'm just insatiably curious, I suppose." And I wanted to clear Hank's name, even if he was doing the wrong thing by hiding.

One corner of Aaron's mouth lifted in a lazy smile. "All right then. Hit me. I have no idea what went down that night, but I have known Jack a long time, so maybe I can help. What do you want to know?"

I suppressed the urge to clap. "Did he have any enemies or a recent argument with someone?" I asked. "From what I've heard, everyone loved Jack. It's so hard to imagine anyone would want to hurt him."

"I can't think of anyone." He tapped a finger to the back of my open laptop screen. "Are you researching?"

"I'm waiting for a page to load. I have painfully slow internet here."

His small smile grew a bit. "Pretty and smart."

Heat crept senselessly over my cheeks. Why did he have to be tall and attractive and make me blush? He didn't live in Blossom Valley, and he was too sad to think of as a potential date. Not that I was looking to date.

Was I looking to date?

"I think what you're doing is interesting and comes from a good place, unlike the news channels," he said. "You're like a cider-making vigilante. Shop owner by day. Justice seeker by night."

"Thanks, but I'm not all that altruistic," I said. "A murder at my new cider shop isn't great news for business, and our livelihoods depend on the success of this orchard." I motioned between myself and Granny, busily loading more rolled apple slices into baking dishes. And that wasn't all. "I've had a scare or two of my own lately, at home and out with a friend. Then another body showed up yesterday, and the sooner we figure this out, the sooner everyone will be safe."

"There you go, saving the town again."

If only I could. I wet my lips and considered my next words carefully. I wasn't sure I could trust Aaron, but he was the only person I knew who knew Jack personally. I crossed my fingers behind the counter and took a chance. "The guy found in the forest was Chad Denton. Does that ring a bell to you?"

Aaron's eyebrows rose. "The news crews are calling him John Doe."

"I know."

He sat back a bit, watching me. "You knew him?"

"No. I thought you might recognize the name. Maybe a friend of Jack's or a friend of someone who'd come into town for the wedding."

"It doesn't ring a bell, but I can ask the Warrens when I get back to the lodge," he offered.

"That would be great."

An older gentleman strode through the open door, drawing my attention. Wisps of white hair floated above a mostly bald head, and he pressed a porkpie hat to his chest. "Hello, Penny," he said.

Granny snapped upright and spun wide-eyed to stare. "Kitty whiskers," she whispered, then shoved the final apple trays inside the oven and shut the door.

I recognized Owen Martin from his press badge. I lifted a finger to Aaron, indicating I needed a minute, then I rushed over to stand between Granny and the older gentleman. "Hello," I said. "I bet you're here to collect your nametag."

"I am," he said, extending a hand for me to shake. "Owen Martin."

"Winona Mae Montgomery. Here's your badge." I placed it on the counter between us and waited for him to go.

He beamed back at me, tucked the badge into the pocket of his tweed trousers, and chuckled affectionately. "You look just like your grandmother. Pretty as a picture."

Granny elbowed her way around me and frowned at him. "You have your badge. Try not to lose it again."

"Excellent advice. Thank you." He glanced at me, then Aaron, before setting his gaze back on Granny. "You don't seem to be too busy, Penny. Maybe you'd like to take a walk with me. Get some fresh air and sunshine."

"No, thank you."

I eased away. The tension was palpable, and I didn't want to be caught in the explosion when Granny erupted.

Owen slid onto a stool at the bar, clearly unable to take a hint. "Well, then, I might as well have a bite to eat and sample a glass of this young lady's apple cider. It's all anyone's talking about."

A little hard to believe given the two recent murders, but I let him have that one.

# Chapter Sixteen

Granny softened toward Owen, and they talked until she finished her apple wraps and other pastries. Then he walked her back to the orchard to meet a tour bus. I closed up at five instead of waiting until my usual closing time of seven. I'd run out of things to do, and Aaron had been my one and only customer, unless I counted Owen, but neither of them had paid. Aaron and I had a good talk too, but it was what I'd learned when my webpage on Chad Denton finally loaded that convinced me to call it a night and head back to where Wi-Fi was speedy and I could freak out in peace.

I hurried up the front steps, dreaming of a hot shower, comfy pajamas, and a late night of online reconnaissance. Shockingly, my porch was empty. Kenny Rogers and Dolly were almost always curled in front of my door in the evenings, waiting for their dinner and a nap on my couch.

"Kitty, kitty, kitty." I called, turning the key in my lock and swinging the door wide. Maybe closing early had thrown off their schedules. "Here, kitty, kitty."

"Meow."

I started as Kenny Rogers stared up at me expectantly from the living room carpet. Dolly came to rub on my legs a moment later. Had I forgotten to let them out with me this morning? It would be unusual, but it was possible. Hadn't I snapped a picture of them chasing grasshoppers outside the barn around lunchtime? I supposed that might've been yesterday.

Before I could retract my key from the lock, a delectable scent wafted up my nose. I spun and stared at the man in my kitchen, flipping burgers in a skillet. "Hank!" I hissed, flipping the deadbolt behind me, then checking through the curtain to be sure no one was outside to hear. "What are you doing here! You promised me you'd leave!"

"I did leave," he said, looking ridiculous in my frilly vintage apron, a folded kitchen towel tossed over one shoulder. "Now, I'm back. Are you hungry?"

The cats ran around my ankles, mewling and rolling at my feet. There was fresh food and water in their bowls.

"I brought them in when I got here," he said, nodding to Kenny Rogers and Dolly. "I heard them on the front porch. They seemed to be starving, so I fed them and refilled their water."

"Why are you here?" I asked again, trying and failing to make sense of his continuous reappearances. "And how are you getting in?" I raised my palms and shoulders, then let them fall dramatically. "I've made a point of double-checking my door and window locks every day since the wedding."

He pushed two juicy burgers around in my favorite cast-iron frying pan, unmoved by my exasperation. "Key."

"Key!" I stage whispered, wanting to scream, but not wanting to alarm my grandma or her tour group if they happened to be anywhere within earshot. "How did you get a key?"

He pointed to the four-letter plaque by my door. K-E-Y-S. Where I kept my spare sets to everything on the orchard, including Sally and my home.

I opened my palm to him. "Give it back."

"I put it on the rack," he said, giving the pan a wiggle. "Check for yourself. Also, you're almost out of Swiss cheese, and your mushrooms are looking questionable."

I snagged my spare house key from the little hook beneath the K and put it in my pocket.

Hank arranged slices of baby Swiss cheese on the burgers, then removed the lid from the smaller pan on the next burner. Rich and salty scents of onions, mushrooms, and butter lifted into the air, and I drooled a little.

My stomach hollered in excitement and Hank grinned victoriously.

"My girl loves her mushroom Swiss burgers," he said. "I never forget something like that."

I set out two plates and opened a hamburger bun on each. "I'm not your girl, but I appreciate the sentiment." I dug out the condiments and pickle spears, then popped open a bag of chips and dumped a handful on each plate.

He cast me a disbelieving look. "You'll always be my girl, Winnie."

"No," I said. "I won't, and I'm not and you need to stop saying stuff like that. It makes me uncomfortable and it confuses people. We're friends now. That's it, and that's enough." I crunched a chip, then bit into my pickle while Hank slid a burger onto each of our buns and spooned sautéed mushrooms and onions over the cheese.

We carried our plates to the couch and set them on the coffee table while we got comfy on the cushions at either end, then brought our plates onto our thighs. I sunk my teeth into the burger and juice wept from the sides. "Amazing," I mumbled around a mouthful of heaven. "I don't know what your secret is, but this is always an out-of-body experience."

"You're always nicer to me when I feed you," Hank said. "I should probably make dinner more often."

I set the burger down and wiped my mouth on one of the folded napkins Hank had brought along. "I appreciate this," I said, and honestly, it was the least he could do after breaking in twice, "but we aren't making a habit of it. And you still can't stay here. Once you finish eating, you have to leave."

"First thing in the morning."

I took another bite of burger, shaking my head in the negative. "Tonight."

He pressed his palms together in mock prayer. "Can we just enjoy our meal without arguing? Tell me what Aaron had to say. I saw him at the cider shop. He stayed a long time. Do you think he's handsome? He's taller than me, but those super-tall guys are always dopey and uncoordinated when they move."

I had another bite of burger and ignored his blatant self-obsession. "He seems nice, and he's a wealth of information on Jack, which was handy because the only other person I know who knew Jack is still semi-catatonic."

"Elsie?" Hank asked.

"Apparently, and considering I didn't know her outside of planning her wedding, I doubt she'd want to open up to me anyway. Plus no one wants to speak ill of the dead, so even if Jack had been a monster, no one would dare say it now."

"True," Hank agreed, removing the top portion of his bun and layering chips on the mushrooms and onions before returning the bun to position. "So what did you learn from Aaron?"

"He mentioned that Jack's family was super up-tight. They put a ton of pressure on Jack to succeed at everything and kept him stressed out over his need for their approval. According to Aaron, Jack was naturally driven so the added push from his folks was rough on him. He had to have the right grades, get the right degree, own the right home, marry the right girl. And Aaron suspects he had unreasonably high business goals too. He thinks Jack and Elsie might've been arguing about money for the last few weeks before the wedding." It would explain what had happened to their original venue. Maybe it was overpriced, so they cancelled it. An orchard wedding in Blossom Valley had to be half the cost of a traditional wedding and reception in Louisville. Fewer people. Smaller venue. Her mama's home cooking. A borrowed truck instead of a limo.

"What does Aaron do for work?" Hank asked, nearly finished with his burger.

"Home remodeling along the river. He was in construction, then he started flipping houses for profit."

I savored each bite of my burger, trying to recall the things Aaron had said about Jack. "He said he was glad to see Jack finally settling down and that Jack and Elsie had been through a lot together. What do you suppose that means?" I asked.

Hank seemed to think it over, then gave a noncommittal grunt. "Who knows."

"It made me wonder if Jack had cheated on her before. Maybe that was what he'd meant by saying it was nice Jack was finally settling down."

"I don't know," Hank said. "Why kill him at the wedding? Why not just call the whole thing off or get a divorce and take half his stuff?" Hank lifted his pickle spear. "I guess we need to talk to Elsie."

"You can't show your face in public because you're wanted for questioning in Jack's murder, and her mom assumes you're guilty, so I wouldn't go knocking on her door if I were you. I can go, but if Elsie's not talking in general, I don't know why she'd open up to me."

Hank took his plate to the sink and returned with two sodas. He set one on the coffee table for me, then cracked the other open for himself. "Set up a time to talk to Aaron again. Try to find out what he meant by those things about Jack and Elsie. Speculation isn't helping us here."

A slow grin moved over my face as something

else came to mind. I hadn't told him about my more significant news yet. "I know the real name of the John Doe in the forest."

Hank lowered the can slowly away from his lips. "How?"

I told him about my impersonation of the old man with a crush on Granny, then my trip to the crime scene, the chat I'd had with Dot, and about nearly being caught spying by the sheriff himself. "So I looked him up," I continued. I ran to my bedroom to collect my laptop and dashed back to the couch, already typing in the website address I'd finally found while at the cider shop. "Look." I turned the laptop to face him and waited as he read.

Chad Henley Denton of Louisville, Kentucky, had an arrest record ten miles long, but none of the charges ever stuck, and they all reeked of organized crime. Embezzlement. Tax fraud. Loan sharking. Money laundering. "Can you believe it? I think we had a real-life mobster in Blossom Valley." For a minute or two anyway.

Hank set the laptop on the coffee table and expelled a long breath. His eyes were wide as he leaned his forearms against his knees. "How long until his goons come looking for him or whoever killed him?"

"We don't know he had goons," I said, "and I know none of the charges stuck, but that says more about his lawyer than himself. He must not have been a very good criminal to be busted so many times."

"Jack could've borrowed money from this guy then not been able to pay it back," he said.

Exactly what I'd thought when I first read that

webpage. "It's a strong possibility given that this man was from the city where Elsie and Jack live now, and Aaron said they might've been having money trouble."

I still had no idea where the missing bridesmaid fit in, but I could visit the hospital tomorrow and work on that. "Is your pal Sarah a smoker by any chance?" I asked, suddenly wondering if Sarah was missing from her life because she was stalking mine.

Hank made a sour face. "No. Gross. And don't give me that look. I know what you're thinking."

I doubted that very much. I hadn't told anyone about the cigarette butt or my possible stalker.

"She's not a murderer," Hank continued. "She's pocket-sized, for crying out loud. She couldn't kill anyone if she tried. Which she wouldn't."

"A person of any size can wield a gun and whatever was used to whack Chad Denton on the head," I said. "Plus whoever was driving the truck that hit Jack was small. I saw the seat rolled forward. Not to mention, she ran from me, and now she's in the wind. How do you explain all that?"

"That's all circumstantial. I don't know why she ran from you or stood me up at the cabin, but she isn't homicidal, and she hasn't gone on a sudden killing spree. Why would she do that?"

"That's what I'm trying to find out," I said. "I learned from Reese at Sip N Sup that Sarah works at the hospital, so I'm going to stop by the medical records department tomorrow and see if she's there. If not, maybe someone will tell me when she's due for her next shift or direct me to where she's hiding."

Hank frowned. "I could've told you she worked at the hospital."

I glared. "You know I've been looking for her! Why didn't you tell me?"

Realization flashed in his eyes, and his expression turned accusing. "You told Gina where I was. Why would you do that? You could've put her in danger, and now she's in this too."

"She's been in this since the moment her big brother ran away," I yelled, no longer able to keep my cool. "I would never intentionally put Gina or anyone else in danger. She was on my doorstep begging for help, not the other way around. And for the record, every time you show up here, you're dragging me deeper into this too, which is why you need to go."

He pulled his chin back and managed to looked surprised. "I made you dinner. I fed your cats."

"You did those things for yourself," I snapped. "You anticipated this conversation and prepared your ammunition in advance. I know your games, Hank Donovan, and I don't have to play them anymore. I appreciate the dinner, but if you show up here again before this all gets sorted, I'm going to confess everything to Colton and turn you in. I'd rather make him mad than continue to help you do the wrong thing."

Hank stood and pressed his hands to his hips. Anger and disbelief colored his cheeks. "Now you wait just a minute—"

A set of headlights washed over the front window, bathing him momentarily in light through the curtain.

He dropped to the floor like the chicken he was and crawled toward the back door.

"You'd better run far and fast," I called. "Because if that's Colton, there's no way he didn't see you, and you can't hide long from him."

Our sheriff was a bloodhound.

# Chapter Seventeen

I waited for Colton on the porch, intensely thankful for his presence for a number of reasons. For starters, his arrival had gotten rid of Hank, and now that I had all the keys to my home back, he wouldn't be making anymore surprise appearances. Secondly, I was glad to see Colton was still speaking to me after the way he'd stormed out yesterday morning. As I waited for him to exit his cruiser, I realized there was one more reason as well. I'd missed talking to him, and I'd been worried about him. Whatever secret thing had been haunting him lately had also been bothering me, lying ominous and ever-present in my mind. I didn't like knowing that someone as innately good and just as Colton Wise could be made to feel so ill at ease. Colton had been a Marine, a detective, and was the sheriff. Anything that could worry him made me stop and shake in my boots. I wished there was something I could do to help.

"Hey," I said with the lift of a hand as he finally

stretched out of his cruiser. "What brings you by, Sheriff?"

He snorted a derisive sound as he made his way up my front steps. "Thought I'd better check in on you. Make sure you haven't gotten any more scares while I've been wrapped up in the latest crisis."

"No more scares here," I said, opening the door for him and motioning him inside. "Can I get you something to eat or drink?"

"I grabbed something at the station," he said, then stopped to take a deep inhalation of breath. "Whatever you had for dinner smells like magic."

"It was," I admitted. "Swiss burgers with mushrooms and onions."

His attention caught on the pair of plates in my sink, and my stomach knotted. "Company?"

I nodded, rubbed my suddenly sweat-slicked palms down my thighs, then turned for the fridge. "How about some dessert since you've had dinner?" I suggested, hoping desperately to change the subject. "I have cider and a few of Granny's apple turnovers."

He didn't answer, so I prepared the snack instead of turning to face him. I'd threatened Hank with telling Colton about him, but in truth I was the chicken, and I didn't want to. I wanted to pretend that Hank hadn't selfishly shown up here, twice, and put me in this position.

When I turned to pass the glass and plate to Colton, he was gone. "Colton?"

A moment later, I heard soft footfalls in my hallway and panic shot through me. I hurried through my kitchen and living room with a full glass of cider in one hand and a plated turnover in the other. "Colton!"

He stepped out of my bathroom and watched me with knowing eyes. I prayed Hank hadn't left his toothbrush or boxers in plain sight. Actually, I hoped he'd taken his boxers far away and would keep them there. I squirmed under Colton's scrutiny. Surely he saw the sheer panic in my eyes. If he asked me anything, I'd crack like a piñata. I couldn't take the pressure, and I hated lying.

"Thanks," he said, accepting the treats. "I just wanted to wash up before I ate. I've been in the forest all day."

It was polite of him to say so, but my bone-dry sink beside him told the truth. He was as much a liar as I was.

We returned to my living room in silence and sat on the couch.

"Would you mind turning on the news?" he asked, his voice a little confrontational. "I like to keep up with media coverage. Reporters like to twist and sensationalize things. Plus," he said, sipping his cider and suddenly staring right at me. "They have all those cameras. I can only see what I can see, but five or six news crews can see a whole lot. You know what I mean?"

My mouth opened, but no words came out.

He smiled, then turned back to the screen and bit into his turnover. "Any luck finding Hank?" he asked as the weatherman predicted another hot one tomorrow.

"I stopped looking," I said, which was wholly true. "How's the turnover?"

"Good. Here we go," he said pointing to the television screen. "This is what I mean. They played this clip earlier, and I thought I was going crazy at first, but I wasn't. Let's see what you think."

"Oh-kay," I uttered, turning my attention to the news. Colton was acting strangely, even for his new stressed-out normal, and I didn't like it. Hopefully he hadn't seen Hank and Gina on camera and come here to ask me about it. I'd already told him that I helped Gina look for him that first day.

The camera shifted to a bystander answering the reporter's question and caught a distant figure in the background. Someone wearing a red plaid flannel shirt and Mountaineers baseball cap, which both looked a lot like Grampy's, cut through the shot. My stomach tightened. A press badge on a lanyard bounced around the person's neck.

"Huh." I said. "I wonder where that guy was going in such a hurry."

"Come on!" Colton barked. He set the empty plate and glass on the table beside us. "What were you doing out there yesterday? Why would any sane person return to the place where someone shot at them and another person died?"

"Because I'm scared," I snapped back. "I'm on edge all the time, and I'd gotten spooked again that morning, so I behaved a little impulsively. I just wanted to know what was going on and maybe how soon this nightmare will end."

Colton's expression softened a bit. "You put yourself in danger because you were scared?"

"I'm sure it's hard for you to understand, but I can't live in this constant state of anxiety and anticipation forever. I'll go insane or die of heart failure if someone else doesn't kill me first." The truth of the words startled me and I sucked in a breath. I wasn't just endlessly curious like I'd gotten used to saying, I was afraid. No sooner had I acknowledged it than my eyes began to sting. A truckload of awful memories rushed up to meet me in my miserable state. I'd barely survived the last killer in town.

I swallowed a lump of emotion and willed myself not to cry. "I can't change what happened last winter, but I can change the helpless way I'm feeling now. I went to the crime scene because knowledge is power. If there was something there to learn that might help you arrest the killer, then I didn't want to miss it. And I was never in danger," I said. "You were there."

Colton mimed his head exploding. "Was it worth it?" he asked, disapproval etched on his handsome face. "Deceiving me and posing as a member of the press so you could snoop?"

"Kinda," I admitted.

Colton sat back, shoulders slumping. "Great. Why?" He didn't really look as if he thought it was great, or like he wanted an answer, but in the interest of full disclosure after being caught sneaking onto a crime scene, I confessed.

"I heard dispatch give you the John Doe's name."

He rubbed his forehead. "Go on."

"I found him online. He wasn't a nice man. He's been arrested for loan sharking and money laundering."

"He's also been wanted on a dozen murder

charges," Colton said, "but his slippery lawyer gets the cases thrown out of court every time. Did you know that?"

"I only knew his slippery lawyer kept him out of jail for the money stuff."

He lifted hopeful eyes to mine. "And now that you know this mess is bigger than some unfaithful groom?" he asked, eyebrows high.

I was sure he wanted me to say I'd stay out of it, or to admit I was in over my head, but I was still processing the fact that Chad Denton had been a murderer. Not that Colton had asked, but I didn't know how to feel about it. Should I be glad Mr. Denton wouldn't be killing anyone else now? Or should I be adding locks to my doors? "Denton was a killer, but someone killed him."

"Yes."

"So, there's an even more dangerous killer out there now? Possibly still in Blossom Valley?" I pressed a palm to my chest, certain I could feel the hives rising. "We have to figure this out." I could put on coffee and we could brainstorm all night. Sleep when it was dawn and the world was bright instead of dark and cloaked in shadows. "Have you talked to Elsie?"

"Winnie," Colton warned.

"Okay, but hear me out," I pleaded. "If the murders are related, then who committed them? I think Jack borrowed money or made some other deal with Denton, then couldn't follow through on it. Maybe he needed money to repay Denton, so he and Elsie moved their wedding to Blossom Valley to free up some cash. She made all the arrangements here at the last minute, saying the

Louisville venue had fallen through, but never told me exactly what that meant. Also, they probably didn't expect Denton to find them here. They probably thought they'd have a peaceful wedding, escape for their honeymoon, regroup, and deal with Denton later. Denton killed Jack. Elsie killed Denton in revenge." I chewed my lip. "Except Denton was too tall to have driven the truck. And none of this explains what happened to Sarah Burrie."

"Who?" Colton asked, dropping his hand away from his forehead to look at me.

"The missing bridesmaid," I said. Did he not know about the missing bridesmaid? I filled him in while he dug a roll of antacids from his pocket and took a few. "I can't figure out the connection between Sarah and Denton, but I'm thinking she killed Jack over an affair. Maybe she killed Denton because he'd intended to hurt Jack. Believe me, I see the irony, but love is blind."

"That's not how that expression works," he said. "And whoever killed Denton did it before they killed Jack, if," he gave a dramatic pause, "if," he repeated, "the two murders are connected."

"Of course they're connected," I said. "How can they not be?"

"Anything's possible. You think the bridesmaid did it."

"Why else did she run from me?" I asked.

"Probably because you were chasing her."

I narrowed my eyes. "And that was days ago. Where is she now?"

"Probably with Hank."

We stared at one another for several long beats,

neither of us willing to break the silent standoff. I caved first. "I think she's on the run because she killed these men. We know she was at the reception when he died, and she could have easily been the person shooting at me. Maybe she was trying to keep me away from the body she'd hidden in the leaves."

Colton shook his head slowly. "No."

"Well, if she's not the killer and on the run, then where is she?" I felt the blood drain from my face as an unthinkable alternative registered. "What if she's dead?" I whispered the final word, then tried not to be sick. I'd been so busy accusing Sarah of murder that I hadn't stopped to wonder if she was in real danger.

In the end, Colton agreed to look for Sarah Burrie. In return, I'd promised to take a break from sleuthing, stay at the orchard and let him work without the fear I would turn up as the subject of his next murder scene. I'd also promised to find another, less dangerous, way to deal with my fears and anxiety. In other words, I needed to find something to distract me so I wouldn't keep trying to rush his investigation along.

I decided that was a no-brainer. Tomorrow I'd give one hundred percent of myself to the cider shop and refocus on growing my business. I needed a plan to recover from any bad press and remind folks the cider shop was safe and fun.

And I needed to enter that contest.

Granny loaded another pair of pancakes onto my plate, which was still covered in bits of fresh sliced strawberries, whipped cream, and syrup from my first serving. "Can you believe Owen stayed as long as he did yesterday?" she griped. "It's like he couldn't take a hint. Maybe the old guy is losing his ability to read verbal cues and body language. His eyes have obviously already gone because he said I look just the way I did in high school, like Mary Steenburgen." She pushed a hank of straight brown hair behind her ear and rolled her eyes.

"You do look like Mary Steenburgen," I said. "The only one who doesn't see that is you, and you shouldn't call Mr. Martin an old guy. He's your age and you aren't old." I piled strawberry slices onto the new pancakes and sprayed a funnel of whipped cream over them. "I noticed you showed him around the farm and let him help with the tour bus group."

Granny's cheeks pinked. "Well, he was here, so he might as well have made himself useful."

I stuffed my mouth full of pancake before I made a comment she didn't like. For example, I might've pointed out that I hadn't seen her laugh or smile so much outside of needlepoint-night since Grampy died. Instead, I chose a safer topic. "That was the biggest tour group we've had this season. Maybe the biggest we've ever had."

"Fifty-four souls from Pittsburg." Granny smiled over the rim of her steaming coffee mug. "And I'm expecting another like it next Sunday."

"That's great! Now we know those postcard invitations we sent out of state were worth their time and effort. Did anyone buy anything?" This time of year, folks could pay to tour the orchard, see the trees and facilities, but the apples were still on the branches. Guests would have to come back in a couple months to see the harvest in progress, pick their own bushel, or watch the production of Smythe Orchard cider in the press house. That was always my favorite part. Grampy had fitted our press house with machinery that washed, ground, and pressed the apples into thick cloudy cider, then filtered the pulp and left results that were ready for bottling. I used those for the base of my gourmet flavors.

"Those tourists were all interested in your cider shop. Took lots of pictures of the barn and asked about the history. I let them know that you were closed for the day, but that we'd set up a tour of the barn if they came back another time."

I worked on the pancakes, pleased with my life. My cider shop, the historic barn that housed it, and the blessed orchard it stood on were beyond perfection. I was thankful for time with Granny this morning, for her fantastic cooking, for waking to my alarm clock instead of a cranky sheriff, and most of all for no signs of Hank. There was basically no way this day could go wrong. "Do you have any tours scheduled for today?" I asked. "Anything I can help with before I open up for lunch?"

"Nope. I think I've got it all covered. I plan to take my needlepointing outside and get a little sun until someone comes. I'm making a few phone calls today too. We need a harvest crew on the books fast."

That reminded me. "Colton said you might want to hire someone to stay here year-round and manage the orchard. He said an orchard manager could tend to the harvest crews and handle the lawn, basic maintenance, things like that."

She considered the notion a few moments before nodding. "He's probably right, but I'm not sure where I'd start looking for someone like that." Her eyes misted with tears and I knew she was thinking of all that Grampy had done for her and the orchard they loved. "Dot's coming by with a crew to handle the grass this morning. Maybe one of those guys will have experience with farm management."

I wasn't convinced that mowing lawns translated to orchard management capabilities, but I didn't want to be a bummer. I decided to wait and see.

A loud rattling sound echoed up the gravel lane, and we went to the window for a look.

Dot was behind the wheel of an old farm truck and headed in our direction.

"What the devil?" Granny asked.

The truck was pulling a trailer, and from the best I could tell, it was full of some kind of small livestock. "What does she have there? And why's she hauling it here?"

Granny opened the front door and moved onto the porch for a better look. "Maybe it's the equipment for those lawn workers."

That would have made more sense if she wasn't pulling an animal transport. "You'd think a lawn-care crew would have a proper trailer."

Dot swung the truck around and parked in Granny's driveway. She climbed out with a broad smile. Her muck boots were filthy. Her jeans and tank top didn't look much better, and her thick auburn hair was piled on top of her head. The mirrored aviator sunglasses protecting her eyes reflected the shock on my face and Granny's. "Morning!" she called, rocking back on her heels. "Where do you want them?"

"Want what?" Granny said, pronouncing each word slowly.

"Your lawn crew. I thought we'd start in your backyard since it's fenced and you probably want to tend to your flowerbeds, but can't get at them."

"Are those goats?" I asked, peeking through the trailer's slatted windows. The words were rhetorical. There were clearly a half dozen pygmy goats staring back at me. Their beady eyes and scraggly beards gave them an aged appearance, while their stumpy legs and stout little bodies made them seem youthful. I couldn't tell which was true. "You brought goats to mow our lawn?"

"Sure. I told you they come cheap. Will work for food." She grinned. "It'll take them a while to clear five acres, but they can pluck away at it. Once an area is manageable, we'll relocate them and you can keep that part down with a regular mower."

We didn't have time for any mowing, which was how the lawn had gotten so out of hand, but I couldn't seem to form the words. "Goats?" I said instead, not new to the concept, but she could have warned me. I was still adjusting to the two cutie pie kittens she'd suckered me into adopting a few months ago. Those guys already ran my life. I didn't think there was room for goats.

"Don't worry," she said, unlatching the transport's rear gate. "These guys are mine. I'm not trying to find them forever homes, except maybe this one." She pointed at a small white goat and whispered the words before returning her voice to normal. "Without them, who would tend to my lawn?"

She opened the gate and led the first gray-and-black goat down a ramp, then handed his short lead to Granny. "This here is Kenny Rogers. Kenny Rogers, this is Granny Smythe."

"How do you do?" Granny asked him.

"They're excellent at keeping lawns under control. Briars and brambles too, but you'll want to guard your roses and blackberries. Kenny Rogers enjoys both as much as we do."

Dot led the next goat down the ramp to me, then repeated the process between Granny and me until we each had a goat lead in both hands.

"What's wrong with the little white one?" I asked. Why had she singled him out?

"He's adorable," Granny said.

Dot sighed. She reached for the little goat's lead. He took two steps downhill, went stiff, and keeled over.

"Heavens!" Granny gasped.

Dot crouched and rubbed his side. "It's okay. You're all right."

The little goat seemed to shake it off and rolled onto his feet. He bleated and wobbled in Granny's direction, not quite steady on his legs.

"He's a fainting goat," Dot said. "Drives me batty. I swear I get a little heart attack every time he falls over, which is often."

Granny laughed and patted his head.

Dot took the last two goats for herself, then grabbed the little white one's lead as well. "What you need are sheep," she said, falling back into the discussion of our overgrown grass. "These guys will get the job done, but sheep are better for consistency. I only have two right now, and you'd need at least twenty. I thought we could start with these guys and see what you think."

Granny and I followed Dot, each of us leading our goats to Granny's backyard. The space had been fenced in for my protection years ago because I tended to wander. That was still a little true, but the gate no longer helped.

We released the goats into the grass, then watched as they immediately began to graze.

Granny pulled Dot into a hug. "This is a perfect surprise, thank you."

I laughed. "It is definitely not what we were expecting," I said. Though it was just like Dot to come up with an animal solution to any problem. "How long have these guys been mowing lawns?" I asked as seriously as possible. "Granny was hoping you might recommend one to manage the orchard."

"I'd recommend Kenny Rogers," Dot said, giving the goat closest to her a pat. "I've got to return the truck and trailer to Farmer Bentley, but I'll be back to check on these guys throughout the day. They shouldn't be any trouble, and they're pretty good about minding fences until they see something they want outside the line, then they can be a bunch of Houdinis."

Granny's eyes widened. "What do I do if one gets out? I can't chase them."

"If one gets out, he'll just meander. You shouldn't have to chase him. Get him by the collar and lead him back." A small black goat climbed onto Granny's lounge chair, then onto her patio table. "They like to climb," Dot said, "that's normal." She gave the goat's tiny cowbell a flick and the goat bleated. "Don't let them out of your sight when you're close like this. These guys can be temperamental and they like to head butt."

"They seem terrifying," I teased.

"Find out," Dot challenged. "Oh, and for goodness sakes, do not under any circumstance open a snack bag within hearing distance from them. That's what their treats come in. They know the sound, and they'll form a little goat mob faster than you can figure out what's happened."

"A goat mob?" This kept getting better. "Consider me warned."

Granny was already on her knees in the mulch, weeding her overgrown garden with the help of her six new landscapers, the little white fainting goat by her side.

I headed for my barn with immediate plans to get a human grounds crew. I was on edge enough lately without worrying I'd be head butted every time I crossed the lawn.

Thankfully, the walk was warm and invigorating. I fell into an easy cadence, mentally counting steps as I treaded across the property to the cider shop. I had important business to conduct today, and the mere thought of it gave my stomach a swirl of anticipation.

I'd been given a mandatory time out by the local sheriff, and I intended to put it to work for me. Granny's friends had reminded me how important this season of my life was. This was my time to do things and take chances. I'd been putting off my submission to the cider magazine's contest because I was afraid of what the judges would say, but I was tired of being afraid. The contest was too huge an opportunity to ignore, and I had to go for it. My dreams were worth the risk. So, today, I'd choose the perfect cider flavor for the contest entry by asking my customers' opinions.

I'd gotten the idea from the taste test I'd given to Colton the other night. He wasn't a ton of help, but polling every willing customer would be. I'd set up a taste-testing station on the cider shop bar today and offer free samples in exchange for a vote.

I'd set an empty canning jar beside each of three cider dispensers and arranged stacks of little paper cups around a bowl of marbles at the display's center. The marbles would be used to record votes. After guests finished sampling and made their decisions, they would drop a marble in the jar beside their favorite flavor. The flavor with the most marbles would go on to represent me in the contest.

I'd made instruction signs and detailed flavor descriptions last night to be printed and used with the display. I'd posted the signs on all of the cider shop's social media accounts and announced my need for help. Since no self-respecting Blossom Valley resident could resist a neighbor's call for help, I expected to get an abundance of feedback before closing time.

I unlocked the barn doors and pinned them open, then flipped the lights on inside. The flood of peace and pride that washed over me was extinguished as I moved toward the bar to get started.

A pair of long arms clamped around me. One hand gripped tightly across my middle, the other clamped over my mouth. My arms were pinned to my sides. My heart hammered, painful and loud. Before I could gather my wits to kick the assailant's shins or stomp his foot, hot breath washed over my cheek.

"Butt out of things that aren't your business or the next body that turns up in this backwater town will be yours."

The suffocating hands relented in a move so lithe I nearly collapsed without them for balance. In the next moment, a set of sturdy fingers knotted into my hair and my forehead connected with the bar.

Then the darkness pulled me under.

# Chapter Eighteen

I opened my eyes to the continuous thump and rattle of someone at the door. It took several moments for me to acclimate myself in the darkness, but curiously, I wasn't in my bed. I dragged heavy, uncoordinated palms over cool wooden planks and a spark of awareness jolted through me. I was on the ground, and my head was pounding.

I cracked my eyes open to a dark and blurry world. Frigid fingers of fear curled around my limbs, momentarily paralyzing me.

"Winnie!" Granny's voice rang out, keeping rhythm with the loud whir of a power tool which suddenly sprung to life.

A narrow shaft of light bled under the door. I squinted, begging my vision to clear and my eyes to adjust, but the whir of the tool might as well have been working through my skull instead of whatever it was actually doing.

A moment later, the door rattled once more, then swept open.

Colton and Granny closed in on me, talking too loudly and both at once. I shut my eyes against the attack, but Colton peeled one of my lids back open and flashed a light into it. Someone hit the wall switch and the room illuminated around me. We were in my store room at the cider shop.

"Can you hear me?" Colton asked.

I pressed a palm to my temple and cringed. "Shh," I croaked.

Granny fell to her knees near my head. She stroked my hair and kissed my forehead. "What happened? How did you get in here?" The fear in her voice said she knew the answer and it wasn't good.

The fine hairs on my neck and arms raised as I intuitively agreed. I'd been locked in the store-room, unconscious. That wasn't an accident, but the details were hazy at best. I struggled to recall what had happened before my world went black, but nothing concrete was presenting. "I'm not sure," I said, trying to sit up.

Colton grabbed my biceps to steady me. "Take your time," he said, crouching over me and running careful fingers over my forehead. "Are you feeling nauseous?"

My stomach was okay, but an icky sensation clung to my skin like spiderwebs.

"Winnie?" Granny asked.

I turned to look at her, but my mind was elsewhere, struggling fiercely against the cloud that had settled over it.

"Paramedics are on their way," Colton said. "I want a professional opinion before she leaves this barn. The skin isn't broken, but she's got one heck of a goose egg growing, and it's never good when people lose consciousness."

"This person could have killed her," Granny whispered, the words coming out in quivers. "Like the gentleman in the forest."

Leave it to Granny to call a loan shark and murderer a gentleman. "I'm sitting right here," I complained. "You realize I can hear everything you're saying."

Colton's face came into line with mine. He lifted a peace sign between us. "How many fingers do you see?"

I pushed his hand away. "Help me up."

"I don't think that's—"

I grabbed his broad, sturdy shoulders and forced myself upright.

He rose fluidly in the next breath and wrapped an arm around my back. "Fine. You can wait in the dining area for the paramedic, but you have to agree to drink some water and sit until they arrive."

I rolled my eyes and it hurt.

Sunlight crawled across the cider shop floor, stretching toward my feet, then climbing my body as I moved closer to the open doors. I squinted and shrank against the brilliance of a midday sun that seared my aching brain.

I slowed as the space between my bar and the open doors came into view. The harsh reality of my morning crashed into me with a lung-crushing blow. "I was attacked," I said.

Granny and Colton turned sharply to stare. "By who?" Colton asked, as Granny released a heart-breaking gasp.

They lowered me into a chair while I tried to remember something more. I took an internal inventory of my well-being. I was sore and shaky, but okay. My vision had cleared, but my teeth chattered with excess adrenaline. "I don't know."

I opened and closed my fists, rolled my wrists and stretched my shoulders carefully. Considering I'd walked from the store room on my own, I was almost certain the blow to the head was my only true injury. "I don't need a paramedic," I said, accepting the bottle of water Granny had uncapped and pushed in my direction. "I'm fine."

"You were knocked unconscious and locked in your store room," Colton growled. "You are most definitely not all right, and you are seeing a medic." He slid his palms against my cheeks, forcing my focus onto his steady eyes. There was emotion there, heavy and intense, flowing just beneath the surface. Anger? At me for letting this happen? At whomever had attacked me? "What can you remember?" he asked more softly. "There has to be something. If not a face, then a scent or a scar on his hand. Maybe a tattoo on his forearm. Something." He released me suddenly, stepping away to grip the back of his neck.

"He wore gloves," I answered proudly, recalling the fact instantly. "Gloves and long sleeves."

Granny bustled away and returned a few moments later with a freezer bag of crushed ice wrapped in a dishtowel and a pair of aspirin to go with my water. She handed off the gifts, then turned to Colton, who looked like he was chewing nails. "Maybe you should go out and keep watch for the paramedics," Granny said. "Or check the perimeter for perps or clues. Or just cool off."

His tight expression loosened, and he dropped his hand away from his head. He turned his gaze from Granny to me, then walked away.

Granny sighed in his absence. "That man is intense."

"Tell me about it." I set the ice on my head and let it hang over the goose egg on my forehead. "Ow."

Granny took the seat beside me and squeezed my hand in hers. "You scared me," she said, an eerie calm in the words. "One of the goats climbed onto the shed in my yard and wouldn't come down. I called you for help, but you weren't answering your phone, and when I started in this direction, the cider shop was all closed up. I turned back and tried your house. Then your phone again. Nothing." She pulled in a ragged breath before continuing. "I came up here to see if the radio was turned up and you didn't hear the phone, but I could hear it ringing before I opened the door." She removed my phone from her pocket and slid it across the table to me. "It was on the floor, and I thought you'd been abducted. I called the sheriff while I ran around looking for you, hoping I was wrong. Sheriff Wise was already on his way by the time I noticed the storeroom door was locked. I thought that man was going to bust it down with his bare hands." Her eyes went wide. "He was as spooked as I've ever seen anyone. It scared me. If he was losing his cool, then things had to be dire. I started thinking about what happened to you before, and I had no idea what we might find on the other side of the door."

"I'm okay," I assured. "Really." That was more than I could say for my poor store room door. I craned my neck for a look in the direction we'd come. "Did I hear a power tool?"

"Yeah. I thought he was going to break your door down, so I brought him the power screw driver behind the counter."

The one I'd borrowed from Grampy's workshop for hanging shelves. Thank goodness for that.

I wanted to make a joke about the importance of decor when my memory of the day's events hit like a sledge. "I was ambushed," I whispered, suddenly recalling every detail with horrific clarity. "I came through the door and someone seized me around the middle. He put his hand over my mouth and whispered against my ear." I pressed a palm to my cheek, feeling his breath on my skin anew. "Long arms. Big hands." My eyes blurred with tears, and a sob filled my chest.

I was a snotty mess when the ambulance finally arrived.

The paramedics were kind enough not to comment on it.

Colton returned during the exam. He too kept his thoughts about my utter instability to himself. Then he walked the men to their ambulance before returning to collect me. "You think you're up to making a written statement?"

"Why not?"

He chuckled. "That was a joke." He drove Granny and me home in his cruiser. The quarter mile had never seemed so long. I closed my eyes when a goat darted across the grassy lane. Colton honked, and the animal fell over. I stayed in the car while Colton and Granny went to lead it back into her yard.

I really needed to hire a lawn crew.

And maybe some extra help at the shop. I'd barely opened for the day and was already closed. Again. It seemed to me the buddy system might limit my attacks and abductions, and that would be great for business, so the help would practically pay for itself.

I handed Colton my house key when he returned, then let him walk me to my door. Kenny Rogers and Dolly took one look at us then ran to their bowls.

Colton made a sweep of the place before ushering me to the couch and delivering a glass of ice water to my hands. "How's the head?" he asked.

"Hurts."

He took a seat in the chair across from me and leaned forward, watching me intently. He looked exponentially older than the man I'd met only a few months back. "Tell me what you remember."

I sipped the water and released a steadying breath, then rubbed my palms up and down my thighs. "I was thinking about creating a taste test for guests. Something like you helped me with, but on a larger scale and hopefully with more definitive results." I glanced at him, offering a small smile he didn't return. "I unlocked the doors, walked into the shop, and a pair of arms latched around me before I reached the bar. One hand covered my mouth." Currents of fear snapped across my skin like electricity, and I was transported back to the moment. "He told me to butt out of things that weren't my business or I'd be next."

"Did you recognize this man's voice?"

I shook my head, fighting another bout of tears and promising myself a proper emotional breakdown later.

"How tall was he?"

"I didn't see him."

"Can I assume you're not running any other amateur investigations?" Colton asked. "When the assailant said to butt out, could he be referring to anything other than my two open murder cases?"

I glared, the fear and anxiety balling inside me like a fist. "I realize I make you crazy, and I'm always in trouble, but be serious. What else is going on with you? The whole truth this time. No more vague generalities. You've been acting squirrely since Christmas."

His gaze dropped to his hands.

"Go on," I said.

Colton didn't speak for several long beats.

I let my eyes close against the dull drumming in my head while I waited.

"Before I came here, I was a detective in Clarksburg."

My mouth and eyes popped open. He was going to tell me? Something personal? I forced my mouth closed and tried to look casual. "Okay." I'd read all about his time with the Clarksburg PD after we met last winter, but he wasn't one to volunteer much about it, or anything else for that matter. "Go on," I encouraged, when he didn't continue.

"I was young. Fresh out of the military and eager

to protect people as a civilian the way I had as a Marine." He folded his hands. Unfolded them. Crossed his legs. "I rose quickly through the ranks from beat cop to detective. Then I interviewed for a position on a joint task force with the FBI. We did a lot of great things. Took down a lot of very bad people. Saved a lot of innocent lives." Colton looked away. He swallowed long and slow. "Then I screwed up, and my partner died."

I pulled in a silent breath. That detail certainly wasn't online. I bit my lip, willing myself silent. Colton had to know I could listen when he needed a friend.

"I took liberties with some information that came in from an informant," he said, glancing shamefaced in my direction once more. "Instead of following protocols to share the information with the task force right away, I wanted to vet the lead, validate the intel first. So I drove to the location in question with my partner at my side. And I got him killed."

I felt his pain cross the room to my heart. "I'm so sorry. What happened?"

"Ambush," he said flatly, his jaw tightening. "I walked him straight into it, and he didn't walk out. Brandon and I were the same age, but he left behind a wife and two daughters."

This time I heard what he hadn't said. "You think it should have been you."

He gave one stiff dip of his chin. "I was the senior officer, and I ignored protocol. All intel was supposed to be reported to our FBI counterpart. Period. It wasn't a case-by-case situation. There wasn't any room for interpretation, and it sure wasn't my

call to make. But I knew how the other officers
looked at me. They thought I was too young, and
I'd risen too fast. So I let my pride make a decision
that was never mine to make. All because my gut
said I couldn't trust the informant." He gave a
dark, humorless laugh. "I thought he was pulling
my chain to make me look stupid. I didn't want to
get a whole strike team mobilized for some
stoner's hearsay. That would have been embarrass-
ing." He shook his head. "I decided to drive by the
location with my partner first and see if the informant was telling me the truth. It was supposed to
be done under the radar. I had no intentions of
letting anyone know we were there and every intention of calling in backup at the first sign of
trouble." He swore under his breath and hung his
head, clasping long fingers against the back of his
neck. "We never saw it coming."

"You were set up."

He rolled guilty, grieving, heart-wrenched eyes
up to meet my gaze. "I did the wrong thing and it
cost a man his life. A woman her husband, and two
little girls their daddy."

My throat tightened and my eyes stung. "Colton,"
I whispered, my voice unsteady. "It wasn't your
fault."

"It was, and that's why I'm here. I didn't deserve to be there anymore, so I turned in my
badge. This . . ." He motioned to the sheriff's
badge on his chest, "was supposed to be an opportunity for me to get myself together. I came here
to run for office, lick my wounds, and find a way to
keep doing what I love. The crime rate was near
zilch when I got here, but we're working on our

third murder inside seven months now, so I think it's safe to say I'm failing my shot at redemption."

"These murders are completely unrelated to your presence," I said.

"Well, it certainly feels like I could do a better job. I lost my partner in Clarksburg, and every time I turn around here lately, I think I've lost you too."

I smiled. "You think of me as a partner?"

Colton managed a droll look. He stood and paced, muttering something that sounded like *unbelievable.*

"Whatever happened to the people who ambushed you?" I asked.

He worked his jaw. "There was only one guy. Samuel Keller. A hired gun. He'd taken an elevated position, then waited for us to come and be picked off. The FBI matched his weapon to a spent casing and bullet lodged in my Kevlar."

"You were shot?" Pain punched through me at the thought, and I placed a palm over my chest, applying pressure against the pain.

"I was luckier than Brandon. The bullet missed my head."

"But the shooter's in jail," I said, remembering the FBI had arrested him. That was a small silver lining, I supposed. At least he would be held responsible for his actions.

Colton stopped pacing and braced his palms on the back of my couch, towering over me where I sat. "It took more than a year in court, but the FBI matched his gun to a dozen other deaths. The sentence came down last fall. Life in a maximum-security prison."

"Good."

"But he overpowered his security team while being moved to Mount Olive, relieved one guard of his sidearm, then killed them both. I got the call during your cider shop's grand opening party last winter."

I remembered. "You went outside in a near blizzard to take the call." I'd known then that Colton had secrets, but I'd never dreamed he'd share them with me.

"Keller's been in the wind since New Year's Day. He ran the guys in Clarksburg around in circles for a couple weeks, then vanished. The FBI is regrouping, but it's got me on edge. I don't want to see him take revenge on the men and women at Clarksburg PD. I was the one who got his sentence served in maximum security. Even after I'd left the department, they used my files against him. He was expecting to do his time someplace soft and get out of there alive. Now two more cops are dead, Keller's free, and Brandon died for nothing."

I set my hand over his where it rested on the couch behind my head.

He pulled free and came around to sit with me. "I want you to know that this town, your safety, and the resolution of my current cases are paramount to me. Yes, I'm gutted that the monster who killed my partner is free, and yes, I'm doing my best to stay on top of the investigation into his whereabouts, but I don't want you to think for a minute that I'm not all-in on my work in this town."

"I know," I said. "I trust you, and I'm glad you trusted me with the truth about what's been bugging you. It's a lot of weight to carry on your own. You need a friend. Do you even have one of those?" I asked, genuinely curious.

In the months I'd known him, I'd never seen Colton with anyone outside work.

"One," he said, his voice low and his tone a little hopeful.

I smiled. "One's a good start."

Colton stood and collected a neatly rolled quilt from the giant basket on my hearth. Then he scooped a pillow off the armchair and set it on the end of the couch. He motioned for me to lie down.

I obeyed, too tired and achy to argue. I rolled onto my side and tucked the pillow beneath my head as Colton draped the quilt over me. He slid the glass of ice water to the end of the coffee table where I could reach it more easily. "Try to get some rest," he said. "I'm going to take another look around the barn before I go. Make sure I didn't miss anything. You should be safe for now. Whoever did this made his point."

"Colton," I said, as he moved toward my door. "If the one who attacked me was a man, then the killer can't be the bride or bridesmaid."

He nodded. He'd already thought of that, of course.

"A man couldn't have fit behind the wheel of the truck," I said. "Does that mean we're dealing with two killers?"

"Truck seats roll, Winnie," he said. And then he was gone.

# Chapter Nineteen

I dreamed of a modern-day Bonnie and Clyde couple terrorizing Blossom Valley. Sometimes the couple was Hank and Sarah. Sometimes it was Hank and me. I woke with a start several hours later. Granny's face illuminated my cell phone screen as it rang on the table.

"Hello?"

"I'm just checking in," she said. "The goats are doing a fine job, and I'm heading over to the hospital to meet Sue Ellen and deliver some apple turnovers. Lizzie Beth Madison fell, and the doctors think she broke her hip, poor thing. She's too young for that, barely sixty."

I sat upright, a sudden bead of excitement forming in my core. "You're going to the hospital?"

"Mm-hmm. Lizzie Beth's husband thinks they might be admitting her. They're running tests now. The turnovers are for him. He's worried sick."

"Can I come?" I asked, taking a quick internal

inventory before pushing onto my feet. The pain in my head had waned to a dull pressure and the rest of me was only slightly achy. Nothing I couldn't manage or that a good night's rest wouldn't cure later. "I'd really like to get out of here."

Granny rolled her truck to a stop beside my porch, then ran around to open the passenger door for me like I was an invalid. I didn't mind. "You've got bangs," she said, admiring the hack job I'd performed on myself, eager to cover the goose egg while she brought the truck over. Now Granny and I had matching hair to go with our look-alike faces.

I shoved dark sunglasses over my eyes to help with the blinding summer sun and considered a second dose of aspirin.

She took the county road to the hospital with extreme care, per her usual, peeking at me from the corner of her eye whenever I yawned or shifted. When the massive building finally came into view, she spoke. "How are you feeling?"

"Okay."

"You don't seem well. Is there anything you need to say? Do you want to talk about what happened?"

Truthfully, I'd been lost in thought. And nearly asleep again, but that was the price of a head trauma, I supposed. I worked up a warm smile. "I was just enjoying the drive."

"Why are you really coming to the hospital?" Granny asked, eyes narrowed as she turned into the large parking lot outside the visitor's entrance.

"What do you mean?" I turned my face toward the open window at my side to avoid looking directly at her. I caught a glimpse of a black Mercedes in the side mirror. It pulled smoothly into the lot behind us, looking as out of place as possible among the mud-drenched farm trucks and ten-year-old sedans. The tinted windows were dark and intimidating, and there wasn't a front plate. I couldn't see the driver, but whoever it was absolutely wasn't from around here. Except for oil company execs, very few people made that kind of money, and those who did drove trucks and SUVs. The Mercedes was impractical and flashy and no one liked a braggart. Maybe the driver was new or visiting. "Did we get a new doctor or something?" I asked, watching as the small car navigated away, probably aggravated by the creeping pace at which Granny moved us along.

"I knew it," she said, accusation strong in her tone. "You feel worse than you admitted. You're going to try to see a doctor while we're here."

It took me a minute to make sense of her accusation. "Not at all," I finally said, though the long pause had reduced my believability. "I feel exactly as well as I said I do, which is not great, but pretty terrific all things considered." I leaned over and patted her arm as she selected a parking space and wheeled the truck into it. "I'm going to stop by medical records and see if Sarah Burrie is working. She's the bridesmaid I scared away at school. I'm a little worried about her, and I might owe her an apology." Or she could be a maniac, but she wouldn't kill me in a hospital, and if I was wrong, and she tried, at least I'd be in a hospital.

We followed a thick yellow line on the ground until we came to the sliding glass doors outside the hospital's main entrance. Granny and I parted ways from there. She climbed aboard a waiting silver-doored elevator. I headed down the long hall toward a massive overhead sign at the end. MED-ICAL RECORDS.

Granny and I were back in the truck an hour later. The whole trip felt like a bust. Sarah wasn't at work, and more than a dozen women had shown up to provide food and fellowship to Lizzie Beth and her husband, but she was being discharged. The party was moving to her home instead, and I was catching a ride back to the orchard.

I slumped in my seat, scolding myself. I should've stayed home and rested. I could've just called the hospital's medical records department. I had a lifelong habit of jumping the gun, and so far my overeagerness had never accomplished anything good. It had, however, resulted in multiple injuries over my lifetime, several horrendous hairstyles, and all sorts of purchases I'd never used. Mostly fitness related.

"How did it go with Sarah?" Granny asked, wheeling out of the lot and back in the orchard's direction.

"The woman at the desk said Sarah has the flu and called off Monday for the whole week."

Granny wrinkled her nose. "I hope there's nothing going around."

I munched on a mini muffin, unconvinced Sarah was sick. She'd seemed to be in perfect health while she was sprinting away from me like an Olympic gold medalist. "These muffins are amazing," I said, suddenly feeling famished.

"Sue Ellen made a double batch for Lizzie Beth,

but everyone brought so much food, we had to take some back. I gave her a few turnovers for her husband, and she sent half the muffins home with me. Everyone knows how you love blueberries."

That was true. I washed the muffin down with a cola I'd bought from the vending machine. I needed the caffeine if I was going to stay awake until nighttime. Every rattled nerve in my body was begging me to sleep for at least a week, but there was no time for that, so I improvised. Muffins, soda, and Plan B.

I thanked Granny for the ride home and waited patiently as she turned back for the county road, on her way to Lizzie Beth's impromptu welcome home party.

When the coast was clear, I climbed behind Sally's wheel and headed for Sarah's apartment building, or the one I believed she lived in anyway.

I brought the rest of the mini muffins as an olive branch for Sarah, in case she really was sick, but I suspected she wasn't at home or anywhere nearby. When no one answered the door at the apartment and the sedan that had been parked outside before was gone, I bit the bullet and headed to Elsie's. Thinking she'd talk to me, if she was talking at all, was a shot in the dark, but I had to try. If nothing else, maybe I'd be able to tell if she was faking her current condition. Or maybe Mrs. Sawyer could help me find Sarah.

The Sawyers lived at the end of a winding gravel lane I'd never been down before. A creek ran alongside it at the base of a mountain on one side, expansive farmland anchored the other. The landscape was peppered with cows, and in the distance an expansive white barn rose from the horizon.

Sawyer Dairy was painted in loopy white letters across the blue aluminum roof.

I suddenly recalled Aaron saying it was important to Jack's family that he marry the "right girl." I'd assumed at the time he'd meant a woman he'd love forever, but now I had a new idea. The Sawyer family had money. A thriving dairy farm. A legacy. Maybe what Jack's blue-collar parents had really meant was marry *up*.

Elsie was outside as I entered the large turn-around drive. The sprawling ranch home before me was as big as it was beautiful and situated on vast acreage tucked among the hills. An inground pool and guest house were visible out back, along with stables in the distance and an abundance of flower gardens everywhere. A small round table and two chairs were arranged under a large oak in the side yard. Elsie was seated in one chair. A shapeless black dress covered her drooping limbs and dark sunglasses hid her watching eyes. Her head turned slowly as I parked and got out, betraying her effort to seem detached from the world. She watched as I approached. The table was set for two.

"Hi," I said, offering a wave as I drew near. I couldn't see her eyes behind the oversized glasses, but her overall expression didn't change, and she didn't speak. "I hope I'm not interrupting." I stared pointedly at the table and its second place setting. A fork lay over the remains of a sandwich and salad. A linen napkin was tucked beneath the plate's edge. Having lunch with her mother? "I thought I should come by and check in. Granny sent you a little something." I offered her the small container of muffins.

Elsie made no move to accept them, so I put the container on the table.

I examined the other cars in view. Two late-model SUVs outside the garage at the edge of the turnaround, and a distant truck by the stables. No signs of a fancy black Mercedes, though I wasn't sure what it would mean if she did own or have access to one. Only that the car had been to the hospital, where hundreds of people worked and even more were admitted or seeing doctors.

"Well," I told her, "I guess I won't keep you." If she wasn't talking, I'd hit another dead end. "Is your mother inside?" I could still ask Mrs. Sawyer about Sarah.

The side door to her massive home opened, and I jerked my face in that direction. It wasn't Mrs. Sawyer, but I wasn't complaining. Aaron's strides faltered as our eyes met, then a smile graced his lips. "Winnie," he said, a pitcher of sweet tea in one hand. "What are you doing here?" He glanced at Elsie, then back to me, smile unmoved. "We were just getting a little fresh air, per Mrs. Sawyer's orders. I thought something cold was a good idea." His black dress shirt and trousers accented a lean, toned physique. Nothing awkward or gangly there, as Hank had insinuated.

"Sweet tea is always a good idea," I said, returning the easy smile.

"Please, sit." He motioned me to his empty seat, then shoved his dirty dish out of the way and set the pitcher on the table. He took a seat on the grass and stretched his legs out in front of him, crossing them at the ankles. His structured dress shirt was unbuttoned at the collar and an undone black tie hung around his neck like a scarf. I wondered, idly, if he'd only packed clothes for wedding-related events and was now limited to dress clothes and the one casual outfit he'd worn to my shop.

"Have you made any progress on your case?" he asked with a wink. "I was just telling Elsie that you were willing to assist however you could, and that a local's perspective can be priceless in situations like these."

I shot Elsie an apologetic look. "I'd be happy to help however I can, but Sheriff Wise has everything under control. I'm sure it won't be long before he knows the truth."

Her lips wiggled, then pulled low into a frown.

"If you've thought of anything else that might help, I could pass it along," I offered.

"Find Hank Donovan," she said, crisp and clear. "Bring him back here and make him pay." Her voice cracked on the last word and a tear slid from beneath her glasses.

I fell back against my chair, half stunned. She'd spoken! I swung my shocked expression to Aaron.

"She's doing better today," he said.

I turned back to Elsie. Keeping my voice low and gentle, I asked, "Do you have any idea what Jack and Hank were arguing about at your reception?"

"How could I know that?" Elsie asked. "I didn't have a chance to ask before . . ." she sucked in a ragged breath, then covered her mouth with both hands. Tears ran over her cheeks, streaming from beneath her sunglasses.

"It's okay," Aaron said, rising fluidly to offer her a handkerchief. "We don't have to talk about it."

"Um," I said, drawing their attention my way, not quite finished. "Have either of you seen or spoken to Sarah Burrie?"

They exchanged a look. Aaron lifted his brows in question, but Elsie's eyes were invisible behind the dark glass.

The dark glass reminded me of the Mercedes once more, and intuition crawled over my skin. I rubbed my palms briskly against the rising gooseflesh and pressed on. "Sarah called off work for the whole week. She said she has the flu, but I think she's on the run and I'm worried."

Elsie shook her head. She bit into her bottom lip, looking almost as if she might literally be biting back something she wanted to say.

"What is it?" I urged.

"I have to go get ready," she said, rising on unsteady legs.

Aaron reached for her as she passed. "Do you need help?"

"No," she said, pulling her arms across her body, away from his touch. "See Winnie out."

She wobbled away, the kitten heels of her sandals sinking occasionally into the earth as she made her way to the home's front entrance.

"When did she start talking?" I asked.

"Today." Aaron kept an eye on her until she'd disappeared through the front door.

"It looks like she took the time to do her hair, and the dress and heels were lovely." Though her makeup was probably a mess. "Those must be good signs."

"Her mom insisted," Aaron said, taking the seat Elsie had vacated. "Her family's holding a private memorial here in a couple hours. Mrs. Sawyer asked me to come and sit with Elsie while she tended to final details."

That explained a lot, namely his outfit, and Elsie's dress, heels, and hair. I'd unintentionally crashed a private memorial. Or I would, if I didn't make myself scarce before guests began to arrive. No wonder she'd instructed him to see me out. My jean shorts and T-shirt would definitely not make a great impression. "Sorry. I didn't know."

"There's a public memorial in town tomorrow," he said. "Then Jack's family will take him back to Morgantown for the funeral and burial." He released a slow breath and pressed his lips into a thin white line.

"I'm sorry," I whispered. It was too easy to forget that Aaron had lost a best friend.

He nodded. "S'okay."

It also seemed to me that this meant Colton only had easy access to out-of-town guests for another couple of days. Once everyone returned to Morgantown, his chances of finding answers diminished significantly. Assuming the guests from out of town knew anything. I hadn't tried speaking with anyone on the subject who wasn't part of the wedding party.

"Aaron!" Mrs. Sawyer stood on the front porch, posture rigid. "I need a hand with the tables, and Elsie's locked herself in her room again."

Aaron's eye lids slipped shut. "Coming," he called.

I wasn't sure how she'd heard him across the significant distance, but she turned and headed inside, indicating that she had.

He reopened his eyes with an apologetic expression. "Duty calls. May I walk you to your car?"

We moved slowly along the lush emerald lawn toward the driveway where I'd left Sally. Aaron glanced down at me multiple times as we walked, as if he might want to say something too. Hopefully he'd speak his mind, unlike Elsie, and not leave me wondering.

"This is going to sound strange," he said as we reached the driveway.

I turned to lean against Sally's door and look up at him. He blocked out the sun like an eclipse, his features unreadable. "What?" I asked, somehow managing a smile. Did he know something that could be used to catch a killer? Had he seen or heard something he'd originally thought insignificant, but now realized was important? Perhaps something he didn't want to say in front of Elsie?

"Would you like to get coffee with me sometime?"

My mouth opened. Then shut. Opened. "Uh." Did he just? "What's that?" I asked, certain I'd misheard.

"Would you like to have coffee sometime?" He smiled shyly, his brows rising slightly. "With me?"

A shaky laugh rumbled out of me. "Oh. Well. I . . . um. Hmm." My ridiculous thoughts ran straight to Colton Wise. Clearly because he was the sheriff who'd warned me off of asking about Jack's death, and having coffee with Aaron would color me guilty. I forced the silly concern aside. Having coffee with Aaron had nothing to do with Colton.

Aaron raised his palms and chuckled. "You're right. I'm sorry. I knew this wasn't the right time to ask you out, but I thought we had a little chemistry going, and I didn't want to leave town without at least giving it a try. Opportunities lost and all that."

I shook the cuckoo off my ridiculous concerns and smiled. "I'd love to. You just caught me off guard."

"Yeah?"

"Yeah." I nodded. "Coffee sounds nice."

The next day moved slowly as I anticipated the evening memorial for Jack Warren and wondered how the private event at the Sawyers' home had gone. Granny and I planned to attend together tonight and do our best to lend support to a wholly shaken community. It'd been easy to forget over the last few days that a good portion of Blossom Valley had been present at the time of Jack's murder, and we were all horrified about that experience in our own ways.

Memorial aside, my stomach churned continually over Aaron's invitation to coffee. He hadn't said when, but I knew it had to be soon. He only had a few days left in town before he returned to Morgantown for Jack's funeral. It was silly to be nervous over a coffee date that couldn't go anywhere, but I was. I blamed the recent head injury.

The day passed in a blur of cider making, cleanup,

and the occasional handful of customers. It wasn't busy, but it wasn't dead, and I was immeasurably thankful for that. My cider taste-testing display caught everyone's attention, and there was a clear favorite, if the marbles in the jars didn't lie.

Outside my shop, two of Dot's goats made short work of the overgrown grass. Granny had relocated them from her backyard using collars, leads, and posts. Now they each had a little fresh scenery and their own grassy meal to devour. I was sure they could escape if they wanted, but both goats seemed content to munch the weeds and watch the folks inside. Guests thought the goats were pretty interesting too, so I called it all a win-win.

Granny bagged another box of turnovers and sighed. "Another pickup," she said. "Who knew so many people would call in orders for cider, pie, and turnovers?"

I stapled a receipt to the bag and smiled. "I'm just glad the town hasn't written us off as harbingers of death."

Granny gave me a playful shove. "We're harbingers of deliciousness. You ought to put your face right on the cider labels."

I needed personalized labels, but putting my face on them was sure to have the opposite effect than what I was looking for.

I knew why most people were ordering pickups. They were avoiding the shop until Jack's family and friends left town, out of respect for the situation. The few customers who'd filtered in so far had told me so. Some had even apologized for coming. I'd assured them the Warrens hadn't given my shop a second thought, but I could still see the guilt in their eyes as they sipped their ciders.

I wiped a line of sweat from my brow, then carefully tested the tender skin beneath my new bangs. Still sore to touch, but the swelling had gone down, and my head didn't hurt nearly as much as it had yesterday. All excellent signs of healing, but I was tired of being attacked inside my shop. I'd made multiple mental notes to get security cameras and signs announcing those cameras posted everywhere as soon as possible.

Granny stepped outside to check on the goats as an old white Bronco came into view through the open doors, bouncing up the grassy lane to my shop. Large rectangular magnets attached to the vehicle's sides identified it as property of the United States Post Office. The driver honked twice, and Granny waved an arm overhead in greeting. "You've got a delivery," she called.

I smiled. The truck was here for me, but it wasn't making a delivery.

I pulled a small jug of cider from my refrigerator and said a silent prayer over it. Then, I tucked it carefully inside the Styrofoam cooler I'd bought and labeled weeks ago, the moment the cider contest had been announced. I inserted the dry ice packets and sealed the container. It was hard not to feel as if I'd also sealed my fate. Forty-eight hours from now, my chilled cinnamon cider would be in the hands of judges. It was the recipe that had started my journey toward my new business reality more than a decade ago, and it seemed fitting that this flavor should represent me in the competition.

I carried the package outside, handed it off to the mailman, and waved goodbye.

Granny wrapped a comforting arm around my back as the truck rolled away. "You've got this, Winona Mae," she whispered. "I'm proud of you."

I turned to give her a tight squeeze. It was nice to know that even if I failed miserably, Granny would turn the catastrophe into some kind of alternate victory in disguise. She was tricky like that. We locked up and collected the goats around five. Time to go home and change clothes for Jack's memorial. I passed my goat's lead to Granny before we parted ways at the field between our homes. She'd return the pair to their herd in her backyard, then pick me up in an hour.

I gave the beautiful day another long look, admiring the beauty all around. My attention snagged on a small black car passing slowly on the main road in the distance. I told myself it definitely wasn't a Mercedes, especially not the one I'd seen at the hospital, because twice in two days wasn't a coincidence. Twice in two days would suggest I was being followed, blatantly, and by someone who didn't care if I knew. Someone who didn't plan to give me the opportunity to report him before it was too late.

My heart gave a wild kick, and I jerked into a sprint across the remaining distance to my door. No one was following me. That car wasn't a Mercedes. The Mercedes at the hospital wasn't following me either. I was paranoid, and I had to get ready for the memorial.

I took one last look over my shoulder to be sure the car hadn't turned up our driveway and proven me wrong before darting inside my home and locking up behind me.

The tantalizing scent of Swiss burgers filled the room, and fire replaced the ice in my veins. "Hank!" I spun for the kitchen, then stopped dead when I saw him at the stove with Sarah Burrie perched on my countertop beside him.

# Chapter Twenty

"Burger?" Hank asked, casually.

I gaped.

He looked like a man at ease in his blue plaid button-down and fresh pressed jeans. He was clean shaven and freshly showered, with a dish towel tossed across one shoulder. If I hadn't known better, I might've assumed he didn't have a care in the world.

Beside him, however, Sarah looked like a wreck, and she didn't hold my gaze. If my memory served, she was wearing the same clothes she'd been in when I'd seen her at school several days ago.

"What are you doing here?" I asked. Though I knew why Hank was in my kitchen. He was there because he was hard-headed, self-serving, and apparently hungry.

Sarah slid off my countertop. "I'm sorry to just show up like this. Hank said it was okay. I told him I shouldn't but he insisted."

Hank wrinkled his nose as she spoke. "Of course

it's okay. Winnie wants to talk to you. She's trying to figure out what's been going on. Cheese?" he asked.

Sarah glanced at Hank and his hunk of Swiss. "No thanks."

He shrugged, then covered two of the three burgers in my skillet with cheese. "I set the table," he said. "You two can have a seat and get started. Your produce needed to be eaten, so I tossed a salad."

I followed his gaze to my kitchen table. Three place settings. A large bowl with salad at the center. Just like he said. To anyone else, at any other time, the scene around me would seem completely normal. But nothing about this was normal. My guests weren't invited, they were both wanted for questioning in a recent murder, and I thought I'd taken Hank's key! *My key.*

"How did you get in here?" I asked, feeling my frozen limbs begin to thaw. "I took the spare key back." I wiggled my keyring. "It's right here, and it's been in my pocket all day." I looked past him to the kitchen window. "Did you break in again? If you damaged my locks, you're going to replace them."

I made a mental note to get a quote on extreme home security for my place when I called about the same for the cider shop.

"I had a copy," he said, jamming his fingers into his pocket. He pulled out another key. "I made a copy a couple years ago after you gave me a key. When I gave your stuff back, I forgot I had the copy. I had to break into my place and hunt for it."

He shook his head, as if I'd really put him out. "Lucky thing I found it."

"Yeah. Lucky," I said. "Leave it on the counter."

He set the key aside, then turned back for the burgers and shoveled them onto a tray. "Come on. Let's eat."

I moved reluctantly to the table, a thousand questions circling my mind. I slid my gaze from Hank to Sarah. "You ran the last time I tried to talk to you. Now you show up at my house? Why?" I crossed my fingers under the table, praying she hadn't come for nefarious reasons. Was the man who'd attacked me her partner?

"I panicked." Sarah wet her lips, looking wildly uncomfortable. Her makeup was gone, and her hair was in need of a good shampooing. Her delicate features were pale and her eyes red. Wherever she'd been these last few days, and whatever she'd been up to, it had taken a toll on her. I hoped I wasn't wrong to delay calling Colton, but I wanted to hear what she had to say.

Hank piled his burger with onions and mushrooms, then took a giant bite. When Sarah didn't continue, he waved his finger in a circle at her, encouraging her to keep going.

She pulled in a ragged breath and let it out slowly. "I ran into Hank last night when we were both trying to break into Elsie and Jack's nutrition shop in Louisville."

My jaw dropped. Not exactly where I thought she'd start the story, but she had my attention. I dropped an elbow on the table and rested my chin in a waiting palm. These two yoyos had made their way to Louisville, separately, but both with the intent to commit a crime while already dodging police questioning. Maybe they were made for each other after all. "Go on."

"We thought we could get an idea of what was going on with their business, or maybe how their relationship was going. People don't just get murdered at their weddings. Something had to have been brewing long before that night."

"Agreed. What did you find?"

"Nothing." She dropped her palms against the table in evident exasperation. "I found a spare key under her planter on the porch and let myself in, but I didn't know what I was looking for. Then I borrowed a key to their shop from the home office and went there to look around. That's when I found Hank trying to get in through a window. We had no idea what we were even looking for. That's why I let him talk me into coming here. He said you were good at this, and we need your help. I think I'm in danger."

I nearly laughed out loud. I still wasn't convinced that she hadn't been the one who hit Jack with the truck, so the idea she was in danger was borderline nuts, and as far as me being good at investigating, I was a walking train wreck. I'd been attacked at my cider shop while they'd been performing a B&E across the river. Together we'd make a three-ring circus or at least a modern-day Three Stooges. "I think we should call the sheriff and talk it out with him," I said, knowing it was the right thing to do. If these two weren't guilty, then there was nothing for them to worry about.

"No." Sarah shot to her feet and darted a crazy glare at Hank. "You said she wouldn't do that."

"She won't," he said, calmly. "She hasn't even heard what you have to say yet."

I looked to Sarah and lifted my brows in question. Knowing she'd broken into two locations across the river wasn't exactly painting her as an upstanding citizen. "You've been on the run because you think you're in danger?"

She nodded, her eyes glistening.

Hank lifted his palms. "First, let's back up so we're all on the same page. What have you learned so far?" Hank asked, redirecting the conversation to me. "Maybe we can put everything we know together and come up with a better picture of things. "You should start. It's your house."

I wasn't sure that made sense, but my big mouth began to move anyway. "Nothing useful yet, but I'm having coffee with Aaron soon. He might be helpful if I know what to ask. He and Jack had been friends a long time." I checked my watch and calculated the time I had before meeting Granny. "I should run into him tonight at the memorial. I'll see if I can set things up for coffee tomorrow."

"Tomorrow's the funeral," Hank said.

"Afterward then."

He shifted, wiping the corner of his mouth with a napkin. "I can't believe that guy asked you out. His friend just died, and he's leaving town soon."

"So what? It's just coffee, Hank," I ground out his name. "You and I have had dinner twice this week. What matters are intentions. Between friends, dinner is just dinner. Coffee is just coffee."

"Oh, so you and Aaron are friends now?"

I rubbed my temples, then swung my face around to look at Sarah. "The thing is, I want to help, but I told the sheriff that I'd stay out of this. So the two of you really need to contact him, and let him help. If you're afraid of being seen at the station by some outside threat, I can invite him here."

"Hold on now," Hank said, pointing a finger at Sarah. "Tell her what happened before the wedding."

"What happened before the wedding?" I parroted.

"Elsie called me." Sarah's voice was low and cautious.

I leaned closer so I wouldn't miss anything.

"She was in the car and she was crying. I was on speaker phone with them when she told me Jack had fallen in the forest while they were hiking, and he needed medical attention, but he didn't want to go to a hospital because they don't have healthcare coverage. She said they couldn't afford it because they own their own business and can't get insurance through an employer like I do. I told them everyone had to have healthcare, but Jack yelled at me to mind my own business. Elsie said he didn't mean to yell. He was just in so much pain, and they really needed my help."

"Did he hit his head?" I asked, wondering if whoever had given Chad Denton a whack on the head had delivered one to Jack as well. "Where were they hiking?"

"I don't know. They didn't say, and he didn't ask me to look at his head. I waited outside for them, figuring I'd usher them in, clean some cuts, and send them on their way. I thought I might even be the hero." She gave a small remorseful smile. "Elsie wasn't overreacting. When Jack got out of the car he could barely walk. He was covered in cuts and bruises. It looked more like he'd fallen off a mountain than tripped while hiking. When I asked what really happened, he practically bit my head off, and Elsie just cried harder."

"What do you think really happened?" I asked, twisting my napkin into a knot.

"I don't know, but he had bruised ribs, a split lip, and swollen cheek. His hands were wrecked. I thought it looked as if he'd been punching something." She paused again, this time to shake her trembling hands out hard at the wrists, before kneading them back together. Her timid eyes rolled up to meet mine. "There was a deep puncture wound in his leg and it was gushing blood. I didn't have anything for the pain and no training to treat something like that. He needed stitches, inside and outside the wound. My surface stitches are bad enough, that puncture was way over my head. I told them I wasn't qualified, but they made me suture it. I did the best I could, but I shouldn't have. I've only been in nursing school a year. We're still learning the anatomical names for all the body parts and systems."

*Nursing school.* There had been a stethoscope around the gear shift of the blue sedan outside her apartment building.

I pressed a hand to my gut and tried not to imagine stitching up a deep and bloody wound. Then, something occurred to me. "Was this the thing you didn't want to tell Hank?" Sarah had said Jack came over one night, and whatever had transpired had traumatized her. Hank had assumed Jack hurt or attacked her physically, but this was just as bad.

Tears spilled steadily over her cheeks as she nodded. "They made me swear never to tell anyone. I knew Jack hadn't fallen while hiking, but they wouldn't even tell me what I was covering up. I was so scared and angry."

Another piece of the puzzle illuminated then. "Colton said the coroner mentioned recent stitches in Jack's autopsy. He thought Jack might've done them himself."

Sarah groaned. "He probably would've done a better job. I'm going to be a terrible nurse. I cried the whole time. Every stitch."

I nearly reached out to pat her hand, but refrained. Was there a chance she was lying? Covering for her own misdeeds somehow?

"It's weird, though, right?" Hank asked. "Why would anyone go to a nursing student instead of the hospital? That business about a lack of health insurance had to be a lie. People only avoid hospitals in movies and crime dramas."

That was a good point. "Are you sure it wasn't a knife wound?" I asked Elsie. "Hospitals are required by law to report all gunshot and stab wounds. Maybe they were trying to avoid that."

"I don't think so," Sarah said, her skin turning a pale green. "The hole was too jagged and broad. And filthy. It took forever to clean. I was afraid I'd sew dirt inside him if I missed anything." She lifted the closest glass of ice water and pressed it to her forehead. "Elsie gave him a pillow to press against his mouth because he kept screaming. Then, she brought him a bottle of unopened scotch to help with the pain. After that, he was just belligerent. It was awful."

"That's why he brought a flask with him to the reception." I realized. Not because he was upset about something but because he was in pain.

"Probably," Sarah said. "I'm just glad he didn't bleed through his white tuxedo. I tried to keep watch all day, and I warned him about the drinking, but he just yelled at me again."

Hank set his burger down. "Was that when I saw him grab your elbow and snap at you? I thought he'd threatened you. That was what pushed me into confronting him."

"I told you to butt out of it," she said, but the words lacked vehemence.

Sarah Burrie was a victim, not a killer.

I picked at my burger, hoping to think more clearly with a little something in my stomach. "Why did you run when I saw you at school?"

"I thought you knew. People around town said you figured out what happened to Mrs. Cooper last winter. I thought you might've figured out that I was wrapped up in Jack's mess. I didn't want to go to jail as an accomplice in whatever he and Elsie had been up to that night. They said that was what would happen if they were caught, but they refused to tell me what."

No wonder the girl had been afraid. "What about the day you were supposed to meet Hank at the cabin? Why didn't you show up?"

"I got lost. Then I heard gunshots, so I turned tail and ran again. I keep thinking that whoever killed Jack knows that he and Elsie came to see me the night Chad Denton died. Jack's killer could assume they told me what happened, that I know something I don't know and want to silence me. Someone has killed two men and taken shots at the two of you already this week. If he considers me a problem needing to be dealt with, I don't stand a chance."

I watched her carefully, looking for signs of deception, but her expression was clear and genuine. My gut said she needed a friend, so I decided to tell her what I knew. "Chad Denton was a known loan shark, among other things." Including killer. "Did Elsie ever mention him or give any indication that she and Jack were having financial trouble?"

Sarah frowned. "I can't imagine Elsie ever having financial problems. Her parents are loaded. If she needed cash, she only had to ask for it. They'd give her anything. Plus, she and Jack had been making monthly payments on all the wedding stuff for more than a year. It should have all been paid off before now. Which was another reason I was surprised when they moved the whole show here. Why go through all that planning just to change her mind last-minute? I'd assumed the massive changes were just meant to cause chaos and home everyone's focus onto her big day."

*Or*, I thought, *maybe Elsie didn't want her mother to know she and Jack were in debt to a loan shark*. Maybe getting all that wedding money refunded seemed like a better choice than full disclosure to her family. It definitely would have created an influx of cash that could have been used to satisfy a homicidal loan shark.

I went to get my laptop and test my theory. "Do you remember where the wedding and reception were originally going to be held? Maybe we can find out what that venue charged and if they give refunds."

"The place was called The Bell. It's an event center inside an old church, and it was really hard to get into. I'm sure it wasn't cheap. She bragged about her ability to book the place every time we talked."

"How often did you talk to her?"

"All the time," Sarah said. "We were both trying to get in shape for the wedding. Elsie jogged through her neighborhood, and I hit the trails in the national park. We traded photos from our hikes and runs. A little healthy competition. It was fun." Her voice cracked, and she stopped to settle herself once more. "One day I sent a picture and she didn't respond. I didn't hear from her for three days. When I finally did, she announced that she'd had a change of heart, was utterly homesick and moving the wedding here."

"Interesting. She'd told her mom there was an issue with the venue." I felt my eyes bulge as I landed on The Bell's website and navigated past dozens of Hollywood-worthy photos to the package rates page. "The average reception at this place is twenty-six thousand."

"Dollars?" Hank choked. "I'd say there was definitely a problem with the venue. People should get a new car with that rental."

I shut the laptop. "They would have lost their deposit, but they were entitled to their payments back. Assuming the deposit wasn't anywhere near twenty-six grand, I'd say they received a hefty refund from the reception hall alone." I didn't need to look at anything else to confirm the venue change had been about money. "Elsie and Jack must've been in deep to owe a guy like Chad Denton that kind of cash. What if Denton knew they'd gotten all those wedding refunds and he came here to collect? They might've chosen to meet in the woods so no one would see them with him. Then something went wrong. A fight broke out and Jack won."

Sarah's mouth fell open. "A fight would explain the extensive number of wounds, plus the cuts and scrapes on his hands. Oh my goodness." She rocked back in her seat. "Jack killed the John Doe. No wonder he and Elsie were so worked up that night and swore me to secrecy. They dragged me into a murder!"

"It would explain why he didn't want to go to the hospital," I added. "They didn't want any record of his injuries."

What it didn't explain was who'd killed Jack.

# Chapter Twenty-one

I offered Sarah the use of my shower and a change of clothes before I left to meet Granny for the memorial. As usual, I asked Hank to be gone when I got back and advised him to turn himself in while he was out. My exact words were: Stop hiding. Cowboy up. Deal with your problems. But I had a sneaking suspicion he'd be watching the evening news on my couch at eleven.

Given the fact Colton wasn't actively looking for Hank anymore, and he was only looking for Sarah because I'd asked him, I decided it was fine if they stayed with me. Sarah was clearly shaken, and I wasn't harboring fugitives as much as a pair of scaredy-cats. Considering my current status as Scaredy-Cat Club president, I wasn't in any position to judge. It was probably better that I knew where they were anyway.

I surprised Granny by showing up at her place before she could show up at mine. The sun would set soon, and she didn't see well at night, so convincing her to let me drive wasn't difficult.

"You look nice," she said, adjusting her patent leather pocketbook on her lap. Her simple black dress and sensible pumps made me smile. It wasn't often that Granny wore anything other than jeans, and I appreciated the change.

"You too," I said. I'd chosen black dress pants and flats in case I had to run, which was a ridiculous thing to have to consider on my way to a memorial, but there it was anyway. A killer was still on the loose in Blossom Valley, and I didn't want to bump into that person while wearing anything I couldn't make good time in. Running was hard enough all by itself. I'd paired the pants with a cream blouse and added a thin raincoat for protection against the newly predicted rounds of evening drizzle.

I took my time on the winding country roads toward town, savoring the quiet moments and intense freedom that Sally provided. When I was cradled in her seat, nothing bad could touch me, or catch me. For a moment, I considered sharing the peculiar details of my week with Granny and asking her what she made of them. Instead, I chose to put it off and concentrate on the drive. I could confide in Granny later. Maybe even on our way home.

She flashed a knowing look my way. "What?"

"Nothing." I put my attention back on the road. "How are the goats?"

"The goats are fine." She paused for a long beat, probably deciding if she was going to let me change the subject so easily. Eventually, she did. "I wouldn't mind keeping the white one. He's got a hearty appetite and if he tries to get away, all I have to do is blow my air horn, and he'll be down for the count. Then I can go and get him."

"Well, don't let Dot hear you say that," I warned.

Granny smiled. "Did you know she's planning to open an animal rescue?"

I nodded. "She'll be great."

"Yeah," Granny said dreamily. "You know, we've adjusted to Kenny Rogers and Dolly really well. How much more trouble could one goat be?"

"Plenty," I said. "Cats are easy. They go in the litter. They don't get lost or stuck on top of the shed. They never head butt or collapse." They were a bit demanding and seriously judgmental, but easy to care for. "I thought you never wanted animals. You always said we live on an orchard, not a farm. Remember?"

She clucked her tongue and waved her hand dismissively. "I only said that to back your Grampy. I'd always wanted a hound dog."

"I didn't know that." I cast a glance her way, shocked and a little sad that she'd gone without something she'd wanted for so long. Suddenly, I didn't mind keeping the goofy goat if it made her happy. She did so much for everyone else.

"I want a basset like the one on *Dukes of Hazzard*." She smiled, as if the thought uplifted her. "I'd name him Flash and let him ride on my lap in the truck. We could go everywhere together."

It was funny how much I didn't know about the one person I'd spent every day of my life with for years and still saw more days of the week than not. Even funnier that I thought of Colton and the way he'd willingly opened up to me the other night. Part of me hoped he'd be at Jack's memorial.

When we pulled into the corner parking lot at Goody's Funeral Home, the spaces were already full. Folks were parking along the roads on two sides and in nearby parking lots. I dropped Granny off at the door, then circled twice, checking for anyone who might be leaving. I kept watch for exiting guests and checked for a black Mercedes. If the car was here, it would be easy to discover who it belonged to and figure out if I was paranoid or right to worry. I didn't see any fancy foreign cars, but a spot opened up along the road at the edge of the parking lot and I claimed it before it was gone.

Folks streamed in and out of the front doors as I hurried toward the early-nineteenth-century home. The massive estate was butter yellow with white trim and a sprawling wraparound porch. The property had been in the Goody family for generations, but only became a funeral home about twenty years ago when Guy Goody, a mortician in Wetzel County, inherited the place and relocated his business to Blossom Valley.

I ignored the large sign positioned on the lawn between the road and sweeping front steps. *When it's time to say goodbye, make it a Goody-bye with Goody's Funeral Home.* I'd wanted to punch his Goody nose for that slogan while helping Granny plan Grampy's funeral. As if any goodbye that required a funeral home could be a good one. I'd gotten through by reminding myself it wasn't Mr. Goody's fault he had a terrible last name and even worse marketing sense.

Inside the glass doors, someone had arranged a

large easel with an extra-large picture of Jack in his West Virginia Mountaineers football uniform surrounded by a giant gilded frame. Beside the massive photo was a guest book and several people waiting to sign. I slipped past them and into the largest gathering room, where mobility was limited by knots and clusters of whispering people around the perimeter. Only a handful of older folks had resigned themselves to the chairs lined up in the room's center. Potted plants, floral wreaths, and bouquets filled the space at the front near a podium and microphone. Jack's white casket was closed and nearly obscured by minglers. I spotted Granny with Elsie and Mrs. Sawyer at the front, recognized plenty of locals, and noted a cluster of Jack's people near the opposite wall. I recognized them from the wedding guests. Aaron and two bridesmaids were with them.

I went to see Granny and pay my respects to Elsie and her mother first. I slowed as I approached, my dinner conversation returning to me in full force. If everything Sarah had told me was true, and my theory was right, then Elsie had intentionally covered a murder. She'd helped her former fiancé cover a man's body in leaves and left him in the forest for time, animals, and weather to dispose of. She'd gotten Jack treatment for his wounds without alerting authorities, by twisting the arm of a young nursing student she'd once babysat. Elsie wasn't who people thought she was, and she was capable of things I absolutely was not.

"Winnie." Granny pulled me to her side. "There you are. I was just telling Elsie and her mother how sorry we are."

I nodded and worked my suddenly dry mouth into a smile. "If there's anything we can do to ease your troubles, just ask. We're happy to arrange meals to be delivered or schedule help with your cleaning and shopping so that you can take more time for yourselves and heal."

I didn't always attend church with Granny, but I was a dedicated volunteer on the Helping Hands Committee. If anyone in Blossom Valley was sick, lost a loved one, or had a baby and we got wind of it, that person could count on a windfall of casseroles and weekly housekeeping until they felt better or forced us to stop.

Elsie wiped her nose on a tissue then dropped it onto a growing pile of similarly wadded pieces at her feet. "I can't believe he's gone."

Her mama rubbed her back.

I was glad to see she was talking because I needed to know who wanted to kill Jack. If she knew about the loan shark, then she knew what else was going on, and she could no longer convince me that her late husband was as squeaky clean and perfect as everyone thought. If I was right, Jack had been a killer just days before he'd been killed. I only hoped Chad Denton's death had been an accident or an act of self-defense, instead of the alternative. The possibility Elsie and Jack had set a trap for the out-of-towner, lured him into the park, then intentionally murdered him was too much for me to fathom. "It's a lovely turnout," I said, forcing the words from between stiff, smiling lips. "A beautiful tribute to a gentle soul. A man who'd never hurt anyone."

Her gaze flicked sharply to mine.

I started to say more, but my phone buzzed with a call from the funeral home. "Excuse me. I'm so sorry," I said, turning away to answer the call. "Hello?" I whispered, scanning the area for land-lines.

"Winnie, it's Hank."

"Hank!" I whispered. "Are you crazy?"

"Meet us in the foyer." He hung up, and I stared at the screen.

Granny gripped my elbow. "Did you say . . . ?"

I spun to face her and gave a stiff nod. "I'll be right back."

Her jaw dropped and her brows furrowed.

"I'll take care of it," I vowed.

She tugged me close and moved her lips near my ear. "I'll expect an explanation in the car."

"I'll try to come up with one," I said, slipping out of her grip. I offered a soft "pardon me" to Elsie and Mrs. Sawyer before bolting into the crowd. I threaded my way through the people to the foyer, where Hank and Sarah stood in the little hallway to the offices, backs to me and tipped forward, pretending to look closely at something.

I joined them, careful not to draw attention. "What are you doing here?"

Hank pointed at Sarah, clearly even less thrilled about their presence than I was. "She insisted on saying her goodbyes and offering Elsie her condolences. I couldn't let her come alone."

I narrowed my eyes and shook my head at her. "You're supposed to stay hidden. You need to go."

She shook her head stubbornly. "Not without

seeing Elsie. I've had time to think, and I can't believe Elsie was involved in the awful story we came up with. How could she be? It can't be real."

"Oh, it's real," Hank snapped. "And Winnie's right. We need to go."

"I won't let Elsie think I'm the kind of friend who ran away when things got tough, then didn't come back when they mattered most. What if that was your friend up there?" she asked, looking as if she might cry again. "What if Elsie was Dot?"

Her question caught me off guard. Dot would never hurt anyone or anything, but what if she did? Would I stand by her or walk away? At what point do our loved ones lose us from their team? Suddenly, imagining Elsie as Dot, I wondered if I'd been too quick to judge and recalled that my version of events was only that. The truth was that we didn't know what happened in the forest that night. The only one who did was Elsie, and we hadn't asked her.

"Will you at least tell her I'm here?" Sarah asked. "Tell her I want to see her. If she doesn't want to see me, I'll leave, but at least she'll know I came."

I looked back to the crowded room, considering. "I can try, but you need to be careful. There's always a chance that the Elsie you knew is gone, and the grieving widow we see isn't what she seems." In fact, she might be a woman who killed her own husband at their wedding reception to cover her complicity in another man's death. I realized my earlier thought was true. The only person left with the truth about what happened in the forest that night was Elsie.

Sarah swallowed long and hard. "Thank you. If she refuses to see me, will you tell her I'm truly sorry for all she's going through."

I sighed. "Just remember, now that Jack's gone, you might be the only one who can tie her to Chad Denton's death."

I slid my arms out of my rain jacket and offered it to Sarah, "Put it on. Pull the hood up and pretend you're just coming in from outside. Use the hood to shield your face, and I'll try to get Elsie to come to you."

She took off the long-sleeved black cardigan she'd borrowed from me and we traded. The sweater was warm and soft, a good choice considering the temperature inside Goody's was about sixty degrees with the air conditioner blowing.

We moved together into the foyer by the giant picture of Jack. Hank tagged along at our heels, then stopped to shake his head at the picture. "Didn't the guy have a better photo for this? He's been out of college for five years. They didn't want to use something taken a little more recently? Maybe one from their engagement photo session?"

"Maybe whoever selected it thought his best days were behind him," Sarah said.

"Well, that's sad." Hank crossed his arms and shook his big head. "When you get married, your best days are supposed to be yet to come."

I stole a hat off the rack above miles of guests' coats on hangers and stuffed it onto Hank's head. "Keep the brim low and don't make eye contact. Stand close together and pretend the two of you are deep in conversation. I'll be right back."

I reentered the gathering room, and slowed as

Granny came into view, mingling with a group of locals near the far wall. I'd have to approach Elsie on my own without the benefit of Granny to keep Mrs. Sawyer busy with polite conversation. I took a breath, turned, and headed toward the front, only to find Aaron there now. How was I supposed to speak to her without him hearing?

Aaron lifted his chin in acknowledgment when he saw me, then smiled.

I rustled up some backbone and headed his way, chin up, smile sincere. "Hey," I said in greeting. "Anything I can do to help out?" I turned my face to Elsie. "I can get you a cup of water or take a walk with you around the building, if you feel like moving a little?" A new idea struck. "Maybe a trip to the ladies' room." The door to the ladies' room was just beside the foyer where I'd left Hank and Sarah. "You could have a minute of privacy there. Maybe splash a little water on your face?"

"What's wrong with my face?"

Aaron grimaced. "Nothing. You look beautiful." He turned the expression on me. "Are you okay?" he whispered.

"Just trying to help."

Elsie dragged a tissue under each eye, then looked at it, presumably for traces of mascara. "By telling me my face is a wreck?"

"I didn't mean anything like that. I'm so sorry. It's just that a splash of cold water helps me refresh after a long day," I said, backpedaling hard, but hoping she'd agree to the trip anyway.

Elsie jerked stiffly to her feet and marched away.

"I'll go with her," I said, excusing myself from Aaron. "It's my fault she's upset now."

He dipped his chin in acknowledgment, then tipped his head closer to mine. "Coffee tomorrow?"

"Yes, please." I smiled, then hurried after Elsie. When we reached the foyer, Hank and Sarah were gone.

Elsie shoved her way into the ladies' room while I checked behind the coats and the giant photo of Jack for signs of the disguised duo.

"Winnie?" Colton's voice spun me around.

"Oh!" I jerked upright and pressed a palm to my chest, eyes raking the crowd behind him for signs of my raincoat or the borrowed man's hat. "What are you doing here?"

"I came to pay my respects," he said softly, and I noticed for the first time that he wasn't in uniform. He wasn't wearing his usual jeans or button-down shirt either. He was in a black suit and tie with shiny dress shoes and clean-shaven cheeks. I'd never seen him without at least two days' stubble and a pair of dirty boots, uniform or not.

I slid my palm from my chest to my tummy where an uncomfortable tickle of emotion had begun.

"How's she holding up?" he asked, sweeping his gaze toward the ladies' room, where Elsie had disappeared.

"She's speaking again," I said.

"Good." He stepped closer and his shoe nudged my shoe. He leaned forward and his breath caressed my cheek. "Has she said anything I need to know?"

I shook my head, working to find my tongue. Sarah's hope for her friend's innocence shook me out of the momentary stupor, and I leaned closer to ask a question that had been niggling in my mind. "Have you checked to see if Jack or Elsie owned a .45 caliber handgun?"

He pulled back and frowned. "Yes."

I raised my brows, waiting.

"There aren't any guns registered to Jack or Elsie, and no one in either immediate family or the bridal party had a .45 registered to them. Criminals don't tend to register their weapons."

"I hear the sarcasm in your voice, but considering that you already checked on those licenses, I must not be too crazy."

His gaze flicked over my head. "She's on the move."

I turned to see Elsie glaring at me as she exited the restroom. Her mother was moving in our direction, attention fixed on Colton. "I should probably leave you to it," I said, "but let's talk later, okay?" I nodded to punctuate the necessity in my invitation, then slipped away.

I had plenty of information that I needed to share with him, and I needed to share it soon. Adding what Sarah told me to what I'd already learned had resulted in a strong theory about what happened to Chad Denton. Maybe if Colton compiled what I now knew with what he'd discovered so far, Jack's killer would be immediately unmasked.

I caught Elsie before she made it back to her seat. "Sarah was here," I whispered, drawing her attention and stopping her midstride.

"Where?" The venom slid from her expression as she turned in a circle, seeking.

"She's gone again," I said, "but she wanted you to know she's sorry for what you're going through and that she'd be here for you now if she could." I wanted to add that, unlike her friend, I wasn't convinced of her innocence, and I suspected what she and Jack had done to Chad Denton, but I figured I should tell Colton first and let him tell her instead. Showing my hand would only give her time to run, and Elsie had the money to do it. Assuming I was right, which I still couldn't prove. Plus, I had no idea who'd killed Jack or why. Unless that too had been Elsie.

I watched as Elsie continued to scan the crowd. Could she have killed her husband? Had she blamed him for getting them involved with Denton to start with? Maybe she'd been livid that his behavior had ruined her carefully planned, super-fancy wedding in Louisville, forcing them back to Blossom Valley so they could repay Denton instead. Then, to top it all off, he'd made her complicit in his murderous act when she helped him bury a body in the woods.

Mr. Goody approached the podium and classical music filtered through hidden speakers, alerting us that the service would soon begin. I took a seat with Granny and resolved to people-watch and listen. I didn't like the ideas that had been circling in my head. I needed to talk to Colton, but I no longer saw him among the crowd.

Granny and I spilled into the parking lot with a flood of other guests following the brief service. True to the forecaster's word, the world outside the funeral home was damp. Wet streets and cars glistened under the amber glow of a nearly set sun. I hit Sally's wipers and cranked the defrosters once we were safely inside. I shivered at the blast of air.

"Where's your raincoat?" Granny asked.

I looked at my sweater. It took a long beat for me to recall the switch I'd made with Sarah. "I lent it to Sarah," I said.

"Good thing you wore a sweater." She rubbed her palms up and down her arms, craned her neck for a look out the car windows, then fixed her eyes on me. "What on earth were Hank and Sarah doing in there? And why were they looking for you?"

I adjusted the vents to point at Granny, took a deep breath, then delivered the whole of my story about Sarah and Hank and our suspicions while memorial traffic flowed around us.

Granny's eyes widened on occasion, but true to her nature, she stayed quiet and calm until I'd finished. "Why didn't you tell me?"

"I am telling you," I said. "Until I spoke with Hank and Sarah earlier, nothing I'd learned had made sense."

I hit my left turn signal and waited for a break in the traffic. I'd picked the worst spot on the street to park, and would be sitting there forever if no one let me pull out. My perfume wafted from the sweater, amplified in the small space, and I wrinkled my nose against the intensity. Sarah had been a little heavy-handed with my favorite spray. Though when compared with me, she was a little extra in lots of ways. Including her love of social media, specifically selfies.

I stopped my turn signal and shifted back into park, then pulled my phone from my bag.

"What are you doing?" Granny asked.

"I'm going to look up Sarah's Instagram account while we're stuck here. She said that she and Elsie were trading fitness photos right up until Elsie changed wedding destinations from Louisville to Blossom Valley. I'm curious about their interactions before that sudden change." I searched for Sarah Burrie on the app. When I didn't find her, I tried the handle she used via email with Hank. Sarah-BearTwenty-two. "Bingo," I said, scrolling through a million photos featuring the little blonde.

Granny stared forlornly out her window as everyone in line beside us seemed to want to turn left. "Well, we certainly have time." She was right. Without a traffic light at the intersection, it would be a while. "We need another stoplight in this town. One right here would be nice."

I leaned toward her and positioned the phone between us. "Let's look at pictures while we wait." I scrolled through Sarah's public photos showcasing the hard work she'd been doing to look great at her friend's wedding. She'd used hashtags to count down the days, and Elsie had replied each day with support and encouragement of her own. When I reached the end of the fitness photos, I started over. "I didn't see anything interesting. Did you?" All their comments to one another were positive and fitness related. Nothing that should've turned Elsie off from the exchanges the way Sarah had thought.

"Maybe we should look at Elsie's photos instead,"

Granny said. "Maybe whatever stopped Elsie from responding had happened on Elsie's side and had nothing to do with Sarah."

"Good point." I gave the screen one last swipe, prepared to search for Elsie's account, when the background of one of Sarah's national forest photos dropped my jaw. "Is that what I think it is?" I asked, using my fingertips to expand the photo on my phone's screen and zoom in to the seemingly endless field of what appeared to be wild ginseng behind her. Ginseng was a natural substance believed to have medicinal properties. It was used for everything from an aphrodisiac to a way to improve memory and mood. When harvested from the wild, ginseng brought in upwards of a thousand dollars per pound. The roots were so sought after that there were laws in place for the plant's preservation. It had its own hunting seasons, like deer, squirrel, and turkey.

The problem with a major find like the one behind Sarah in the photo was that it wasn't ginseng season. And it was illegal to harvest ginseng from a national forest any time of year.

"Folks would kill for the location of a haul that big," Granny whispered.

And I was suddenly sure that someone had.

# Chapter Twenty-two

While a chunk of locals traveled with Elsie's family to Morgantown the next morning to attend Jack's funeral and graveside service, Granny and I hung our CLOSED signs for another reason. We dressed in our comfiest hiking gear and joined our friends around my kitchen table. I had to be sure what I saw in the picture was ginseng before contacting Colton. He'd be irritated enough to learn I was still snooping without sending him on a wild goose chase. Unfortunately, when I asked Sarah about the photo, she hadn't even noticed the plant and couldn't recall exactly where in the vast national park the photo had been taken. Unlike me, Sarah wasn't a creature of habit. So we were forced to wait until dawn to go hunting.

I invited Hank and Sarah to sleep over, knowing they'd both be ready to talk to Colton soon. No one who knew all that we did would still think Hank had anything to do with Jack's death. And Sarah was beginning to see that what she really needed to stay safe was the sheriff's protection. The three of us had sat up talking late into the night, sharing conspiracy theories and hoping Elsie wasn't responsible for Jack's death, though she seemed the obvious culprit. Theories on what had been going on in our town were vast and occasionally wild as we tried to come up with every possibility. The one that worried me most was that we were wrong about it all. It occurred to me after my fourth cup of coffee that the mushroom hunters could have come across the ginseng. One of them might've fired on Dot and me. They were still there, in the area, that day. They could have killed Chad Denton and attacked Jack, protecting their giant cash haul, and Elsie could've been forced to cover it up because she didn't want anyone to know why they were in the forest to begin with. If that was true, the killer might've already cleared out all the ginseng while we'd been chasing our tails and be on his or her way back to New England. We didn't have any time to spare if we wanted to take a look at that ginseng crop.

Luckily, I knew someone who spent a lot of time in the national forest. I'd called Dot to loop her in, and she agreed to help without hesitation. Even after I'd gotten her shot at the last time I dragged her out on one of my reconnaissance missions. She arrived just after breakfast with a box of donuts and a vat of enthusiasm. "This is Carpenter's Run," she said, spreading a map of the national forest over the table and using my salt and pepper shakers to hold it down." A red circle had been drawn around the area in question. "Does everyone know how to get there?"

Our group nodded.

"Carpenter's Run is a good place for us to start because, now that the mushroom hunters have changed campsites, there's plenty of space for us to park off the road and out of sight. We'll hike out past Hank's family's cabin and the location of the John Doe, then begin exploring from there."

"Chad Denton," I said softly, wanting the man to be remembered as more than a "John Doe." He might've been a bad guy, but he'd been a person and he'd been murdered. It only seemed right to acknowledge him by name.

Dot nodded.

"I can only hike until three," I said. "At that point, I have to head back and change clothes for coffee with Aaron. Hopefully we'll find the harvest before then and be done, but if not, I'll still need to go."

Granny patted my back. She and Delilah had volunteered to come as our lookouts. They would stay in position at the mouth of the hollow while we hiked and watch for incomers.

I'd called Gina too, because I knew she wouldn't want to miss the chance to help her brother.

"We'll stay in touch by text and radio," Dot said. "I brought a bag of long-distance radios because reception's spotty throughout the park. We can't rely on cell phone coverage."

Sarah leaned low over the map, frowning. "What if I can't find the location where that photo was taken? I have no idea where I was that day, and I've never started from anywhere except the main gates. Over here." She dragged her fingertip across the paper, indicating the national park's main entrance, then slumped back into her seat. "I tried a new trail every time I hiked for weeks, and I always left the paths at some point to get a truly impressive shot. The ginseng could be anywhere."

"No, it can't," Dot said. "I know this park, and I've never seen so much wild ginseng, so I can rule out the areas I explore most often." She made Xs in pencil over several broad sections of the map, then looked determinedly at our group, one face at a time. "Chad Denton was found on the eastern side of the park, not far from where Winnie and I were shot at, so I think it's fair to assume you were on one of the trails headed in that direction. The ginseng might not be in that exact location, but I'm willing to bet it won't be far either." Dot circled several of the trailheads winding east from the main entrance. "We'll start with these, but come at them from Carpenter's Run so we aren't seen. I'm sure whoever is after those roots will be guarding the area, unless it's fully harvested."

We all nodded. Hank grunted. "Agreed," I said, speaking for the crowd.

Dot turned to Sarah. "Let's see if we can narrow it down a little more. How long did you hike each day before stopping to take the selfies you posted?"

I turned to Granny and Delilah while Dot and Sarah whittled down the possible search area. "Thank you guys for doing this."

"No problem," Delilah said. "I'm glad for a little excitement. Needlepointing rude things is getting tedious. It's time to break it up with some action." Her eyes lit, then she pulled a stun gun from her pocket and showed me. "I came packing electric heat. Penny wouldn't let me bring my Beretta."

"I'm going to agree with Granny on that one."

"This is just as good," Delilah said. "It'll put a grown man on the ground in a few seconds, and it won't send me to jail. We make a great choice for lookouts. No one will suspect a couple of sweet old broads like us to be so dangerous."

Behind them, Gina signed the cross.

I lifted a shoulder when she caught me looking. "At least we don't have to worry about them."

Granny kicked her feet out before her and crossed them at the ankles, getting comfortable and looking pensive. "It makes sense that Jack would want those roots. With his pharmaceutical background and holistic medicine business, he would know exactly what they're worth, where to sell them, or how to incorporate them into his own product line. It must've seemed like fate when he saw that picture."

I'd thought the same thing. The ginseng was a perfect discovery for Jack, given his chosen profession. Unfortunately, the astronomical value of the find also made it great find for anyone who could use a ton of extra cash.

"All right," Dot called. "Who's ready?"

The group cheered, then formed a line for the bathroom.

Dot piled water bottles into a cooler and waited outside.

We moved in a slow processional over the winding country roads to Carpenter's Run, then lined up our vehicles up like a wagon train between the two mountains. Dot's Jeep was first, then Granny's red truck and Gina's white pickup. Hank and

Sarah had ridden with Gina, Delilah with Granny, and me with Dot.

"We never really talked about being shot at," I said to Dot as we waited for the others to get out and head our way. "Are you doing okay?"

"I have nightmares," she said with a nervous laugh. "In the dreams you get shot." Her grim expression said it all. Seeing me shot would be worse than if it had been her.

I'd had the same thought, though not in a dream. If one of us had been hit that day, the other wouldn't have been able to leave the first behind, and attempting to drag or carry the injured friend would only have resulted in both our deaths. We could have died and been buried in the leaves like Chad Denton.

"I tell myself to suck it up," she said. "Look at all you've been through and you keep going." Her gaze darkened and dropped to my side, the location of a near-fatal injury I'd received last winter. "Yet, here you are, trucking along, looking for the truth regardless of risk."

"I never meant to get so wrapped up," I said. "Originally, I'd only hoped to overhear something I could share with Colton to help things along. Then Hank was missing and I worried. I got sucked in. I should've stopped."

"But you didn't because you're brave."

"I'm hardheaded and you know it," I said with a grin. "Luckily, I have very brave and amazing friends to talk me up when I'm feeling especially stupid."

She hugged me across her Jeep's console. "I love

you," she said, "but if someone shoots at me this time, I am never coming here again."

"Deal."

Outside the vehicles, Hank hugged Gina to his chest. She looked small in his arms, but she was fierce. They were the kind of siblings that made me wish I'd had someone to share my childhood with. Though Granny would probably have a head full of gray hair by now if there had been more than one of me. Plus, Dot was a perfect sibling stand-in.

Delilah and Granny hauled two camping chairs and a portable firepit from the back of the truck and arranged them near the mouth of the hollow. They had a cooler with snacks and drinks for props to support their facade. Delilah's stun gun was in her pocket, and her attention was fixed on the road, already watching for uninvited guests.

"Do me a favor," I said, suddenly fearing for unsuspecting hikers as well as Granny and Delilah, should a truly dangerous person come their way. "If you see someone who seems to be up to no good, don't stun them. Call and let me know someone's headed our way." Then I turned to Granny. "While Delilah calls me, you call Colton. Okay?"

The women exchanged a glance before nodding in agreement.

"Thanks." I kissed Granny's cheek and hugged Delilah.

"Saddle up," Dot called, passing out the bottled waters.

I jogged in her direction, wishing we had horses. The hike to Hank's family's cabin was long, mostly uphill, and the temperature was nearing ninety.

Dot led the way with her folded paper map tucked beneath one arm.

"It was nice of your Granny and Delilah to sit watch," Dot said when I reached her. "They'll save our hides if trouble comes."

"I asked them to call us and Colton if they see anyone who gives them cause for concern." I just hoped they'd stay safe in the process. "How horrible am I to have dragged them into this?"

Dot rolled her eyes. "Like anyone has ever made either of those women do anything they didn't want to do. You asked, they answered, and honestly, I think they'd be here even if you hadn't asked. I don't think hell or high water could've kept them out of this."

I shook off the awful images of masked gunmen performing Hollywood-style drive-by shootings in fancy black cars. "Have you seen a black Mercedes in town recently?" I asked, lifting my voice to address the group.

The answer was a collective no.

My shoulders relaxed at that. The car was likely one more thing that plagued my paranoid mind unnecessarily. *Like the smoking stalker I'd suspected of lurking in the trees.* I smiled at the silliness. It had to be one or the other. Was I in grave danger? Or not? I lived alone in the country. Anyone who wanted to hurt me had hours of opportunity to do it every night, and yet no one had.

I stepped over a fallen limb in my path and searched for happier thoughts to busy my mind. "Did I tell you how much Granny is enjoying your goats?" I asked Dot. "They're doing a great job, and I think she's getting attached to the little white one."

Dot's expression lit up. "Do you think she wants to keep him? He's so sweet, but I can't take all the fainting. Freaks me out, and sometimes I think the other goats scare him on purpose. He'd make such a good pet for her."

"I think she's considering it," I said, enjoying the little boost my news had put in Dot's step.

"I can't wait to talk to her about it when we get off this mountain. He's an absolute doll. He'll be so happy to know she wants him."

I laughed. Dot always made it sound as if the animals she'd been temporarily spoiling somehow knew they were all just waiting for a forever home. "Taking him in would fulfill my obligation to adopt one more animal, right?" I asked. "And if so, can I get that in writing?"

She shook her head in the negative. "Not a chance."

Eventually, Hank's family cabin came into view, and we moved quickly past it. Fifty yards later, we rushed past the place where Chad Denton had been found. I was glad for Dot's brisk pace. The familiar locations caused my stomach to twist.

A few yards later, Dot cleared her throat and projected her voice over our group. "Several trails will become visible in another few minutes. We can try them all together or we can split up. What do you think?"

"We should definitely not split up," I said. "Even if it takes all day, we'll be safer together than apart."

Dot smiled broadly. "Says the woman who has reason to dump us for coffee with a handsome entrepreneur in another couple of hours." She waggled her eyebrows.

I snorted. "The poor guy is at his best friend's funeral right now." I should probably have rescheduled our coffee appointment so he could take the rest of the day to decompress, but I hoped to learn more about Jack from him, maybe something to wrap up this whole case.

"Stick together it is," Dot said, stopping to look at her map.

"Wait a minute," Hank interrupted. "I've been on the run for days. I want this to be over. I say we split up. Cover more ground. Call in the sheriff and share our ideas."

I pressed my hands against my hips. "What if whoever picks the right path interrupts the killer while he's digging up ginseng?"

Gina's eyes widened. She gripped her brother's arm. "No splitting up."

Dot refolded the map, then pointed into the trees. "I think we should head this way for a while. We'll come out beneath the cliffs. Most hikers climb to the top for the views, but the area beneath could be a great environment for ginseng. The spot I'm thinking of is off the trails and surrounded by some fairly rough terrain." She looked to Sarah. "Let me know if anything starts to look familiar."

We hiked onward in silence for half an hour before Sarah gasped. "I know this tree!" She beetled over to a towering white oak and ran a palm down the smooth side where a buck had shorn the bark with his antlers. "I took a picture here." She brought up the photos on her phone and scrolled to a selfie of her beside the tree. She'd puckered her lips and drawn a heart on the photo with her initials and P.C.

"Who's P.C.?" Hank asked.

"Prince Charming. It's a joke I have with Elsie. She liked to tease me for all the time I spend in the forest. Like Snow White."

"Wasn't Prince Charming Cinderella's husband?" Hank asked.

I broke away from the pack, leaving them to debate whether or not Snow White's prince was ever named.

Dot moved away as well, scanning the forest in the opposite direction.

All we needed was some sign that someone else had been there. Then we could follow the signs to see where that person had come from or gone. If it was Sarah's trail, we would be exactly where we needed to be.

"Whoa." I stutter-stepped as a sea of ginseng leaves came into view much sooner than I'd imagined possible. The slope of the land had made them invisible from the trail, only a dozen yards away. The seemingly endless expanse was like a rippling ocean of green leaves in the breeze.

"Hot dog!" Hank stage-whispered, scrambling into the waving plants. He lifted his arms skyward in victory, a thousand-watt smile on his handsome face. "It's the holy grail."

Dot hurried to my side, the rest of our group in

her wake. Her jaw nearly unhinged at the sight before us. "There are so many. I can't even see where they end."

It was a million-dollar view that someone had killed for.

# Chapter Twenty-three

We walked the sun-dappled sea of green, mesmerized. How had all this ginseng been here so long? Untouched and allowed to grow, uninterrupted. It was amazing, especially with the increasing bounty on these roots.

"Unbelievable," Dot murmured. "I've never seen this or even heard rumors about it."

Gina took a seat in the sun and cracked open her bottle of water. "Do you know how many consecutive strokes our granddaddy would've had at a sight like this?" she asked. "He loved to look for ginseng. He walked miles every day searching for signs of it. Just for the thrill of the find, I think. He never brought anything home but stories."

"That's because he had to dig it to buy food most of his life," Hank said. "Ginseng hasn't always been worth what it is today, but it's always had value. When he couldn't find work, or when the coal mines were closed, Granddaddy hunted ginseng for survival. All the years we knew him, he just went looking. Maybe some form of nostalgia. Maybe just habit. He didn't dig it anymore because he didn't have to, and he probably knew the next person to come across it might need it."

That was the realest story of life in Blossom Valley I'd heard in a long while. We were a community with a long history of financial struggles. The big oil company in the next county had helped with our employment rates lately, but we were still a collection of farmers and blue collars at our core. And we were proud of it.

"Winnie?" Sarah's small voice called from a distance. She'd wandered the perimeter of the ginseng once we'd found it, and was now over the edge of the ridge. "Look."

Hank, Dot, and I headed in her direction. I said a silent prayer that she hadn't found another dead body. We stopped when Sarah's discovery came into sight. Someone had been digging, but it wasn't a grave.

"Someone's been harvesting the ginseng." I moved in closer, pulse racing. We'd been right. The earth was turned up near the far corner of the ginseng grove and a pile of plants lay wilting on the ground. The roots had been carefully removed.

I snapped photos, then sent them to Colton with the single bar of cell service I found on top of a massive boulder at the edge of the hill. I sent a brief explanation of the photos and our GPS coordinates so he could find us quickly, before whoever had dug the other roots returned.

I hopped off the boulder and returned to the dig site. The area had been heavily trodden and

was crisscrossed with footprints. Leaving such blatant evidence at the scene of a crime seemed careless, but I supposed the culprit never expected
anyone to happen across it.

My phone buzzed with a response text from
Colton. I'M IN THE PARK. GIVE ME THIRTY MINUTES TO
FIND YOU. DO NOT MOVE.

I rolled my eyes, then switched to my camera
app and took a few photos of the footprints.
"Colton's on his way," I warned the others. "Careful not to get your prints mixed up with the crime
scene."

Everyone took a step back and checked the
ground beneath their shoes. Luckily, the earth was
solid and covered with leaves outside the dig zone.

I lowered my phone for a clear look at one distinctive print left among the others. It was small in
comparison and had a familiar pattern of dia-
mond shapes in the tread. The trademark of a
brand I'd only dreamed of owning. I hovered my
foot beside the print and took a photo. Exactly my
size.

Sarah crouched beside me. "Those are Zig
Zags."

"Just like the muddy sneakers Elsie left at my
barn following the reception." She'd been here. Il-
legally harvesting a million-dollar crop of ginseng
only days before her wedding. And based on a second set of larger, wider prints, she hadn't been
alone.

Dot joined us, examining the other prints. "These
are deep. The sheriff will be able to cast a mold and
identify the shoe. He'll probably be able to match
this soil to Jack and Elsie's shoes."

"The soil Hank left on my kitchen floor had traces of mushrooms through it."

Hank lumbered in our direction, running his pocketknife down the edge of a leafy branch he'd cut from a nearby sapling. He plunged it into the ground to mark the dig site. "There's a patch of morels behind the cabin. This whole area is peppered with them." He turned on the flashlight app on his phone to face the sunken spots near trees and rocks, searching, then moving along in the wake of the light. "They grow near the dead trees, places where the ground is moist. By ashes, oaks, elms . . ." He turned his light off and pushed the phone into his pocket. A moment later, he was on his way back to us with a handful of tall yellow mushrooms. "It's late in the season, but they're still good. Morels sell for about twenty bucks a pound at the grocery. It's a little funny those mushroom hunters came all the way out here looking for these guys when nature's winning lottery ticket was right under their noses."

"Except the ginseng is illegal to cash in on," Dot reminded him. "Not much of a lottery ticket."

He shrugged. "It's still funny."

I smiled and checked my watch. "I've got to head back so I'm not late for coffee. Can you guys hold down the fort until Colton gets here?"

They agreed, and I headed back the way we'd come. I sent Colton a text saying we could talk soon and asking him to keep me posted.

His response was instant. I HOPE YOU'RE KIDDING.

I wasn't.

I filled in Granny and Delilah on everything when I returned to the mouth of the hollow. They agreed to drive me home when I realized I was stranded, having ridden with Dot. I sent Dot a text to confirm Colton had arrived to meet them while I was hiking back off the mountain. She confirmed, so I assumed it was safe for Granny and Delilah to leave their post.

We loaded up the camping props and climbed into the cab of Delilah's pickup. She sat behind the wheel, Granny claimed the spot beside the passenger door, and I got sardined in the middle.

"So, Elsie was in on the heist," Delilah said. "Probably hoping to pay back the loan shark."

"That's what I'm guessing," I said. "Though the money she'd saved by moving the wedding to Blossom Valley had to have been significant. How deep in debt could she and Jack have been?"

"Deep enough that the loan shark crossed state lines looking for them," Delilah said.

I watched fields and livestock rush past the windows between massive hay rolls and stately barns.

Delilah made the turn back through town, brows furrowed, apparently putting things together on her own. "The news said the man in the woods died before the wedding. Based on the bride's muddy shoes and that print, we can assume Elsie was involved with that man's death somehow."

"Yep," Granny answered before I could. She seemed heartbroken by the thought. I didn't blame her.

"And the man was a criminal?" Delilah asked. "You said he was a possible killer himself?"

"According to Colton," I said. "I think he came here to collect or to kill Jack. Maybe Elsie too."

"Explains why Elsie was such a mess," Granny

said. "She'd been under so much pressure. Scavenging for cash to pay a loan shark, changing all her wedding plans, getting married while on the run from a dangerous criminal."

*Burying his body in the woods.*

"So who killed Jack if Denton was already dead?" Delilah asked.

*That*, I thought, was an excellent question.

Granny and Delilah dropped me off at home, then headed over to see Elsie and Mrs. Sawyer. They took a casserole and apple pie as an excuse to go inside and visit. What they really hoped to accomplish was establishing a timeline for Elsie since she'd arrived in Blossom Valley. What had she been doing, exactly? And who with? Bonus points if they discovered any last-minute guests who weren't from around here.

I changed into a blue-and-white gingham blouse and jean shorts with sandals, drove a lip gloss wand around my lips, and dashed my lashes with mascara, then hit the road.

Aaron was making a right turn into the Sip N Sup parking lot as I was making a left. He smiled and waved over his steering wheel, then followed me in and took the space beside mine.

I climbed out and locked Sally, then went around to admire his impressive work truck, a maroon Ford F-350 with tool boxes, belts, and a cooler in the back, George Strait on the radio, and an NRA sticker in the window. I smiled. These were the calling cards of a successful, working-class country boy.

He pocketed his phone and keys before climbing out to meet me. He was in another set of black dress pants and shoes. His button-up shirt was open at the collar, and he'd rolled his sleeves to the elbows. His smile was kind and pleasant despite the awful way his day had started. "You came."

"Of course."

He motioned me ahead of him, then accompanied me to the front of the diner in amiable silence.

Aaron opened the diner's door for me, and a blast of icy air poured over my shoulders, sending a shiver down my spine. "Booth or table?" I asked, falling easily into hostess mode, a job I'd performed countless times.

"Hey, y'all," Reese interrupted before Aaron could answer. She waved us to her with a welcoming smile. "Sit here in my section. I want to say hello."

We slid into a booth against the wall and gave Reese our coffee orders before she sashayed away.

"Thanks for meeting me," Aaron said genuinely. "I drove Elsie home from the cemetery and almost stopped by your place to see if you wanted to ride together, but I figured you were busy at the cider shop. I didn't want to interrupt your day twice."

"You wouldn't have interrupted," I said. "I didn't open today, but I might not have been home either. I was out with Granny and some friends."

"Do anything fun?" he asked.

I smiled, debating how much I wanted to admit, then decided to err on the side of too little instead of too much. "Not really."

Reese returned with the coffees, and I pressed mine to my lips.

"I hope it was a nice service," I told him. "Sorry I wasn't there. I was torn about attending, but I didn't know Jack, and I don't know the Sawyers well. I didn't think I belonged."

"It's fine," he said. "The place was packed and a little tense."

"Tense?"

He sighed, stretching his long legs beneath the table. "Jack and Elsie's families aren't big fans of one another. There was a definite line of division between them today. The Sawyers and their people on one side with Jack's business friends. Jack's family and their friends on the other. Both sticking close to their own. Evaluating. Whispering. It was weird."

"It must've been strange for Jack," I said, "to come from a family that struggled financially, then to suddenly have whatever he wanted."

Aaron offered a sad smile. "Jack didn't have whatever he wanted. Elsie's family practically disowned her for marrying him. That's why she moved the wedding here at the last minute," he said. "She was looking for a little peace between warring clans."

"Their families were fighting?" So, I'd been wrong. She hadn't moved the wedding to Blossom Valley to cash in on the payments already made. "She moved the wedding to please her mother?"

"Their families have this kind of cold war going," he said stirring cream into his coffee. "Jack's family thinks Elsie isn't good enough for him because she's never had to work for anything. They as-

sumed she'd leave him if times ever got truly tough.
Meanwhile, her family said Jack would never amount
to anything and he would only drag her down."

"But his business was thriving," I said, adding a
little positive inflection to my voice and trying to
sound as if I meant it. "Both families must've been
happy about that."

"That was all smoke and mirrors," Aaron said.
"Their business was struggling like all new businesses. It didn't help that Jack worried about appearances all the time and thought spending
money was the best way to prove they were on top.
He'd been running crazy trying to prove his worth
to the Sawyers for as long as he'd known Elsie. It
was exhausting to watch."

My mind spun his opening phrase around, trying to decipher his intention. "So Jack wasn't
doing as well as he pretended?"

Aaron gave a dismissive snort. "Jack was borrow-
ing from Peter to pay Paul. He even came to me
for help. More than once. I did what I could, but
I've got crews to pay or the houses don't get finished. If the houses don't get finished, they can't
be sold. If they aren't sold . . ."

I nodded, understanding. If he couldn't sell the
houses, then he didn't get paid. And he would be
struggling too. "So you aren't a one-man show?" I
asked. "I thought you flipped the houses on your
own like those guys on television."

"I started that way," he said, lips curving into a
lopsided smile. "These days I'm more of a fore-
man. I scope the properties, buy them, and deter-
mine a budget. I've got a bunch of crews who
come in and handle the individual jobs. Drywall.

Floors. Roofing. Whatever needs done so I can get the home back on the market."

"Total reconstructions."

"Sometimes." He nodded. "Especially when there's been flood damage from the river. Some of the worst homes are infested with every manner of snake, rat, and you don't want to know what else."

I forced my lips into a deep frown. He was right. I really didn't want to know what else.

My thoughts circled back to Jack. "It must've been hard for Jack to ask anyone for money, especially with all that pressure to be successful." I bit the insides of my cheeks, not wanting to offend Aaron, or insult his dead friend, but needing to know. "Do you think the man they found in the woods could have been here for Jack?" The news stations had all begun to report the facts. Chad Denton was a criminal from Louisville with a lengthy and intimidating record.

Shock crossed Aaron's face. "Not Jack."

"Sorry," I backpedaled. "That was rude and speculative of me. It's been a long week."

"It's okay. This whole thing is a mess. I just wonder . . ." he shook his head. "No. Never mind."

I leaned my forearms on the table, scooting in close so I wouldn't miss a thing. "What?"

He glanced around the room, as if to be sure no one was listening. "Elsie's mom told me that Elsie had barely kept in touch with her throughout the wedding planning until she suddenly changed locations. She said that up to that point, Elsie had refused to take any money from her. Maybe trying to prove she was independent or that Jack was worthy. I don't know. I didn't ask. But what if it was

Elsie who borrowed money from that man? Not Jack."

I ran through the unexpected scenario, flipping my money-borrower from Jack to Elsie. Maybe it was even harder for someone who'd grown up with money to suddenly go without. Maybe it gave her motivation for finding money elsewhere. That scenario also fit the squeaky-clean perception everyone seemed to have of Jack. "At the cider shop the other day, you said Jack and Elsie had been through a lot. Was he unfaithful or unwilling to settle down earlier in their relationship?"

"No." Aaron dragged the word out for several syllables. "It was never Jack. Elsie made him jump through hoops to earn her affection. I thought he was crazy when he proposed, and it shocked me when she said yes, but I was happy for him. It was all he'd wanted for a very long time."

I curled my fingers around the edge of the seat cushion beneath me. My world tilted as reality shifted in my head. Could Elsie have been behind all this from the beginning? It made perfect sense, but I'd been more than willing to accept Jack as the villain and see Elsie as the unintentional accomplice. "Do you think Elsie could have borrowed money from Denton?" Could she have met him in the forest that night? Hit him on the head while Jack fought to protect her? Had Elsie insisted that Jack go to Sarah for medical attention instead of a hospital so she could cover her own criminal behavior?

"It's easier than imagining Jack doing something like that."

Fear lodged in my throat as a new, more horrible thought occurred to me. "You drove Elsie home from the funeral?"

"Yeah. Why?"

"Why didn't her mom drive her?" Blood whooshed in my ears as I waited for the answer.

"Because she went on to the Warrens' house for food and a small wake. She said she wanted to be there to represent her family."

And that meant Elsie, the possibly homicidal maniac, was home alone.

"We have to go!" I jumped up and tossed some ones on the table to cover the coffee.

Aaron followed me out of the building at a sprint. "What just happened?"

"Granny and Delilah are on their way to see Elsie. They think Jack killed Chad Denton, but I think it was Elsie! She wanted to cover her tracks. Keep her relationship with a loan shark a secret. She might've even killed her husband to make sure the truth never got out."

Aaron uttered a cuss, then bypassed me in long, loping strides. He beeped his truck doors unlocked as he ran. "Get in! I'll drive."

I dove into the passenger side of his truck and buckled in. My heart hammered and my eyes stung. I couldn't live with myself if Granny was hurt because of me. "Hurry," I begged.

I opened my small clutch purse and fumbled for my phone, which had gotten buried under the two-way radio I needed to return to Dot. I swiped my screen to life, desperate to let everyone know what was going on and to warn Granny and Delilah not to go to Elsie's. If they were already there, they needed to leave.

The truck swerved and my phone fell onto the floorboards.

I leaned forward to retrieve it and something hard poked against my ribs.

"Sit up," Aaron growled, all pretense of the easy-going guy gone. "Leave the phone where it is."

I sat slowly, mouth gaping. My gaze dropped to the weapon digging into my side. "A Smith and Wesson Governor," I whispered. Small, light-weight, easy to carry.

The Governor shot a .45 caliber round.

Aaron's brows rose, but he didn't speak as he maneuvered out of the crowded lot.

"Grampy had one just like it," I said. Actually, most folks had something darn close. Something they'd call a trail gun. I groaned as the final realization hit, snapping everything else into place. Trail guns were simple, effective protection against dangers a person might encounter while doing something like field work, hiking, or remodeling abandoned homes by the river. "I suppose that gun isn't registered."

"Do I look stupid?" he asked, looking downright deadly.

"You were the one who shot at Dot and me, and you killed Chad Denton. You covered him in leaves and left him to rot."

"Elsie and Jack did that," he said coolly. "I followed them into the forest after Jack made a flimsy excuse to cut out of his bachelor party early."

"They led you to the ginseng." My mind boggled. How had I never seen this coming?

Aaron paused at the next intersection to make eye contact with me before returning his attention to the road. "You know about that?"

I nodded, then he hit the gas.

We barreled away from town, up a winding ribbon of road. "Of course you do. Which makes this easier for me."

I swallowed a boulder of fear. "You recognized the ginseng."

"I'm the one who spotted it in Sarah's photo," he said hotly. "That was my find. I followed Elsie and Sarah on Instagram once the wedding date was set. I liked their monotonous exercise posts and endless selfies out of duty and manners, until one day, there it was. When I called her on it, she had no idea what I meant, so I dropped the subject and asked Jack if he'd noticed. He hadn't. Neither had Elsie. In fact, none of those morons had a single clue. I had to spell it out for them. I told Jack that he could help me harvest it and we'd call his debt to me even. But we had to dig now, before anyone else came across it, then wait until it came into season and sell it. He agreed, and we made plans to meet here on the last day of their honeymoon. Jack was going to tell Elsie he wanted to visit her hometown. Then I'd come by and invite him out for some night fishing. We'd harvest through the night, and no one would be any wiser."

"But you weren't the only one Jack and Elsie owed," I said. "Being free from your debt wasn't enough."

Aaron's gaze grew dark, and he tightened his grip on the wheel. "Jack told Elsie about our plan to hit it big, and she told him she was in debt to Denton. She talked him into cutting me out so they could take care of her problems instead. They changed their wedding plans and came here to collect the ginseng themselves."

"You confronted them and fought with Jack in the woods," I guessed.

"No, I stayed hidden while Denton confronted Jack, then beat the snot out of him. It seemed like karma to me, so I let it go on until Denton had him out cold and Elsie hit Denton over the head with a rock. She covered him in leaves, then managed to get Jack on his feet and off the mountain. I went to check the guy's ID. I'd gotten the gist of who he was by listening to them argue. Then I kept the ID to cover my tracks since I'd already touched it. He grabbed my wrist while I was trying to recover him."

Bile rose in my throat, rolling and pitching in my gut. "He wasn't dead, so you shot him."

"I had no choice. Afterward, I knew Jack and Elsie wouldn't be back for a while. They had two days packed with wedding-related events, and Jack was pretty messed up when he left. So I made the best of the situation and went after the bounty myself."

"And you killed your best friend."

"Only because Jack was losing it over what Elsie had done to Denton. He thought she'd killed him and they'd covered it up. He was day-drinking and guilt ridden. He was sure someone else would come after them next. To avenge Denton's death or collect Elsie's debt. I saw a way out, and I took it. I knew Elsie would never return for the harvest if Jack was dead and she blamed herself."

I glared at him, unable to speak and desperate to turn the tables. I just didn't know how.

"I was on my way off the hill with a load of roots when you and your friend showed up. I gave a couple shots to turn you around. I couldn't let you see me up there. It would've raised suspicions. Plus I couldn't let you happen across the ginseng."

"So you shot at Dot and me, killed your best friend, and let Elsie believe she killed a man." How had I been so utterly blind? How had I ever believed him a decent human being?

"Your friend was right," he said. "You're not a bad amateur detective. I'll give you that, but it's the end of the road for you." He turned into a narrow hollow, bouncing over the remnants of a long-forgotten road, and parked his big truck in the shadows of a thousand towering trees.

He reached behind the seat and unearthed a shovel, then motioned me out of the truck with his gun. "It's time for one last hike through the forest."

# Chapter Twenty-four

I dug into my purse as Aaron exited the truck and rounded the hood to my side. I palmed the two-way radio Dot had given me, then turned it on. I slid a ponytail holder over its middle and crushed the big orange button to stop any sound from exiting the device, and hopefully allowing anyone still on my channel to hear what was going on. I shoved the radio into the waistband at my back and dropped my billowy blouse over it just as Aaron yanked open my door.

He snatched the purse from my hands and threw it into the trees, then scooped my fallen cell phone from the floor boards and chucked it too. "You won't be needing those anymore. Now march."

"Where are we going?" I shuffled forward, dragging my feet and staring desperately toward the mouth of the hollow. I just needed one distraction. A mushroom hunter or hiker or bear. Anything, so I could run.

"Where do you think?" He pushed the shovel in

my direction, and I wrapped my hands around the handle, wishing there wasn't a gun pressed to my ribs.

"What's the plan?" I asked. "Bury me in the woods?"

Aaron curled one set of strong fingers around my bicep and towed me into the trees. "You're going to that dilapidated shack where your run-away friend was staying. Everyone already thinks he killed Jack. He nearly confirmed it by running away when he found the body. Idiot. Now, we're going to make it look like he's killed you too. The shovel's for me to get as much of that root as I can before I leave town. I'll have to come back for the rest once news of your death has passed."

"No one will believe Hank killed me," I said, dragging the shovel behind me, hoping to leave a trail.

"You're wrong about that, pumpkin. You've got a serious reputation as the town snoop. It seems fitting that you'd go looking for Hank, the killer, and wind up as another one of his victims."

I winced as sticks and stones jammed into my skin through the open-toed sandals. The slick soles slid on loose earth and decaying leaves. "I'm not a snoop," I groused, trying to stay upright while he hauled me forward at a too-brisk pace. "And don't call me pumpkin."

"Yes, you are, and everyone knows it. They also know you've been turning over rocks looking for Hank, so the discovery of your body at his cabin will fit perfectly. The timing couldn't be better," he mused. "Elsie's mom is hiring a private detective to find Hank, so her daughter can have closure. I'll make sure it looks like you found him first." The levity in his voice increased with each word, as if the plan was coming together perfectly as he spoke. "I'll be sure to wipe my gun clean and hide it nearby. Then, the cops can charge Hank with Denton's murder too."

"This is preposterous." My racing mind hung up on something else that barely mattered considering I was about to die, but I couldn't let it go. "You moved the seat after you hit Jack with the getaway truck to make it look like someone my height was behind the wheel."

Aaron shot me an incredulous look, then jerked me up a small embankment. "Smart, right?"

I groaned internally. Colton had told me as much, and I'd been hung up on that small detail anyway, as if it was the one that would break the case wide open.

"Try to keep up."

I wasn't sure if he meant physically or mentally, but at the moment, I was struggling to do both. "I can't believe you'd kill your best friend over money," I said. "You're worse than Jack. You thought he was so terrible for trying to seem more successful than he was. Well, what do you think of yourself? You killed him!"

"I'm someone who knows how to work hard, scrimp, save, and build a business from the roots up," he snarled, tightening his grip on my arm until I whimpered in pain. "While Jack was bragging and showing off at parties, I was knee-deep in river muck, restoring abandoned properties on my own. I made them mansions, and now I keep my crew's families in paychecks too. I take that seriously. It's something folks respect."

*Folks like the Sawyers.* The proverbial lightbulb snapped on bright enough to blind me. "You wanted Elsie."

"Shut up." He yanked my arm until I was sure the shoulder would dislocate.

I nearly dropped the shovel I was dragging from the burst of pain. But the shovel was my lifeline. I dared a peek over one shoulder, verifying the trail left behind us. It was spotty but visible for someone who was looking.

"What are you doing?" Aaron snapped.

I turned a hot look in his direction. "This is about your petty jealousy," I said. "You did everything the right way, but Jack got the girl. That's why you've been hanging around in Blossom Valley, checking on Elsie every day when you could have easily returned home by now. You're no better than Jack. I bet you thought you'd be the hero when you loaned him money. You thought Elsie would see you as the bigger, better man, but she didn't even notice. Did she?"

"Shut up!"

"Elsie had had her own problems to worry about," I droned on, hoping he'd stop walking before we reached the cabin, before we were too deep in the hills to be found. "That's why you shot Denton. You had to be sure he wouldn't come after Elsie again because you wanted her, not because you wanted to frame her."

"Shut up, pumpkin," he warned, emphasizing the final word, provoking me with it because I'd let him know he could.

My words came faster, tumbling over one another as all the details began to make sense. "You've been positioning yourself as her closest confidant and ally so that when she pulls herself together again, you can take your best friend's place in her life. You'll have all the money from the harvested ginseng, and a thriving business to boot. Elsie won't have to go looking for cash ever again. Because you would provide it."

Aaron planted his feet and spun to face me, his cheeks red, eyes flashing with fury. He pulled his gun-wielding hand back with a snap, and I braced for the hit that would come. "I said shut up!"

"I wouldn't do that if I were you," a furious tenor advised. Leaves crunched in the distance as Colton's voice rose like mist through the forest. "Jefferson County Sheriff. Release Miss Montgomery. Drop the gun and get down on your stomach so I don't have to shoot you."

Aaron released me, his face pale as he scanned the trees for Colton. He didn't drop the gun. Instead, he used his free hand to stabilize the weapon. He locked his arms as he turned to search for the voice.

I raised the shovel onto my shoulder, overcome with relief at the sound of Colton's voice and still fuming at the way Aaron had grabbed and taunted me. So I swung. "And I said, don't call me pumpkin!"

The impact reverberated through me as the metal connected with Aaron's lean, muscled back. He pitched forward, the gun flying, and I ran.

Behind me, Colton spoke again, this time louder, closer, and infinitely angrier. He faced off with Aaron as he struggled back to his feet, fists up and preparing to fight.

"You probably shouldn't add assaulting the county sheriff to your lengthy list of crimes," Colton said, "but I wouldn't mind if you tried."

Stupidly, Aaron went for it. His long arm snaked out to punch Colton in the nose, but Colton dodged the hit, barely moving. Aaron swung again with the same result. Livid, he launched himself at Colton, who caught and spun him into a choke-hold before slamming the taller man onto the ground and pressing a boot to the back of his neck.

"Dumb," Colton said as he pried Aaron's arms behind his back and secured them with cuffs. "You can come out now," he called.

And people began to filter from the shadows and trees. *My people.*

Granny and Delilah, Hank and Gina, Sarah and Dot. Plus a bunch of park rangers and a pair of deputies climbed the hill in our direction.

I covered my mouth, tears blurring my eyes, then ran into the fold. Joy and adrenaline fueled my flight until suddenly I collided with one broad chest. I hadn't intended to run to anyone in particular, but I'd landed hard against Colton's body, and he'd caught me.

His strong arms enveloped me. One hand pressed me closer. The other hand cradled my head against his shoulder. "Sorry I was late," he whispered.

My friends piled in on us, forming a massive group hug. Their voices came in a beautiful blur.

"What are you all doing here?" I sniffled, detaching myself from Colton with a jolt of shock and embarrassment.

Dot pulled me against her. "We were already

here, silly. Trying to figure out what to do about the ginseng. When you called us with your walkie, we figured you cut your date short." Her gaze cut to Aaron, being hauled off the forest floor by his cuffed wrists. "You had the button depressed so we couldn't radio back."

Hank tugged me away from Dot and into his arms where Sarah and Gina took turns hugging me too. "We heard it all," Hank said. "He said he was taking you to the family cabin, so we headed this way. Sheriff Wise was with us, so he took the lead."

"Actually, I told you all to stay where you were," Colton corrected.

The group chuckled, but Dot and Granny were wiping tears.

"Come here," Granny said.

I squeezed her middle as Delilah patted my back and freed the radio from my waistband.

"Dot called us when your radio came on," Granny said. "She stayed on the phone with me while we made our way here from Elsie's place. She told us you were headed to the Donovans' cabin. So, we headed this way too."

Delilah's eyes were wide. "This was thrilling. I was happy for the chance to be a lookout, but seeing a killer cuffed is so much better."

"I'm just glad us old birds made it in time. We knew we'd almost caught up with you when Sheriff Wise started hollering," Granny said.

I turned for another look at Colton.

His gaze cut to mine from where he spoke with his deputies, as if he'd somehow known I was looking.

"Sheriff Wise?" a park ranger called.

Colton watched me another long beat before turning to answer the ranger's call.

"You nearly scared us all to death today," Granny said softly, hooking her arm around my back and leading me to a nearby fallen tree for a seat.

Delilah watched Colton closely as we climbed atop the broad, curved trunk. "I think that man in cuffs is lucky there were so many witnesses. Your new sheriff looked fit to kill when he saw him raise a hand to you. Trust me on that," Delilah said. "I spent forty years surrounded by military men. I know that look when I see it."

I watched Colton more curiously, wondering if she was right and how I felt about it if she was.

"Well?" Dot asked, climbing onto the tree with us. "Tell us everything. What did you learn? When did you know he was the killer? How did he know you knew?"

I pulled in a shuddered breath and retold my harrowing tale in extreme detail to my beloved friends. Then I cried.


The Fourth of July in Blossom Valley was a week-long event, jam-packed with parties, barbecues, bonfires, and parades. American flags lined the streets, cemeteries, church lawns, and ball fields. "Land of the Free" signs popped up in every front yard. Red, white, and blue banners stretched over Main Street and local radio stations played marathons of similarly themed country music. There was no place in America more patriotic

than our town. Whatever they did to celebrate in
big cities or even in D.C., it couldn't compare to
the spirit of camaraderie, pride, and love of country found among my people.

Granny and I had been on Main Street since
sunup, scouting out our spots for the parade. We'd
set up camping chairs, brought a cooler and
plenty of sunblock, then settled in for the best day
of the summer. By noon, both sides of the road
were lined in locals six deep, all decked out in
their red, white, and blue finest. Generations of
families stood proudly, cheerfully, waving at the
floats, bands, scouts, and veterans as they marched
along to a medley of "Yankee Doodle" and related
classic songs. Children raced into the street to collect candy tossed by the firemen and homecoming
queens.

"I'll be right back," I told Granny. "Don't let anyone steal my spot." It was hot as blazes and we were
running low on cold drinks. It was time I splurged
for a pair of sweet teas and a boat of watermelon
slices from the nearest vendor.

Hot summer sun beat down on my tan limbs as I
rushed through the crowd, hoping not to miss anything good and praying the line wouldn't be too
long when I reached my destination. I stopped behind a family with a little girl seated on her daddy's
shoulders and a baby packed into a sling across the
mama's middle. Snow cone syrup dripped onto the
daddy's head while the mommy tried not to wake
the baby with her laughter. I'd watched many parades from Grampy's shoulders, and the memories
were some of my favorites. For one quick heart-

beat, I allowed myself to imagine being in the mama's position, enjoying a parade with my kids and a husband who made me laugh.

The family stepped aside and the vendor called out to me.

"What can I get ya?" the man asked from his place beside the cart.

"Two sweet teas and a quarter watermelon, sliced."

He nodded and began to put the items together.

I tapped my toe and closed my eyes as wind danced across my face.

"Ten dollars," the man said.

I opened my eyes to find a familiar hand trading cash for my treats.

"Keep the change," Colton said, scooping the drinks off the counter.

"Hey." I beamed. "You didn't have to do that."

"Wanted to." He passed me a cup, then collected our paper boat of watermelon slices. "I hoped I'd see you here. How've you been?"

Colton had texted and called to check in, but he hadn't been around much the last two weeks. He'd been busy building an airtight case against Aaron.

"I've been good, thanks to you," I said, squinting up at him against the midday sun. "You've saved my life twice now, you know."

"And you didn't even need an ambulance this time," he teased, "so I guess I'm getting better at my job."

I bumped my hip against his as we made our way back to Granny. "How'd it go at the deposition yesterday?"

"Aaron's lawyer tried to make a deal, but I have an airtight case. This thing will go to trial." He grimaced. "You might be asked to testify."

"It's okay." I shrugged. "I can do it."

"I have no doubt.'

We stopped at Granny's chair, and Colton passed her the sweet tea and watermelon with a grin. "How's the needlepointing going?"

She made a sour face. "The Stitch Witches are stealing our patterns and making us look like fools. Plus they took our interest in partnership for the convention as a sign of weakness and are making memes online about us."

He widened his eyes and mouthed the word, "Wow."

She nodded. "I'd like to put a needle on each of their chair cushions, but I suppose they'd retaliate."

"Well, if you're taking orders, I wouldn't mind a PLEASE SEAT YOURSELF sign for my bathroom."

I barked a laugh, and Granny gave him some side eye.

"Oh!" I rocked onto my toes. "There he is!"

Granny gasped, then stood for a better view at the upcoming group.

"Who?" Colton sounded significantly less than enthusiastic than Granny. His palm brushed protectively against the small of my back as he moved into place beside me, staring down the street at the next group of marchers.

"Boo," Granny said. "He's my new goat. He's kind of small and he falls over a lot, but he mows my lawn and Dot said I can keep him."

"He falls over?" Colton asked.

"He's a Tennessee fainting goat," I said, fighting a grin. "So he gets to ride in a wagon while the others . . ." I hadn't finished my sentence before the high school marching band rounded the corner on a high note and Boo went stiff. "And down he goes."

"He can't help it," Granny said. "It's genetic."

A broad smile curled Colton's lips. "I bet Boo does a nice job when he's upright, but I have some human contacts for you too." He pulled a folded scrap of paper from his pocket and passed it to Granny. "If you're interested in an orchard manager or a grounds crew, these folks might be a good place to start. I did some research, ran some background checks, called a few references. I wouldn't mind coming by during the interviews if you want."

Granny accepted the paper. "I might take you up on it. Boo can only eat so much grass."

I sipped my drink and waved at Hank and Sarah across the street. They were holding hands and looking strangely smitten.

"What do you think of that?" Colton asked, his voice low and tentative.

*Better her than me,* came to mind, but I kept it to myself. "They look happy. I think that's nice."

"What about you?" Colton asked. "Are you happy?"

I turned to face him and tipped my head back for a good look at his face. "At the moment? Quite."

He smiled and the crowd seemed to fade. "Have you gotten any news on that cider contest?"

"Not yet. Soon, I hope. If I wind up in a national magazine, I'm going to need to hire someone to help at the cider shop. I don't suppose you have a reference list in your pocket for that."

"I can make one," he said, still smiling.

It might've been the heat, but Colton seemed to lean forward a bit, and his gaze dropped away from my eyes. To my mouth?

My phone buzzed, and I jumped. "It's Dot," I said, breathlessly as I checked the screen. "She probably can't find us in this crowd." I read her message and frowned. "She's not coming."

Colton tensed. "Is everything okay?"

"One of those mushroom hunters lost their truffle hog near the national park, and she's been called in to help locate it. Bummer."

Colton shifted, sliding long fingers into his pockets. "A truffle hog?"

"Don't ask," I told him.

I checked to be sure the folks around us were watching the parade instead of looking our way, then I wet my lips. "What were you saying before?"

His gave an impish grin.

And his phone buzzed.

"Sorry. Give me just a second." Blood seemed to drain from his face as he checked the message.

"What is it?"

"Keller was spotted in Jefferson County early this morning." He turned his phone to me, showing a grainy image of a man crossing a gas station parking lot.

"He's here?" My stomach churned and my chest tightened. The prison escapee who blamed Colton's team back in Clarksburg, and possibly Colton himself, for his lifetime sentence was in our county? "Are you safe? Is he here for you?"

Colton rubbed his mouth and swore. He scanned the crowded streets then tipped his head toward an empty patch of sidewalk several yards away.

I handed Granny my drink. "I'll be right back."

"If he's coming for me," Colton said, his voice low and cautious, "that could be good or bad. If I see him first, he's going to jail for life. No amount of good behavior will erase killing those guards during his transfer."

"And if he sees you first?" I asked, heart pounding as I imagined the worst.

"Let's hope I see him first." Colton pressed his lips into a thin white line, looking slightly uncomfortable and wholly miffed. A low growl rumbled in his chest.

"What?"

His expression went cold and the muscle along his jaw twitched. "If he's coming for me, he'll want to hurt me in a way that'll make it last."

"Like torture?" My stomach pitched in revolt at the thought of someone hurting Colton like that.

"More likely he'll try to do that by hurting you."

"Me?' My stomach lurched again and my pulse hit a sprinter's pace. "Why?"

Colton's phone began to ring, and he lifted a finger.

"Wait," I said. "I can watch for him. How will I know if I see him?"

Colton grimaced at the ringing phone. "He's tall. Late thirties. Likes to dress in black. He'll stick out like a sore thumb here. And he always drives obnoxious expensive sportscars." He raised the phone to his ear as images of the mysterious black Mercedes crept through my mind. "Wise," he said, accepting the call.

My world tilted as the possibility solidified in my head.

"Be there in twenty," he told whoever was on the other end of his call, then shoved the phone into his pocket. "I've got to go. I'll call you later," he said, reaching out to give my hand a squeeze. "Remember what I said. Stay safe. Keep your eyes open."

I nodded, forcing memories of the shadow near my tree line out of my head. Keller hadn't been to my home. Stalked my property. Been in the forest with me. That was impossible. I was still shaken from my run-in with Aaron. "Tall. Dangerous. Fancy car," I said. "Anything else?"

Colton palmed his car keys, already moving away. "He likes to gamble, drink, and he's a chain smoker. Call me if you see anyone who looks suspicious. Trust your gut. You see him, you call. You got it?"

I nodded woodenly, swallowing a boulder of fear as he jogged away.

Then I raised my phone and dialed Colton's number.

# Recipes

## FRIED BOLOGNA FOR THE SOUL

*Ingredients*
    Butter
    2 slices white bread
    Mayo
    Mustard
    2 slices bologna
    1 slice American cheese
    Lettuce, tomato, onion (optional)

*Directions*
    Melt a pat of butter in a medium skillet over medium heat.

    Spread butter on one side of each slice of bread. Lightly toast the buttered sides of the bread in skillet.

    Remove bread and spread mayo on untoasted side of one slice. Spread mustard on the untoasted side of the second slice.

    Make slits or small Xs in the center of each slice of bologna to stop it from curling, then place bologna in buttered pan and fry 2–3 minutes each side, until the edges are wavy and brown.

    Place cheese on bologna in skillet until it begins to melt.

    Remove bologna and cheese from skillet and stack on one slice of bread. Layer with lettuce, onion, or tomato, as desired. Top with second slice of toasted bread.

Serve with chips and a dill pickle spear for a down-home country lunch.

## SUMMER CIDER SLUSHIE

*Ingredients*
   Apple cider
   Ice
   Cinnamon
   Nutmeg

*Directions*
   Fill a blender with apple cider and ice. Add cinnamon and nutmeg to taste.
   Blend for a refreshing summer treat with all the fun flavors of fall.

# EASY APPLE DUMPLIN'S

### Ingredients
2 apples, peeled and cored
2 cans crescent rolls (8 rolls each)
¾ c butter, melted
2 Tbs cinnamon
½ c sugar
Vanilla ice cream (optional)

### Directions
Preheat oven to 350°F.

Peel and core apples. Slice each apple into 8 wedges.

Divide crescent rolls into triangles, then cut each in half to make 16 triangles. Wrap each apple wedge in a half-crescent roll.

Spray a 9"x13" baking dish with cooking spray. Line wrapped apple wedges in dish. Pour melted butter evenly over wedges.

Mix cinnamon and sugar together. Sprinkle evenly over wedges.

Bake at 350°F for 32 minutes, or until golden brown.

Serve warm. Add a scoop of vanilla ice cream, if desired.

# ACKNOWLEDGMENTS

Thank you, dear reader, for joining Winnie and Granny Smythe on another Blossom Valley adventure. You make my dreams possible. Thank you, Norma, my brilliant editor, and the amazing Kensington crew. I'm humbled and honored to be a part of your team. Thank you, Jill Marsal, my beloved ninja of an agent, for believing in me and my stories. Thank you, Jennifer Anderson and Danielle Haas, my infinitely patient critique partners, who make my pages better. Thank you, Darlene Lindsey, the world's greatest mother-in-law and my biggest fan. I couldn't have come this far without you. Thank you, Mom and Dad, for the unending gift of your limitless love and support. Finally, thank you family, Bryan, Noah, Andrew, and Lily. You are my greatest adventure.